THE WITHERING

J. BRIAN BALLINGER

GRAVESIDE PRESS

CONTENT NOTES

Please note: it should be assumed that basic horror tropes will apply. These include death, gore, and violence.

For a list of other potentially triggering subjects,

please refer to page 260.

CHAPTER 1

Eleven emaciated bodies lay scattered about the church, gasping for breath. The longest residing patients of the makeshift infirmary inhaled with what little strength they had left, their cracked lips pulling only meager sips of air.

High above the heads of the sick, at the summit of their sanctuary, the old church bell rang; well-worn hands pulled the coarse rope to make it play. Sixteen times it tolled over the quarantined town, four rings to mark the top of the hour and the rest to confirm it was midnight, each ring cascading over the surrounding dwellings. For the healthy few within the church, the deafening noise brought respite from the constant wheezing of the infirm.

The same calloused hands wiped themselves across holy robes and set about tending to the ill. Father Martine Donadieu dutifully saw to the needs of his congregation; his aging frame had rebelled little that day.

Incense and candles burned within the church. The former served to calm the ill and their visiting kin. However, the woody, floral scents were lost to Donadieu's scarred nose, and the smoke burned his lungs. He detested smoke, it always wafted back a memory he preferred forgotten. Candles, however, were invaluable. Donadieu remained wary of the flames, but he needed their flickering light to navigate the pews upon which the villagers lay.

Donadieu was serving a late meal, and the gaunt parishioners who were able to slurped back the stew he'd prepared. He glided through the rows of his frigid church and carefully steered his spoon into the mouths of those whose arms would not work. Children breathed easier when the restless caretaker was near, their hair tousled by tender hands.

Cramped and cold, the village church stood in the center of the commune. Stone walls greedily absorbed the cooking fire's heat, leaving little for those sheltering inside. Unusually early frosts carried by the approaching autumn winds crept in through the cracks and stabbed at the ill, wool blankets serving as their only shields. Adorned solely in his robes, the priest's deeds were sufficient to keep him warm.

While he made his rounds, a peculiarity caught his eye. A formerly common occurrence turned rare from recent events; the confessional curtain had been pulled shut. Donadieu did not recall seeing or hearing anyone enter the building, but this was not unusual, as he was easily lost in his work. The ringing bell and the fluttering shadows may have concealed the sinner's entrance.

Worry crawled down his throat and nested unwelcome in his chest. The number of people who came to give confession seemed to halve with each new victim residing within the church. There were now so many in need of his care. When members of his flock did come to make confession, they were usually driven by an overwhelmingly burdened conscience. As with most nights of late, he stopped to reassure himself, "This evil persists, but so do I."

Still, he was grateful for the opportunity to sit. His black robes trailed as he slid the spoon back into the cauldron and advanced towards the beckoning curtain. When near to his private booth, his legs anchored to the ground. For the first time in his life, a powerful instinct begged him not to set foot in the cabinet's maw. He could not distinguish whether the imaginary force that repelled *him* emanated from the curtained chamber, from his mind, or somewhere else entirely. What he did know was that he did not *want* to go. All day he had cared for others' bodies, but now when his duty demanded caring for a soul, he hesitated.

In the end, devotion won.

Father Donadieu entered the cubby and eased himself into an uncomfortable wicker chair. Relief washed over his blistered feet when he raised them from the stone floor. With one last hesitation, he turned to his side and drew back the confessional slide, pulling harder when the wooden contraption stuck. His soul ached as sobbing greeted him through the lattice. The priest sat in silence while the man sputtered and wept. Brief pauses dotted the crying, but they did not last. Donadieu's mind floated back to the grounds of his family's manor. It did that a lot as of late. It had to. All the misery of this ancient town funneled into the ear of the weary priest.

Eventually, snot gurgled, and the whimpering waned. A broken voice filled the void, and the ritual began.

"In the name of the Father, the Son, and of the Holy Spirit. Amen."

"May God, who has enlightened every heart, help you know your sins and trust in His mercy."

"Bless me, Father, for I have sinned. It has been forty days since my last confession." The man's voice barely bested a whisper and maneuvered with a thick rural accent common in the north of France.

"I am glad you have come, my son. Pilgrimage to the confessional can, at times, be a journey. You made that journey alone. From here, I walk the path of grace at your side."

The kneeling man's voice remained a whisper. "As you know, Father, Louise became afflicted three months back, one of the first. She withers more every day. I fear it will spread to the children. Every night when I return to care for them, they ask, 'When's Mother getting better?' This last month, all she's done is gasp for air. I don't know how she still lives."

Donadieu recognized the sinner's voice, a potter named Thomas who worked at a small shop in town. "The sickness weighs on us all, my son. But you did not come here to discuss your family. Tell me of your sins."

The man sighed. "God has ripped the very soul from her body. Her smile is gone and all that remains is a husk. Nightly, I curse Him for it."

Father Donadieu heard countless confessions as a man of the cloth. Now, the hair on the back of his neck stood at attention and a spark lit behind his eyes. Something was wrong. This confession was hollow.

"Why are you here, my child? You did not make the journey for blasphemy alone."

Thomas cried anew. Between outbursts, he continued. "It was too much, Father. *It was too much.* Every day I feared I would return to a cold bed, and every night her breath hissed in my ear. Never blinking, never speaking, never eating. She was already dead, and still she breathed. My will collapsed last night, and I was corrupted. I laid awake for hours and listened to her. God had taken her soul, and all He left was a breathing corpse.

"I remember the moon shone through our window, and that the thin layer of clay on my hands looked black in the pale light.

I retrieved a spare blanket from the chest, and I walked to where she lay. My darling Louise, now but hollow skin and bone. I held the blanket to her face, Father, and I pushed it down with all my strength," the man wailed at reliving the memory. "My soul left me that moment, Father, and it has yet to return. I held that blanket there as long as my arms would allow. Even on that bitter night, I dripped with sweat before I relented. When I removed the gag from her face, she breathed on."

"My son—"

"I shivered as I gazed down, the frigid air clawing at my flesh. Desperation pushed me further. With tears clouding my vision, I cast the blanket aside and gripped at her throat with my bare hands. I squeezed with such force my palms nearly met. Anything to stop the awful hissing of her breath.

"I am a coward, Father. I admit. As I committed that mortal sin, I closed my eyes and turned my head. I could not watch what my hands attempted to achieve."

What little stew the priest had eaten threatened to come up. Bile burned the base of his throat. Conflicting emotions swirled in his head, and he was grateful it was not his responsibility to judge. Carefully, he weighed his options on how to proceed. The scales in his brain teetered back and forth. At last, one option weighed the lightest of them all.

He spoke slowly and calmly. "Murder is a mortal sin. The path ahead will be difficult for you and I am sorry for that, but you must confess this to the authorities. Your penance will be great, and you must pay quickly; it is likely they will take you to the noose. Fear not, my son; God forgives all sins if you repent, and I know—"

"But Father," the weeping man said, "she would not die! I held that blanket as long as I was able and choked her even longer. It didn't matter how long I withheld air, when I released my grasp, that horrid breathing resumed."

Donadieu's voice softened. "Was this, perhaps, all a dream?"

There was a brief pause before Thomas continued. "She wears a necklace of bruises."

Hope drained from the priest. How he longed for the last few months to have been a dream, but like the man across from him now, he knew the horror was real.

"Have you any other sins to confess?"

"No, Father." The man's crying eased. "I am sorry for these and all my sins."

"God has taken mercy on you, and you should rejoice. He spared your wife and saved you. Your penance is to abstain from all food but bread and water for thirty days and repeat Psalms every morning and night for the duration. Take this miracle from God and reflect upon your misdeeds. It is time for closing prayers."

All crying had stopped, only sniffles remained. "My God, I am sorry for my sins with all my heart. In choosing to do wrong and failing to do good, I have sinned against You whom I should love above all things. I firmly intend, with Your help, to do penance, to sin no more, and to avoid whatever leads me to sin. Our Savior Jesus Christ suffered and died for us. In His name, my God, have mercy."

The prayer of absolution followed. Donadieu's voice remained steady, but opposing desires ripped him in half. He wanted to flee from the man and this evil, to hide in the darkest corner of the church and pretend the disease had not cast a looming shadow over his town. And he wanted to console the man. To bound from his booth, tear back the indifferent curtain, and comfort Thomas with an embrace.

Inhibitions meant he did neither.

His duties nearing completion, the priest continued, "Give thanks to the Lord, for He is good."

Thomas replied, "His mercy endures forever."

"The Lord has freed you from your sins. Go in peace."

A rustle of cloth and fading footsteps informed Donadieu when the penitent had left. He reflected on the harm this unholy curse, the Withering, had on the bodies of his flock, and more importantly, their souls. Especially those not yet afflicted.

The demanding nature of spiritual healing left him sapped of energy. His body refused to remove itself from that cramped booth and hard chair. Donadieu wrestled with what he had heard and felt hollow when reliving the tale in his mind. He wondered, had sections been added, perhaps misremembered? The confession couldn't be true in its entirety, yet the passion with which it was told churned uncertainty in the priest's mind. The potter, at least, believed his own words. Donadieu was certain of that.

When he finally recovered his strength and set to resume his chores, new footsteps clacked on the stone stairs outside the church entrance. A woman entered where the man had left. In her arms, a slack child lay. It had been a long day and Donadieu's resilience strained like a single hair suspending a boulder, but it held.

"Sleeping?" he asked, nodding at the child.

The woman shook her head no. Her eyes were stained red from what must have been a hefty flow of tears, but now her mouth held a stoic, flat line. "Can't wake her."

"Bring her in, Camille. Set her on any free pew. I'll look after her as best I can."

A forced smile tilted the edges of Camille's mouth, but her eyes refused to acquiesce to such a falsehood. With heavy footsteps, she brought the sagging child into the temporary ward and gently laid her upon an open seat. "Thank you, Father. With Benoit and her sharing the room, I couldn't risk it spreading."

Donadieu tried his best to leverage a genuine smile; Camille's face did not show if he succeeded. "Of course. Your daughter will be safe here."

Camille's eyes worked up and down the priest's old robes. "Your clothes need mending," she said. "I can't remember the last time you brought them to be patched. If you're not careful, they'll disintegrate around you. That wouldn't be very modest for a priest." She made no effort to hide the emptiness behind her eyes.

The absurdity of the joke brought forth a laugh from the priest in spite of himself. "Go home, Camille. Look after Benoit. Josephine is safe in my care."

"Thank you, Father," she said again. Camille cast a long stare toward her daughter and then retreated into the bitter night. Donadieu watched as she disappeared into the blackness.

Would any more misery appear before dawn came? As he waited, his mind wandered again, this time to less fond memories. The fire. His excommunication. The scars they had left on his body and his soul. He thought of the letters he'd sent begging for assistance, and how he hoped aid would come soon.

Before long, a guilty conscience forced him back to work.

CHAPTER 2

One Month Later

Outside the nearby city of Lille, Pierre Laflamme trudged along the fringes of a swamp. Mud clung to his leather shoes and with each step it cemented his feet back to the ground. Adding to his effort was the stubborn old mare he coaxed along with a lead. The horse was enjoying her day splashing through the wetlands and was in no rush to be hurried along by the muddy man.

Pierre savored the rural air; its herbal and mossy aromas charged his lungs. Birds sang from the swamp's trees and insects buzzed overhead. The sweltering summer had long passed, and refreshingly cool autumn winds invigorated him. A long ride awaited, and this knowledge left him determined to enjoy the country stroll, even if the horse and mud slowed it to a crawl.

As he tramped along the water's edge, pulling his feet from the greedy muck, a familiar shrub caught the young doctor's eye. He glanced back to the horse, who was chomping on some swamp grass, and began to collect leaves from the plant. Pierre crushed them in his hands and sniffed the pulp to confirm his identification. Whiffs of sap and a subtle sweetness tickled his nose. *Bog-Myrtle*. To repel insects he rubbed the leaves onto his skin and collected more for later medicinal use.

Pierre was so concentrated on the plant he did not notice his animal companion move. Now, it was Pierre who lingered behind, and the horse had much less difficulty in getting the other to budge. Yanked by the rope wrapped around his wrist, Pierre let out a yelp as he was dragged into the water.

His head emerged from beneath the murky bog, and he began to retch dirty water and pond scum. The acrid flavors of rot forced their way into his startled mouth and caused him to gag. His boots barely reached the soggy ground and when he tried to stand, they dug only deeper into the mud.

Panicking, Pierre grasped for whatever land he could reach, but the peaty earth crumbled in his clutches. Rescue only came when the horse decided she would prefer to leave the swamp after all, and the same tight lead pulled Pierre free. Feigning ignorance about all the noise, the mare looked back as though curious about the commotion.

"If you were my horse, I'd smack you for that," Pierre said. Both parties knew the threat was empty.

His woolen clothes, now completely soaked, weighed heavily upon his thin frame. Their march to circumnavigate the bog took the better part of an hour, thanks to the suction of the ground and a certain stubborn party. When they finally arrived at their starting point, Pierre watched the animal exit the water and smiled when he saw the bounty they'd collected.

Together they wandered toward the shade of a nearby oak, where Pierre fetched the jar he'd left there before the hike began.

Indifferent, the horse began to graze. One by one, the engorged parasites fell from the horse and the doctor quickly scooped them from the ground and placed them gently into his jar. There would be no shortage of leeches on this trip.

Once satisfied there were no more to collect, Pierre led the mare back to her home at the farm, wafts of hay and manure guiding him toward his destination. When they returned, they were greeted by a pair of hearty laughs and Guillaume, the master doctor, beckoning them over.

"What's the point of renting the mare if you're just going to splash around to find them yourself?" his mentor jested. "How many did you get?"

"Twelve."

"Thirteen," Guillaume corrected, pointing to the fat leech dangling off Pierre's arm.

"Ugh," Pierre said. "Must've stuck on when the horse pulled me in." He gave his arm a shake and the plump leech released. He gathered the parasite off the ground and added it to the collection.

"Old Belle here would never do such a thing, isn't that right, girl?" The farmer winked at his beast. "I best get her back to the stable. Anything you folks need before you head off?"

"If you'd allow us," Guillaume said, "we'd appreciate a final walk around the land to gather any herbs we may find. We've been applying our trade heavily of late and our stocks are low. The plants look healthy here."

Pierre handed the lead to the farmer. Guillaume tossed him his coin, adding an extra copper for good measure.

The farmer grinned. "I doubt the lord would shed a tear over some missing weeds. Help yourselves. What are you folks doing out here in the middle of nowhere? Nothing but mud as far as the eye can see."

"We're doctors," Guillaume said. "Just came from Lille. Seems a local village has taken ill, and they've requested help. We were the ones chosen to go; a place called Bastion, I believe."

The farmer's face lost its tan complexion, replaced by the white of heavily milled flour. "There's nothing you can do there," he said. "You'd be wasting your time. Turn back." The farmer clicked his tongue and started Belle toward her stable, shaking his head along the way.

"What do you suppose that was about?" Pierre asked.

Guillaume shrugged. "Doubt we'll ever know."

Pierre watched the disgruntled farmer and his horse walk toward a roughly built shelter and wondered if perhaps the farming life would have suited him. Air that was free from the stench of the city and land overflowing with food. An honest life. Most importantly, no one died if he made a mistake.

"—eye out for nettles, centaury, specifically the root, and rosemary we can dry. Those are what we lack the most, and the walk in the sun should give you a chance to dry off before the ride. Also, grab any wildflowers you find for our masks. Sage especially; it's strong and in season. I've yet to meet a miasma that could penetrate a fistful of sage."

"Pardon?"

Guillaume rolled his eyes. "Walk the grounds and look for herbs."

Pierre nodded sheepishly, and the two parted ways.

When master and apprentice met at the far extent of the property, their pouches looked as though they may burst from their bounty. They eyed each other's satchels, and a friendly competition fired between the two. Walking back through the field, they glued their eyes to the ground and grabbed every herb they could, with some playful shoving for good measure. Once back at their mobile residence, they laid out the plants for inspection.

"You've got a fine eye, kid," Guillaume said. "Everything you've picked is exactly right. Not quite as plentiful as me, mind you, but still impressive."

Pierre could not help but blush at the praise. Guillaume was not shy with compliments when deserved. He crawled in the back to stow the goods in every corner of their covered wagon. Their transportation was a rather standard affair: four wooden wheels pulled by a young mount named Hippocrates. Hippo for short. Every square inch of floor in the cramped abode was spoken for. Boxes, trunks, and tools littered the interior of the wagon. Above, taught wool acted as covering.

"How long until we reach the commune from here, do you think?" the apprentice asked.

"Several hours' ride, at least. The local priest has been sending letters to the college for a quarter year now, but the town's so far out of anybody's way that no doctor has been free to go round. I guess he's given up on the idea that God's going to fix things for him and he's decided to call the professionals." Guillaume snorted at his self-indulgence.

"Did the letter say what ails them?"

"No. Not that a small-town father would be able to tell the difference between summer asthma and plague." He laughed to himself, hardier this time. "With the contagion going unchecked for so long, I'll bet most everybody's dead, or they've worked their way through it. I'll make sure we get paid either way." Guillaume winked at Pierre. "I doubt we'll be there long. Hop in the back and make a few remedies, just in case. I'll steer."

Guillaume hoisted himself up into the driving seat with a few puffs of exertion. Every year, his gut extended slightly farther than it had the last.

The apprentice looked up at his mentor, worry wrinkling his forehead. "I've never made them by myself before. I'm not sure I should."

An impatient sigh blew from the lips of his mentor. "Pierre, you've read the codices on how to make them more times than I've actually done it. I promise I'll look them over when you're done to make sure they're alright, but if you don't start making them now, then when? When you're a doctor out on your own, you'll need to be able to do these things."

The young man looked at his feet for a moment before glancing back at Guillaume, whose attention had already shifted to ensuring his comfort on the hard wagon seat. Pierre opened his mouth to make a rebuttal, but thought better of it and reluctantly slunk to the back of the carriage.

"Ready?" Guillaume called back.

"Ready," Pierre replied.

A crack of the reins, and Hippocrates started to trot. The wagon lurched into motion, the inertia gently shoving Pierre. The vehicle crawled; it was a lot of weight for one horse, but Hippo was strong, and the doctors never pushed him. Together, they plodded along.

The steady pace allowed Pierre to get to work. He recovered his books from their hiding nooks and opened them to relevant pages. Laid out in a semicircle on the floor, he studied the texts until convinced he could replicate their instructions. In a mortar and pestle, he ground together carefully selected bundles of herbs to make poultices and salves. Tonics and teas were brewed on a small, specially mounted stove hanging off the back of the carriage. The range hid a tiny flame fed by softwood twigs and allowed tinctures to gently boil away, or to be used for heating on the coldest of nights. The occasional hole in the road jostled his concoctions, once spilling an unfinished mint oil over the wooden floors. Despite the setback and the now aromatic interior, steady progress was made. When they identified what ailed Bastion, at least one of his medicinal creations would surely be of use.

After hours of work, Pierre sat back, satisfied. He proudly surveyed the pile of vials, tins, and small metal pots full of medicine. With intent to return to the front of the vehicle, he crawled over the oddly stacked boxes and crates of supplies which littered the wagon. The doctors always insisted they would organize better at their next destination but had yet to find the time. Contorting himself to reach the helm, he joined Guillaume and sat in the passenger's seat.

Guillaume looked over and raised an eyebrow. "They good?"

"They should be," Pierre replied. His quiet voice revealed hollow confidence.

"Take the reins; I'll go back and take that second look." Guillaume carefully handed over the worn leather straps to Pierre and started crawling over the seat and into the back. There were a great deal more grunts as Guillaume made the climb.

Vials clinked in the back as each was inspected by a careful eye. Pierre took the opportunity to enjoy the fall scenery along the rural thoroughfare. The autumn colors were at their most brilliant, and the musky-sweet aroma of fallen leaves traveled with the breeze. Late blooming wildflowers dotted the roadside. He tried to identify as many as he could and recall possible medical applications for the ones deemed safe to consume. Occasionally, they passed other farmsteads and shared waves with the farmers or their children as the wagon rode by.

Farther along in the center of the vacant road, an unusual shape piqued Pierre's curiosity. Before he could identify the object, there came a deep sigh from within the wagon. He knew that sigh. He'd done it again. The noise compressed his lungs and shame bowed his head. Pierre waited like a statue for Guillaume to crawl back through the wagon. The cart's suspension bobbed from his effort and gave one last bounce when he plopped himself onto the empty seat.

"Pierre," he said, but the apprentice could not bring himself to meet the man's gaze. "Pierre," Guillaume said again, and this time Pierre shyly tilted his head to meet his mentor's eye. "You've read every book on medicine since Hippocrates himself walked the Earth, probably twice, and that knowledge is essential but…" Guillaume trailed off, and Pierre could see he was working the phrasing over in his mind. "Sometimes you need to close those books in order to apply what you've learned from them."

Guillaume raised a pair of tins used to store balms with a frown. "I saw the recipes you were attempting to create from the opened manuscripts. You were paying too much attention to the pages and not the work. You've swapped ingredients halfway through, confused one recipe with another. The technique was good, but you lost focus and mixed the wrong materials. We can't use these now." He tossed the two containers into the back of the wagon.

Pierre dabbed at a watery eye. "I'm sorry."

Guillaume sighed again, this time pitying rather than chiding. "The execution of the medicine was perfect; you just need to pay more attention to what you're doing and not what you're reading."

"I know," came the soft reply. The two sat in silence as Hippo carried on and the carriage bounded along the road. As always, Guillaume had been merciful in his corrections, but Pierre still wanted to wrap the blanket around his face and hide in the back with the crates.

An uneasy silence hung over the two, broken when Guillaume asked, "What's that ahead?"

Pierre slowly lifted his head from his hands, his gaze following to where Guillaume pointed down the road. He strained to look at the object he had noticed before, squinting to bring it into focus. About twenty wagon lengths ahead of them stood a sign in the center of the road. The curious duo waited for the text to come within reading distance. When it was, they knew they were close.

BEWARE PLAGUE
QUARANTINE AHEAD
TURN BACK

A skull had been painted onto each corner of the sign to convey the message for those who could not read. Farther yet up the road, a second warning sign stood with the same message. This one, however, was enforced.

Soldiers sat on either side of the quarantine checkpoint, each adorned in army blue, muskets at their sides. Near the soldiers, swaying from the sturdy branch of an oak hung the body of a man; a bloody hole the size of a fist had been punched through his chest. Dangling from his neck, there was a sign that read: DESERTER.

"Looks like he caught a base case of lead," Guillaume joked. "Real rough on the lungs, I've heard."

Pierre did not laugh. Thus far his medical career had been tending to colds and minor infections, but a visit to a plague town was in an entirely different league. Insecurity brought about a nervous sweat that slicked his hands.

Steadily, the wagon approached the perimeter guards, and Pierre spotted two more marching along the boundary through the woods.

"Stop," one of the guards commanded, his hand held toward them. "The town of Bastion is under quarantine, so ruled by His Majesty the King. None who enter may leave until the quarantine is lifted."

Guillaume leaned forward to address the man below. "And how will you know when the quarantine is safe to lift?"

"We send a scout every other week," the soldier replied. "Should anyone still be ill, the enforcement remains."

"I guess we have our work cut out for ourselves. Thank you for the warning, but this is why we are here. We're doctors."

The soldier shrugged and stepped aside. "Your funeral. Godspeed, and good luck."

Guillaume thanked him and Pierre snapped the reins. He did not know if it was just his mood and the foreboding circumstances which soured his perception, but the formerly vibrant landscape now appeared to turn to ruin. In the distance, fields lay fallow. Rot covered the land from an unharvested fall crop, and the air tasted stale and uncirculated.

As they continued along their path, fewer and fewer trees retained their colorful foliage, and the dying trunks began to press claustrophobically against the sides of the road. Hippo kicked up clouds of dust from the drought-stricken road. This lingering haze of floating dirt obscured vision for the doctors and tinted the landscape an unpleasant brown. Around them, the sounds of nature quieted. Only the sky refused to bow to the hostile land; radiant sunshine cut through the gloom and led them along their way.

Thirty minutes of riding passed until Guillaume spoke again. "We must be getting close now. Best you should climb in the back and change. We don't want to enter a plague town unprotected until we know what we're dealing with."

Pierre nodded. The shame he carried from his failure now darkened into an all-encompassing dread. They rode into a forsaken place, and he carried his worry like a ball and chain.

Within the confines of the covered wagon, Pierre tossed aside his recently dried wool and readied his costume. Long, black linen robes, skintight leather gloves, a doctor's cane and a dark hood contributed to the look, but they were not what made it special. That was the plague doctor's mask. Pierre held up the piece and stared into the non-reflective eyes. The glass stared back. He shuddered.

When he'd stuffed the beak with the morning's fresh flowers, he fastened the straps to fit snugly around his head. Wearing the mask too long always resulted in headaches, but annoying as the aching was, the diseases they treated would have been far worse.

Pierre emerged from the tented wagon reborn. Again, he took the reins and Guillaume slipped into the back to complete his own transformation.

Hippo dragged them up a small hill, and ahead through the hazy glass eyes, Pierre could see a lone, old, and decrepit barn standing in the middle of a field. The walls of the structure slanted as though it would topple from the force of a sneeze.

Following the barn, the outskirts of a town came into view. *Must be Bastion,* Pierre thought. Its buildings stood in better condition than the barn, but only slightly. Shingles dangled from roofs and shutters hung at odd angles. Mildew grew freely on the facades, and many had shattered windows. At least these homes stood straight. Despite the number of houses, the village appeared deserted.

Kicking up plumes of dust, their carriage rolled into the dozing town. When the commotion of their wagon became audible to the homes, the sleepy village began to wake. Shutters creaked open, and the townsfolk peeked out to have a look at who may dare to roll into their forsaken home.

Then they began to yell.

CHAPTER 3

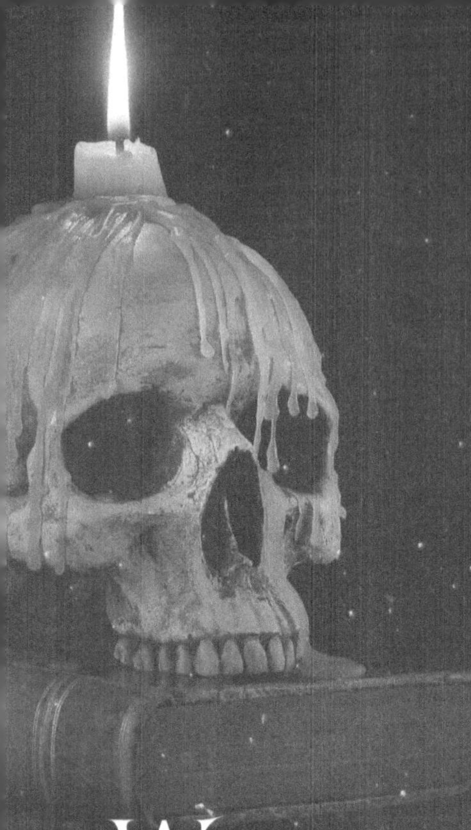

With a splash, Father Donadieu dropped his bucket into the spring on the north side of town. He took care not to completely fill the vessel when he pulled it out; it had been years since he could carry that much weight in a single trip. With a groan from the effort, Donadieu brought his prize up and rested it against his stomach. After a few cautious steps testing the load, he poured a bit of water onto the ground to get the weight right. Satisfied, Donadieu clicked his tongue approvingly and turned to travel the short path back to town.

As the babbling noises of the water faded behind him, he became aware of a new sound: a growing ruckus to the east. Curiosity churned in the priest like the water in his bucket. Disturbances rarely occurred when the sun was preparing to set; folks usually ate dinner before they lost the light.

Despite his awkward load, Donadieu hobbled faster, hoping to find the cause of this unusual commotion. He didn't have to travel long, for when he reached the main street, there came an unfamiliar horse strolling toward him. Towed behind the animal was a covered wagon. It bounced along on the unevenly cobbled street and the clacking noise of the wooden wheels bounced off the walls of the village homes. Seated atop the carriage were two men dressed all in black. Most eccentric of all, their dark outfits came topped with masks that had protruding beaks. Plague doctors.

Relief cascaded over the priest and the tension wound tight in his joints began to uncoil. Donadieu stood straighter than he had in a long time, the bucket now no heavier than an apple in his hands. Finally, help had arrived. The old priest was ready to share the load he bore alone for the ailing town.

A handful of shouting townspeople followed the wagon as its entourage, in its entirety, the spectacle resembled some form of bizarre parade. What Donadieu initially assumed to be a cheering crowd welcoming their medical friends revealed itself instead to be a riotous mob. Rocks and other trash were thrown at the carriage, the debris pattering off its taught covering. Folks cooking dinner opened the shutters to their homes and joined the fun by throwing stale bread and old fruit at the newcomers.

The unruly rabble was a collection of locals known to the priest, members of his congregation. Disappointment stung his chest when he saw the violence his people threatened. The local carpenter waved his hammer menacingly at the doctors. "Begone omens, bring your death elsewhere," he yelled.

"We don't want your kind here," Screamed a teenager following the mob, a cruel smile on his face.

"Leave our families alone," Shouted a woman from a townhouse window, "God will save us from the Withering, and from the likes of you."

Donadieu flushed with embarrassment, set down his bucket, and waved the doctors to where he stood. When the locals saw the physicians being beckoned by the priest, they muttered amongst themselves but continued in their pursuit.

Addressing the crowd, the priest began to yell, "Every night we pray to God that He rid us of our struggles, yet when He sends men to carry out His divine will, you yell at them and curse them away?" The crowd paused in its pursuit and allowed the carriage to break ahead.

"Their ilk brings death; we don't need more strife!" Someone at the back of the gathering yelled. Nods and whispers from the mob carried agreement and they resumed their stomping march.

Undeterred, Donadieu replied. "The bible tells us, 'Carry each other's burdens, and in this way, you will fulfill the laws of Christ.' These men come to help carry our burden. To turn them away would be to turn away the teachings of Christ himself."

The villagers again paused to argue, harsh murmurs rippling through the crowd. Although Donadieu had only lived in Bastion a decade, his opinion carried weight as though he were born there. Slowly, the throng began to quiet, but they were not convinced of the outsiders' benign intentions. Nearly silent, they stood and watched with suspicious eyes.

All the while, the carriage continued to approach until it reached just a few paces short of where Donadieu stood. He swayed nervously as the birds gazed down upon him and he began to sweat in his heavy robes. As happy as he was for their presence, he understood the locals' fear. The doctors' soulless eyes pierced straight through him.

The priest gave the doctors time to alight from their carriage before addressing them, and he was glad he did; much of his anxiety fled when one of the physicians, quite a plump man, struggled comically in his dismount. The fellow grunted and huffed as he wriggled his way to the ground.

The thinner doctor had no such troubles and dropped with something like grace. Together, they approached the priest, the larger doctor first and the taller in tow.

"I'm Guillaume," said the lead, his voice muffled and coarse behind the heavy mask he wore. With a flick of his head, he added, "Thanks for calling off your dogs. This here's Pierre and behind him is Hippo."

Donadieu smiled at all three of his guests individually. "I'm dreadfully embarrassed about all that," the priest said. "We're a small town, just shy of a thousand inhabitants now. They know we need help, but when you finally arrived, it seems fear got the best of them. I'm Father Martine Donadieu, by the way. It's a pleasure to make your acquaintances." He extended his hand.

"Pleasure is ours, and no need to be embarrassed. We get that reaction most anywhere we go." Guillaume said, allowing the priest's hand to linger in the air. It was the second doctor who stepped forth to complete the greeting, but not before the gesture grew awkward.

"Right, well," Donadieu said, "I suppose it's getting later in the day now. I don't think anyone would protest if you stayed in the Auclair house. I can show you the way. It's been empty for over a year, before the Withering came."

"The offer is appreciated, but for the time being, we'll sleep in our carriage. Hippo's a great sentry, and nothing beats your own bed. Even if it's just some straw on a board."

"Of course," Donadieu said. "There's a small courtyard behind the church if you'd like to camp there. Granted, the lot is next to the town cemetery, but I'm not asking you to treat anyone buried there." He smiled but could not tell if his joke made it through their masks. "The church is where we're currently housing most of the ill. It'll put you right next to the action."

"That'd be perfect," Guillaume said.

"Excellent. I'm just heading back there myself after collecting some water." Donadieu picked up his bucket, whose contents sloshed from the motion.

"Pierre," Guillaume cut in. "Grab a sample of the water, please. I want to take a whiff later when free of this mask to make sure it smells clean. Sometimes people become immune to tastes and smells that are omnipresent, no matter how egregious."

The tall doctor walked to the rear of the wagon, his ornamental cane clacking on the ground as he walked. Murmurs from the watching crowd grew as he produced a large satchel from his effects and rifled through its contents.

Curiosity got the best of Donadieu, and he too craned his neck to get a peek at what Pierre was doing. After straining a little too far, he caught the dead eyes of the other doctor's mask staring back. Donadieu withdrew his outstretched neck and awkwardly coughed.

When it was clear nothing exciting was about to happen, the crowd began to lose interest and disperse. A teenager in the group half-heartedly threw an underhanded rock toward the wagon. A stern eye from the priest caused the young man to frown before he also returned to his home.

A sparkle of light brought Donadieu's view back to the tall plague doctor who held an empty vial, its glass shone in the afternoon sun. With movements that looked clumsy to the priest, possibly a result of the protective outfit or maybe a consequence of the man's long limbs, Pierre uncorked his tube, filled it with water from the bucket, and sealed it again before tucking it back into the doctor's pouch.

"After you," Guillaume said, gesturing to Donadieu.

The priest nodded and led the men through town. Pierre with horse and wagon secured the rear. For many years, this place had been Donadieu's home, its charm and familiarity carved its way into his soul. He'd been delighted when he'd first arrived at his posting. The humble stone buildings haphazardly placed around the town never stood greater than two stories high, and their roofs were topped with fired clay shingles to keep the rain and snow at bay. The quaint houses were much smaller than the manor he grew up in, or the enormous cathedrals where he studied, but they had an endearing, homey quality. This feeling was always lost in larger abodes. He had developed a theory from his travels: the smaller the home, the humbler the occupant. Donadieu preferred humble folk.

"If you don't mind, Martine, we'd like to ask you about the disease that afflicts your town," Guillaume said as they followed the priest.

Hearing his first name spoken aloud surprised the priest. As long as he could remember, he had been Father Donadieu. It bemused him so greatly that the slight failed to garner any of the intended indignation. "Of course, I'll help any way I can."

"Pierre," Guillaume said, "write his answers down so we may consult them later if needed. First, we need to understand the mortality of what we're dealing with here. How many of the ill have you buried?"

"None," Donadieu replied.

Although the priest could not see him, a lengthy pause conveyed Guillaume's confusion and annoyance well enough. "You don't bury the dead? No wonder you have such a problem. What do you do with them?"

"We have no dead," Donadieu replied. "People ought to die, but they don't." He turned to the doctors, hoping to be able to judge their reactions through the costumes. Instead, he found they'd stopped some ten paces back, their beaks pointing toward him like accusatory fingers. Sheepishly, he retraced his steps, and Guillaume continued the interrogation.

"You mean to say you wrote a dozen letters to summon physicians and *nobody* has even died? This is a lot of excitement over some food poisoning. You are aware of our fee, correct?"

"I can assure you this is more serious than some bad food. And yes, I have your fee prepared. I've been saving for months."

"We take ten percent up front."

Donadieu grimaced. "I understand." He fumbled through his robes and presented a small pouch of coins to the two. Guillaume accepted the offering and handed it directly to Pierre, who fingered the coins inside and then nodded.

"Excellent!" Guillaume said. "I have a few more questions."

"Anything."

The party resumed their walk.

"Has anyone noticed or complained of any peculiar or foul smells since the onset of the sickness? We need to know if the illness is humoral or miasmic."

"Forgive me," Donadieu said, eager to learn more. "You'll have to explain what that means to a layman like me."

Guillaume chuckled. "Of course, it would be entirely too much to expect a cleric to know of the ways of modern science. Disease is spread one of two ways: Miasma, a sort of devilish cloud often identified by foul smells, or through the unbalancing of the body's natural humors. Sometimes one can compound upon the other."

"Fascinating," Donadieu said. "But to answer your question, there have been no odorous complaints that I'm aware of. As you may guess from the scars across my face, I'm unable to smell."

"That's good," Guillaume replied. "Miasmatic illnesses require both destruction of the miasma's source and balancing of the humors. Humoral diseases are usually much easier to treat. How long has the illness been present in the town and how have you been treating them?"

"It's been four or five months now since the first was stricken with the Withering. That's what we call it; you'll understand why when you see them. As for treating them, I've been giving them somewhere to rest and feeding them soup when they have the strength to eat, dripping water in their mouths when they don't."

"Interesting. Lots of hot and wet foods. You've likely imbalanced their blood. We have leeches, so we should be able to remedy that; with the little buggers, we'll drain the excess fluids out."

Hope sparked within the priest. "It'll be that simple?"

Guillaume shrugged. "It could be."

The party rounded a bend and there, magnificent and tall at the end of the street, stood the church, Bastion's looming monument to God. It was by far the tallest building in the village. Its spire stood highest of all, a cross held aloft for all the region to see. Its old stone walls were weathered but solid as a mountain.

A field wrapped around the east of the church and extended a few hundred feet before it hit more city dwellings. To the west stood a cemetery enclosed by a low wall. A few dozen rows of headstones and crosses jutted haphazardly into the sky, memorials to Bastion's long dead. Before it all was a small garden, but the bitter air had long since killed the flowers, leaving it an ugly stretch of brown. Despite its ailing occupants and its haggard appearance, every time Donadieu looked upon the familiar building, a feeling of home welcomed him.

"That's it ahead," he said. "There's a one-horse stable round the back; you can hitch your companion there."

"Perfect. We'll park the wagon in the lot and get to work. One last thing before we begin: as we left Lille, a messenger asked us to deliver some letters. None have dared approach the borders of the quarantine, and I think rightly so; the guards looked quite unforgiving. The letters had been accumulating for quite some time, so there seems to be a reasonable stack. Pierre, get the notes for the man. I'm sure he'll help us deliver them."

Donadieu watched as the tall doctor wrapped around the back of the wagon and then emerged shortly after with a hefty pile of papers. Pierre handed them to the priest, trading him for the bucket he still carried.

"Thank you," Donadieu said, both happy for the letters and the relief from the heavy weight. "I'm sure some people have been waiting for these for a long time. I'll see them delivered tonight."

"Thank *you*," Guillaume replied. "We'll take the bucket inside, make sure everyone gets a drink. Now if you'll excuse us, we'll do some initial investigations tonight and continue in the morn." Without waiting for a response, he turned toward the church.

Against his better judgment, Donadieu found himself compelled to know more about his unlikely associates. "If I may be so bold, Doctor. Is it safe of me to assume you do not consider yourself a man of God?"

Guillaume answered without turning back, his voice carrying the assurance of someone who'd waited a great deal of time to answer a question they'd thought long and hard about. "I've spent my life cleaning up the plagues that God has sicced upon the earth. I'll be damned before I worship Him for it."

Donadieu frowned, certain that working with a man who defied their very creator would pose challenges. "And you, Pierre?" he asked, hopeful he could find a connection with at least one of the men.

The tall doctor swiveled his head between Guillaume and Donadieu before answering the priest. His voice took Donadieu by surprise on account of its youthful character. "My grandfather died at the St. Bartholomew's Day Massacre."

Embarrassment heated the priest. Although he himself had not been present, the religiously justified executions at the hand of his Catholic peers twisted his gut with shame.

"Senseless killings!" Donadieu called after Pierre turned to follow Guillaume.

The priest shook his head and muttered to himself as he looked at the stack of letters in his hand. *You knew you shouldn't have asked. You just had to poke, you stubborn old mule.*

With the doctors now tending to their task, Donadieu set off to complete his own. A drizzle began to patter across the town, but he didn't mind. He enjoyed the soothing nature of rain, and the land needed some relief from the recent drought. Bastion had only received a handful of such showers all summer; this light rain would not cure the parched land, but it would help. Perhaps these doctors were a good omen.

He wandered about the streets and delivered the mail house-by-house. Donadieu enjoyed the brief social interactions as he handed over the letters, pleasantries largely absent since the Withering struck town. The small talk rejuvenated him in ways he had not thought possible, but the merriment he gained from his brief visits fled entirely between them. The roads of Bastion, once lively and full of life, remained empty. This surreal vacancy of such a public place stood the priest's hairs on end.

Donadieu had only delivered half the stack of letters before the sun revoked its light; in its stead rose a waxing crescent moon. The thin sliver of celestial light was not enough to read the names of the letters' intended recipients. He resolved to resume in the morning.

He tucked the remaining papers into the interior of his robes and set off toward the steeple of his church. Halfway across town, the pious monument jutted high above the modest residential homes. It should have been an easy five-minute stroll, but while on the way, he found his feet unexpectedly anchored to the ground.

A malevolence hung in the surrounding air, but as to its source, he could not tell. Suspiciously, he eyed his uncooperative feet and then his surroundings. He was standing outside the house of Thomas the potter. A parishioner, he noted, who hadn't been to confession in almost a month.

Once refreshing, the rain began to chill him through to his core. The droplets stung like ice when a breeze blew across him. Open shutters battered against the house in the wind, curtains danced and, when the breeze blew just right, revealed glimpses into the inky black interior. Many of Bastion's homes had deteriorated quickly after the Withering struck its inhabitants, but this one oozed a tainted aura from every crack in the masonry.

The chains binding his legs released when he accepted that he must visit the home. He swallowed hard and timidly approached, his right hand slipping into his pocket to fiddle with his rosary beads for comfort. Two sharp knocks from his bony knuckles sent echoes cascading through the house. No response.

In Donadieu's grasp, the handle felt cold as death. It gave no resistance as he pushed, and the unlatched wooden door creaked slowly open. A pittance of light lazily crept into the room and a chorus of buzzing assaulted the priest's ears. He swatted the air as an army of flies animated from the commotion.

Donadieu's throat burned as two unwelcome insects were caught in the draft of a shocked inhale. He hacked for minutes to dislodge the invaders, covering his mouth all the while to prevent further molestation. By the time he recovered, most of the flies had escaped into the night.

When the moonlight revealed what had attracted the insects, he became thankful for his lack of smell. Before him, draped over a small table in the center of the room, was the potter. Dark puddles of dried blood coated the floor, and splatter from arterial spray painted the walls. Nearby to the corpse, a carving knife. Even though the body had started to rot, brutal and uneven slashes across the man's forearms made it clear the death was self-inflicted.

Instinctively, the priest signed the cross and muttered prayers as he looked over the consequences of the mortal sin. When the shock of his discovery had abated, Donadieu stepped to the table and shooed the remaining flies by sweeping a hand above the corpse. He picked up the instrument of death and studied the blade. A tingle crawled up his spine when he discovered the knife's edge was chipped and dull. Either the man had butchered himself in deathly silence, or the neighbors heard him scream while he carved and had refused to intervene. Donadieu's stomach turned at the thought of either scenario.

Concerns for the rest of the potter's family—a wife and two boys, if Donadieu recalled correctly—caused him to scan his surroundings. The abode was modest and adorned with only the essentials. An unlit hearth indented the wall to his left. Plates and bowls, the potter's handiwork, remained scattered about. On the far side of the house, he was able to make out a pair of doors, undoubtedly connections to the home's bedchambers.

Donadieu pushed deeper into the darkness, willing himself to overcome his instinctual desire to flee. His shoe squeaked when he pulled it free from the sticky floor, the noise rippling gooseflesh across his skin.

Only one of the bedroom doors was already open, so he made that his first stop. He peered into the room and a void peered back. Again, he fought an urge to run, wishing desperately to return to the cold and pale moonlight. Instead, he stepped gingerly into the darkness. Arms outstretched, the priest fumbled around the edge of the space, hoping to find what must be a densely curtained window. He knew the window existed, for he could hear the tapping of the rain against the pane.

As he made his way through the gloom, he noticed the sound of pathetic lungs whispering gasps of air beside him.

The revelation paralyzed the priest, terrified by whatever may have been watching him in the darkness. All at once, the shock relented, and he tore through the room in a more frantic search for the window. His fingers slid against the cool stone walls until a sharp object punctured his leading finger; Donadieu yelped from the pain. A splinter from the windowsill had pierced him.

He withdrew his injured hand like a wounded paw and pulled back the curtains with the other. Moonlight stumbled into the room as though it were unsure what it should touch and what would be best left in darkness.

Donadieu spun with the light, desperate to spot the creature with which he shared the room. When he saw what had made the noise, Donadieu sighed in indignation, annoyed with himself over his baseless panic. The breathing came from the two young boys, both sleeping in a shared bed. Apart from their short, raspy breaths, the children's emaciated bodies lay unmoving, an unmistakable symptom of the Withering. Gently shaking their shoulders elicited no response and confirmed the priest's fear. He sighed and said a quick prayer above them, but did not hold much hope for a result. Prayers had not yet been effective in turning back this evil.

With little else to be done for the children, Donadieu continued on to the house's last room to check on the potter's wife. He opened the door and found the moonlight already comfortable inside.

Immediately, he wished the light had not been so bold.

The bedroom's sole occupant lay unmoving. Donadieu knew the comatose woman, Louise. When he beheld her, the air caught in his throat. Her haggard body resembled a mummy dragged from the muck of a distant and forgotten swamp. Dry as leather, her skin stretched around her limbs. The hair upon her head looked rough as straw and wildly unkempt, and patches of her scalp were entirely devoid of any at all. Fingernails resembling claws protruded from her fingertips long enough to be extra digits. Eyeless sockets epitomized gateways to a horrific, unknown plane, a route happily traversed by the flies which crawled upon her body. A splotchy purple bruise wrapped around her neck, seemingly tattooed into the leathery skin. Even the longest residents of the church's medical ward had not deteriorated to such a horrendous extent.

Her vibrant yellow nightgown served to accentuate her body's decrepit condition. It remained brilliant in even the pale moonlight, its vibrancy drawing attention to her decay.

It was not her horrific appearance, however, which robbed Donadieu of his breath. It was the rhythmic motions of Louise's own chest. Her sternum rose and fell, accompanied by a terrible gurgling with every strained breath.

Overcome by revulsion and an overpowering sensation that he did not belong, Donadieu retreated from the room. When clear of her door, he turned and sprang toward the street as quickly as his legs would allow. Only when he emerged into the spitting rain did he release the air from his bursting lungs, unaware he had been holding his breath. The cold rushed into his chest as he breathed deeply, hands on his knees. He could not shake the feeling of a man having just narrowly escaped being buried alive.

The priest again glanced at the house, half-expecting to see a horrific face staring back through the open windows. The dancing curtains revealed nothing but darkness.

With quivering legs, Donadieu resumed his trek to the church and traversed the town in record time. He thought as he walked of the state of that poor woman, and the fates of all those afflicted. Upon arriving at his home, he pushed open the doors and was greeted by a cacophony of wheezing and coughing.

Among the ill, Donadieu noticed medical instruments lying scattered about. The metal devices were unfamiliar to the priest, but he assumed they had been left with purpose and was in no mood to investigate. The absence of the doctors meant they had retired, and he decided to do the same. He had no stomach for dinner that night.

Weaving through the church, the priest stole himself away to the modest back room where his bed and a few personal effects were stored. To distract himself, he removed the remaining letters from his robe. Studying the names of those to whom he still had to deliver, he plotted a delivery route for the following day. Donadieu raised an eyebrow when he read the name on the penultimate letter. It was addressed to him. The letter was from the bishop.

Hopeful, Donadieu tore into the letter. For weeks he had sent messages with the soldiers every time they came to check upon the town. Each text begged the clergy to send a relic to Bastion. The latent holy power contained within the religious artifacts was said to perform miracles that were impossible through prayer alone.

As he read through the letter, his hope transformed to scorn, and he pressed his eyes shut; there would be no relic. Any hope of a recovery for the ailing town now lay on the shoulders of the doctors alone.

Tomorrow he would send the groundskeeper to collect the body of the potter and arrange to bring Louise and the kids under his care. For now, all Donadieu could do was kneel and bow his head.

"Lord, I pray tonight, as I do most every night, for Your blessing and the protection of Bastion and its people. I see Your hand behind the doctors who arrived today, and I pray You guide them as they set about their purpose. I know they are not dutiful to You, as they ought to be, but they seek to rejuvenate their fellow man whom You so lovingly created. Let their medicines work quickly and their care restore the spirits of the ill. This I pray in Your name. Amen."

CHAPTER 4

"Senseless killings!" the priest called from behind.

Pierre did his best to scrub the religious inquiry from his mind and set about his work. The question of faith came unexpectedly and unwanted. The not-too-distant Wars of Religion remained a tender spot in the nation's collective psyche. He hoped the father would spend most of the evening delivering letters, so they may be left to work unbothered by Catholic preachings.

After he parked his wagon in the field and secured Hippo in the stable, Pierre moved with a hasty stride toward the main entrance of the church after Guillaume, who had already wandered inside. On his way, and with nothing left to distract, his mind was fixated on their mission within Bastion.

All at once, the gravity of his responsibility pulled him to a stop and the fear of failure sent his mind spinning. Guilt and embarrassment consumed him as he imagined the consequences of another of his novice mistakes. The anxiety left him swaying with indecision. Only when Guillaume called could Pierre continue, his action more a response to the summons than a gathering of courage.

As soon as he entered, Pierre was overcome by the place. Grand tapestries depicting the piety and purity of saints hung from the rafters, seeming to mock the over two dozen infirm who lay scattered on the pews below. The ill sputtered and coughed into the air, wheezing as they breathed. Pierre inhaled deeply in response, proving to himself he was not subject to whatever this plague may be. The powerful scents of botanicals and herbs rushed through his nose, stinging his nostrils with their potency.

Pointing his beak as he looked around the place, he wondered how long he and Guillaume would remain. The church was old and, despite its height, smaller than its facade suggested.

A decorative rug stretched along the aisle that ran through the building, now so dirty that only faint splotches of its natural color remained. The pews on either side of the aisle reached to the walls, and beside him the building's ornate confessional booth drew his attention. The cabinet's brilliant red curtains dangled open, beckoning him to step inside.

Central to it all stood a podium from where the priest gave his sermons, but behind the modest pulpit loomed an ornate window easily ten feet high. The stained-glass mural depicted a crucified Jesus, and Pierre couldn't help but stare. He shuddered when a villager's hacking cough broke his concentration.

"Are you done sightseeing?" his mentor jested from across the room. "We've got work to do. Let's start observations, you take notes. We'll spend the evening trying to identify any clues to the cause of the malady, and tomorrow we'll begin the treatment. Between the texts in the wagon and those stored in your head, we should be able to figure out something." The acknowledgement gave Pierre a needed boost. No one could deny he was well read.

Without waiting for a response, Guillaume approached the most densely populated section of pews; unrelated by age or profession, these victims would provide an excellent sample.

Guillaume dictated as he assessed the patients. Pierre, ever astute, took exemplary notes.

"No boils nor pustules present on the bodies, unlikely to be bubonic," Guillaume began, poking a comatose patient with his cane. "Only visible symptoms are protruding bones and tight skin resulting from lack of sufficient nutrition." He placed his wrist upon the forehead of a sleeping child. "Temperature is normal. Flesh is flush. Circulation regular. Haggard breathing is the only identifiable sign of distress."

A comforting familiarity overtook Pierre as he scribed for the master physician. No judgments were forced upon him and no life-or-death decisions to make, only the simple task of recording dictation.

"Are you Death?" rose a quiet voice from within the church. The doctors turned to a sickly child peering above a distant pew.

"Quite the opposite," Guillaume laughed. "We're doctors."

The child looked confused by the response, but a coughing fit overtook him and he returned to his blankets.

Guillaume continued, unbothered by the interruption. "I suspect the humors here to be quite unbalanced, as predicted. I might guess too much yellow bile, and perhaps extra blood, is to blame for the malady which attacks this town. A combination of the region's drought and excessive soup consumption has skewed their balance too hot. This would explain the cough. There have been no reports of miasmatic odors, so the risk of widespread contagion seems low. The populace here is starved for cold. Fortunately, we have plenty of mint and the winter approaches. Tomorrow we will reduce the bad blood of the ill and dose with foods to reset the balance. I predict the recovery will be swift, inevitable really with the coming winter. This should be an easy one."

Pierre smiled underneath his mask as he copied the analysis. Pride swelled in his chest at the competence of his mentor, and he aspired to one day be so proficient. It took but half a day since their arrival and Guillaume had already prepared a remedy in his mind.

"Let's lay out the tools for tomorrow and hit the hay," Guillaume said. "We'll run a few separate tests until we can determine exactly what ails these people, just in case. Any thoughts, Pierre?"

Pierre blushed beneath his mask at the notion he may accent Guillaume's expertise. "Nothing to add. I'll follow your lead."

Together, they pulled tools from their satchels and arrayed them neatly on unoccupied rows. Jars of tonics and balms sat beside menacing hooks, bone saws, and knives, all with well-worn handles. The dried blood and rust on the old steel gave Pierre a glimpse into the past of each object, and he secretly hoped the equipment would recall their past victories and aid in guiding his hand when it came his time to wield them. He prayed that time would not be soon.

As they finished their preparations and headed to the door, Pierre remembered the bucket he had taken from the priest and wished to apply the inspiration gained from Guillaume. "You go ahead. I'll give the water to anyone who will take it and meet you in the wagon. I'll make sure it's cold, even I can't mess that up."

"Don't be so hard on yourself," Guillaume said. "You're on the cusp of becoming the finest doctor I know. Just need some practice. I'll lay out some food for when you arrive." He rested a hand on Pierre's shoulder, squeezed, and exited out the church's side door.

Pierre watched the door close behind him. Outside of casual study and observation, this was the first time he'd witnessed his mentor work in earnest. Watching the man's mastery of the medicinal arts infused him with conviction. Tomorrow, they would begin to cure this poor town and, days later, ride off as heroes. He could already taste the sweetness of their coming victory.

Elated with his indulgent predictions, Pierre turned to face those for whom he would care. He surveyed the empty church, and his smile faded behind his mask.

With Guillaume at work, the walls had radiated an aura of hope and healing. Now alone, they seeped despair to match the wheezing of the infirm. The air spun him with imaginary gusts, and his muscles threatened to cramp when he tried to move. The panic of responsibility began to overtake him. He steadied himself on a pew, breathing slowly until he regained his composure. The water must be doled. The sooner he began, the sooner he could leave.

Pierre hoisted the bucket and got to work. Some of the ill lay unconscious, others slept, but a good many lay awake, their eyes crawling over him as he worked. With an unwieldy ladle, he scooped the water into the mouths of all those who retained the ability to drink, even if they could not speak, and they gulped down the refreshment. For those who could not indulge, he placed sparse drops of water on their lips, hydrating even the most excessively inflicted. The task took only a handful of minutes to complete, but to Pierre, it seemed like hours. When he finished, he returned the ladle to the bucket and headed straight for the door.

The cool day had turned into a frigid night, and a light rain pattered across the field. He breathed deeply and removed his mask before staring up into the cloudy sky. His hair was damp with sweat, and a biting wind wormed across his scalp. He rubbed his hands through his hair as he followed the glow of their wagon.

There was no fanfare to the doctors' nightly ritual. They shared a meal of biscuits, cheese, dried meat, and each a cup of wine. They indulged in conversation about the day to come and the day that had passed. As the discomfort from his time in the church faded,

Pierre's eyelids grew heavy. They readied a mountain of blankets and exchanged a simple, "Goodnight," before laying down their heads to rest.

Pierre awoke with a start, panting into the crisp morning air. Plumes of vapor spewed from his mouth. The surrounding field brought the aroma of frost and dying leaves, which mixed with their stove's faint wisps of smoke. He squinted as he looked toward the opening of his home; the sun's glow crept above the horizon, announcing its pending arrival. *Too early,* Pierre thought. He closed his eyes and settled back into his bed. Outside the wagon, something rustled the frosty grass.

Just an animal, he tried to assure himself, but his heartbeat quickened all the same. As the noise grew louder, a vise began to compress his chest and his breathing grew shallow. He'd heard tales of doctors being chased from towns by pitchforks and torches, their presence misunderstood by the uninformed masses and their masks confused with the source of disease, rather than the cure. Their reception the previous day gave weight to such claims.

Closer and closer, the shambling came. With his eyes wide and his motion slow, Pierre crawled from his bed to peer out at the noise before any such siege could be laid.

Slowly raising his head above the seat at the front of the wagon, he spied out on the lawn toward the church. He saw nothing but frost-coated grass. Behind him, Guillaume snored.

Just the wind, Pierre thought and laid back down to rest. Despite his intention to sleep, he could not bring himself to close his eyes. He stared at the wagon's ceiling and listened carefully for the noise to return.

He did not wait long before he heard it again. Louder now, closer. It seemed to stir directly beside him, only separated by the wagon's woolen walls. It sounded like the buzzing of insects, or *whispers?* He could not discern.

The vice around Pierre began to crush his ribs and his limbs petrified under the blankets; he dared not stir. Despite his best efforts to the contrary, a whimper escaped his lips. The pathetic noise floated lazily in the air. Although hardly above a whisper, to Pierre, it felt the loudest noise he'd ever made. He waited, frozen in fear, for his utterance to rally the unknown attacker and begin his demise.

To his great surprise, the sound vanished. Pierre heard no retreat from whatever lingered outside the wagon, but the noise did not return.

After many more minutes of cautious breathing, the vice released its captive, and Pierre exhaled a pressurized sigh. His fluttering heart slowed, and he regained the function of his limbs, all while unsure if he'd truly heard anything at all. To dismiss his fright, he turned his mind to the day ahead and fantasized about all those he would help, and how he and Guillaume would save the day. Shortly thereafter, the church steeple began to ring.

The commanding vibrations from the bell shook the carriage, their proximity made the gongs deafening. Guillaume jumped up beside him and began to curse and yell and plug his ears. When at last the bell finished its auditory assault, ten rings in all, the doctors stretched and blinked lazily at each other.

"Sleep well?" Guillaume asked.

"I did," Pierre lied, knowing the puffy bags beneath his eyes would give his secret away.

Guillaume pretended not to notice and retrieved some food to be their breakfast. Salty bread appeared from a basket, and he poured them each a cup of watered-down wine. "Eat up," he said. "We have much work to do today."

Pierre greedily accepted the offering. He ripped the stale loaf and dipped it into his wine to soften. As he ate, he could not stop his mind from reliving the panicked frenzy that had happened mere minutes before. He became so lost in thought as he chewed that, before he knew it, he found himself following his mentor into the church, fully dressed in his protective clothes.

Guillaume pushed the side door open with authority and strode into the church. Pierre scampered behind. Already awake and walking through the pews, Donadieu was hydrating the ill with the remaining contents of the bucket.

The priest smiled at the doctors when they entered. It was an honest smile and, despite their awkward encounter the day before, Pierre genuinely felt welcomed. With its caretaker present, the church looked whole. Donadieu set down his bucket and came to greet the doctors. Guillaume maneuvered around the priest and inspected their tools.

"Well," Donadieu said, turning to Pierre. "Anything I can help you with?"

"I think we'll be alright," Pierre replied quietly from behind his mask.

Donadieu nodded thoughtfully. "Just to sate my curiosity, can you explain to me what you plan to do here today?"

"As Guillaume mentioned yesterday, we are operating under the assumption their humors are imbalanced, likely skewing too hot and dry, but we aren't certain. In unknown cases such as this, we split the infected into groups and treat each section differently to see which medicine yields the best results. Most will be left entirely alone for a control."

"How wondrously thorough," the priest replied. "Is this standard for all treatments, the Black Death, for example?"

Pierre worried the conversation may drag on longer than he would like, but the priest was their benefactor, and he wished to remain professional. "Such experiments are not needed for known diseases like bubonic plague. Onions help to correct the humors, and the smell drives away the miasma. Not unlike the incense here in the church, actually."

"So that pungent smoke may have a use after all," Donadieu said, stroking the white stubble on his chin. "And for these tests, what do the treatments entail?"

"We'll feed them cold foods such as mint, cabbage, or lettuce." Pierre peered over Donadieu's shoulder at Guillaume, who stood with his arms crossed, looking his way.

"Fascinating. Would you use leeches for treatments such as this?"

Increasing the speed at which he spoke, Pierre replied. "Not always, but in this case, almost certainly. If we suspect one has too much blood and not enough black bile, we use leeches to drain the excess, leaving room for the lacking."

Donadieu's eyes turned to the heavens as though lost in thought. "The miracles of modern medicine," he said while shaking his head.

Guillaume walked past the two, intentionally brushing against them both as he made his way back to the wagon.

"Well," Donadieu said, "I feel I may be in the way if I linger while you work. Perhaps I'll finish delivering the letters I didn't get to last night. Don't hesitate to ask if you need anything."

"Your hospitality is appreciated, Father," Pierre replied, relieved he might finally begin.

The priest briefly disappeared into his room and returned with the stack of papers. "One last thing before I'm off."

Pierre's eyes rolled behind their lenses.

"I checked in on one of my parishioners last night, and she

is…entirely unwell. Perhaps later in the afternoon, would you be available to make a house call with me to take a look?"

The thought of practicing alone terrified Pierre. "I'll check with Guillaume," he stammered out.

The priest looked disappointed. "Very well. Please let me know when you two have time. May God bless your efforts today. I'll see you later." Donadieu smiled and left through the front entrance of the church. Guillaume returned not a moment later.

"He's gone then?"

"Yes, to deliver the rest of the letters."

"Good." He handed an armful of supplies to Pierre. "I've brought some chalk and the canes. Mark the groups and we'll each take one to start. You try cold foods, I'll take dry? We'll use the leeches last."

Pierre received the supplies. "I'd be a fool to argue."

Bending over, Pierre chalked the floor as instructed. Designations in place, he and Guillaume each approached a patient. Pierre's ward was a gaunt old man with a scraggly beard that stretched past his chest. The man breathed slowly, and his eyelids pressed together. Concerned the elder may lash out at being woken, Pierre raised his cane like a fencing sword. With a few cautious jabs, he poked at the wrinkled ribs. When the man did not stir, Pierre breathed easy, knowing he would not have to work on a conscious patient; he hated working on people who watched.

The apprentice began by examining the man's skin, pushing away tattered clothes with his cane. He searched for any signs of pustules, bubo, rashes, or any other outward signs of disease. As was the case yesterday, he found nothing. A coarse gasp erupted from the old man, and Pierre jumped as though lightning had struck beside him. Guillaume chuckled only a few steps away. The apprentice eyed his sleeping ward suspiciously. Another quick jab proved he remained unconscious.

It surprised Pierre that, despite such a profound humoral imbalance to cause a coma, there were no physical manifestations on the body. The results of their experiment should prove to be most interesting.

He uncapped a small jar of mint jelly and took a dollop upon his finger. With a delicate touch, he smeared the cooling jam across the gums of the sleeping man, wary that he may bite, as a fingerless doctor once warned him.

He then repeated this test upon a young boy and a middle-aged woman. The woman, being conscious, was able to willingly partake in a greater quantity of jelly. Much better for their study.

Guillaume and Pierre continued to apply humoral remedies as ordained by the chalked markings. Foods that balance hot, cold, dry, and wet were fed to the ill; they need only wait to see which remedy performed the best.

The final test required Pierre to collect the leeches. They needed to ease their wards from the burden of excess blood. He retrieved the heavy ceramic jug from the wagon, the dense contents pulling his hands low. When he reentered the church, his mind wandered back to the mystery of his morning disturbance. He could not shake the feeling of imminent danger he'd experienced, despite his best attempts at dismissing the ordeal. Distracted by the memory, he misjudged his step and slammed his foot into the corner of a pew.

Pain bolted up his toe and arched through his leg as the leech jar flew from his fingers, its glazed exterior refusing to be recaptured by his grasping fingertips. A shattering crash echoed through the church, as did a thud from Pierre's own collapse. The impact pressed the air from his lungs and, as he looked up, the parasites writhed on the wooden boards before him.

"Pierre," Guillaume said, concern softening his voice. Pierre would not hear the rest. Thoughts of ceaseless blunders caused by utter incompetence consumed him. The crushing weight of his constant failures compelled a retreat from the scene of his latest atrocity. "Pierre!" Guillaume called after him, but he was already stumbling out the door.

Already obstructed by the mask, his vision further clouded from the tears welling in his eyes. The word *useless* echoed around the walls of his skull. Lost in a world of despair, Pierre wandered aimlessly through the nearly vacant town. When people passed, they jeered or threatened him while gawking at his mask; one even threw rotten produce at him, missing his face by mere inches. Gutted and depressed, he tucked himself down a small alleyway between a pair of battered houses. He found a tipped over barrel upon which he sat and began to sulk.

His head bowed, and he caught it in his gloved hands, his beak nestled between forearms. Now alone, he allowed his woes to overtake him; his breathing shortened to spasmodic contractions and a whimper left with each exhale. He was roused from his misery only when a delicate voice carried from farther up the alley.

"Are you alright?"

The voice startled him and all but replaced his sorrow with surprise. Gazing down the alley, he saw the small creature which had made the noise. It was a child, no older than ten. Her honey-brown eyes looked ancient from worry, but her hair still sparkled with the temporary blonde of youth. The blue and white dress she wore was covered with an assortment of garish patches.

"What's your name?" Pierre asked, raising his voice an octave above his natural tone.

"I'm Marianne," the girl replied proudly. "Are you a monster?"

"What? Oh, the mask." Slowly, to ensure he would not be perceived as a threat, Pierre slid the mask from his face. "Just a regular human. See?"

Marianne furled her eyebrows. "Why are your eyes all red? Are you sure you're not a monster?"

"I've been having a little cry," Pierre said, offering a sniffle as proof.

Marianne stomped her foot and squinted at him with accusatory eyes. "Daddy told me grown-ups don't cry. Are you lying to me?"

He feigned a smile at the child. "Sometimes we just can't help it, and I'm only *just* a grown-up."

Marianne took her time to study Pierre before her expression softened, and her voice lost its confrontational skew. "What'cha crying about?"

The question took Pierre off-guard, but he supposed the answer was simple enough. "I'm not very good at my job."

The girl climbed the barrel beside him. At first, she struggled, and Pierre attempted to help her up, but she rebuked his help by muttering, "I can do it myself." He tried not to laugh at her awkward flailing, but credit due, she made it up.

"I'm bad at lots of things too," the girl said, turning to face him. "But Momma said as long as you keep trying, you never get worse, and it's true! I've never gotten worse at anything that I've kept trying."

Pierre ran a hand through his sweaty hair and met the girl's eyes. "You have a very smart mother, you know that? You should listen to her."

Marianne stopped looking at Pierre and turned her gaze to her dangling feet. "Momma doesn't talk anymore. All she does is lie in bed. I cry about it. I think Pappa cries about it, too, but he also pretends he doesn't."

A stake of sorrow pierced Pierre's heart. He wiped at his eyes and the surging need to help this young girl left him dumbfounded. "That's why I came here. I'm supposed to help make people feel better."

Her eyes grew wide, and a broad smile revealed a missing front tooth. "You can help my mommy?"

"I'm certainly going to try."

She turned and hugged Pierre, all her strength amounting to a gentle squeeze, but it was exactly what he needed.

"Pierre, I presume," carried a familiar voice down the side street as its owner approached. "And little Marianne, what a pleasant surprise."

"I'm not little," Marianne protested. "I'm nine!"

"My apologies," the approaching priest said. "I did not mean to offend the young lady."

"Hey, Mister Bird," she said, "did you know that Father Donadieu got his scars from a dragon?"

Donadieu chuckled. "His name is Pierre, Marianne. And yes, it's true, a great dragon attacked a monastery once when I was younger, but I fended him off." The old priest mimed fighting invisible foes with an imaginary sword.

The girl giggled delightedly beside Pierre, kicking her feet into the barrel and clapping for the show. Pierre, having nearly recovered from his episode, grinned ear-to-ear despite himself.

Donadieu stood up straight and reached around to brace his lower back. "Those adventurous days are behind me now, I'm afraid. What are you two doing out here, anyway?"

Pierre stood and offered a hand to help Marriane down from the barrel, but she knocked it away and jumped down. "I came to find you, Father," Pierre said. "I'm ready for the house call. I can't promise anything, but I'll see what I can do."

"Marvelous!" Donadieu said. "Marianne, it's probably best you go home to your papa now. The good doctor and I have some work to attend to."

The child tilted her head and looked at Pierre, who caught her gaze while he affixed his mask. She grinned. "You're gonna do great."

CHAPTER 5

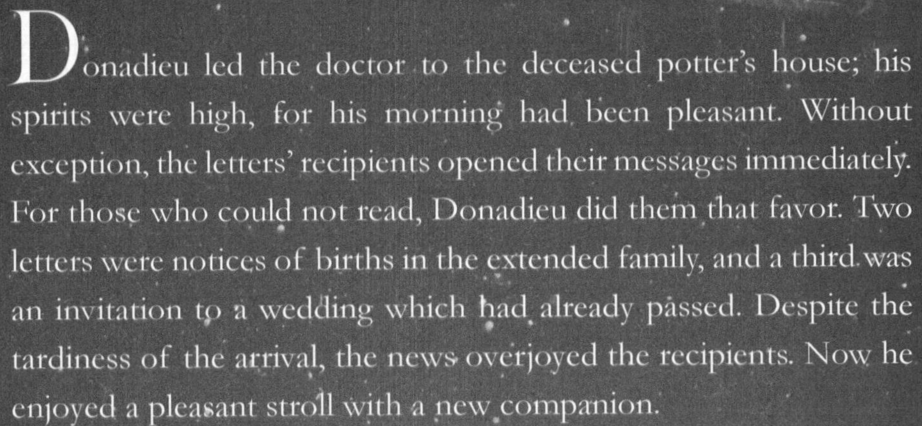

Donadieu led the doctor to the deceased potter's house; his spirits were high, for his morning had been pleasant. Without exception, the letters' recipients opened their messages immediately. For those who could not read, Donadieu did them that favor. Two letters were notices of births in the extended family, and a third was an invitation to a wedding which had already passed. Despite the tardiness of the arrival, the news overjoyed the recipients. Now he enjoyed a pleasant stroll with a new companion.

Only the knowledge of their destination sullied the priest's mood. Like a creeping shadow growing longer in the evening, the closer they got to the house, the more somber he grew. His own body staged a protest against the destination by stiffening his knees, as though it were a crew in mutiny against their deranged captain's course.

Doing his best to ignore this rebellion, Donadieu chatted with Pierre as they sauntered along.

"So, have you fought many dragons, then?" Pierre asked.

The quip put a smile on the priest's face and helped to ease some of his dread. "Just the one, actually. And between you and me, it was more of a building than a dragon."

"How did it happen?" Pierre asked. "The fire, did you get trapped inside? What kind of building was it?"

"The flammable kind," Donadieu replied with a wink, and then he steered the conversation from the uncomfortable topic. "How are you enjoying your stay in our little town?"

Farther up the street, several people made obscene gestures toward the doctor. If Pierre saw, he pretended not to.

"I must admit the reception has been…lukewarm," he said at last.

Embarrassed by his people, Donadieu decided it would be best to drop that subject too. "Just around this corner now," he said and led them with his outstretched arm.

They rounded the bend, and a new street opened before them. On the old roads stood a man in dirty clothes, heaving to pull a handcart behind him, its contents covered by a thin dusty sheet.

"Ah," Donadieu said, "Pierre, meet Pascal. He's our groundskeeper at the church. He maintains the garden and digs the graves."

"Pleasure." Pierre smiled from habit, but Pascal could not have seen behind his mask.

Donadieu gestured toward the sheet. "That's him then?"

"Aye." The grubby man cast an expectant eye at Donadieu. The priest retrieved a pair of copper coins from within his robes and placed them into Pascal's waiting hand, who snatched them back as soon as the coins clinked.

"You didn't go into the back room, did you?" Donadieu asked.

"You told me not to," Pascal replied and began to haul his cart away.

Donadieu grimaced at the reply.

Pierre turned to the priest. "I thought you said no one died from the disease?"

Donadieu hesitated briefly. "This was something different. Shall we go inside and check on the patients?"

"Lead the way."

The priest approached the building, and all the goodwill and cheer he banked throughout the morning was spent as he pushed on the cast iron handle. Hinges creaked as it swung open, and the paws of rats skittered across the floor, fleeing to escape the light. As he entered the late Thomas's house, the priest was grateful to be exploring the building in daylight and with company. Stepping aside to allow Pierre to view the macabre scene, he said, "This was the 'something different.'"

Donadieu allowed Pierre time to digest the scene before proceeding. A faint, "After you," floated from behind the doctor's mask.

The heat dissipated immediately upon entry into the rustic house, an eerie cool replacing it. All was as Donadieu remembered from his last visit, with the exception of the missing potter, who was now in the back of Pascal's cart.

"Let's start with the children," he suggested. "They are in better health. Follow me; it's the door on the right." Donadieu led the way through the house and around the blood before standing beside the entrance to the children's chamber. The room remained illuminated by the window he'd opened the night before.

Like those in the church, there lay two shriveled bodies gasping for air. Flies congregated around the loins of the children who appeared to have soiled themselves ages ago. Donadieu eyed Pierre's mask. Medical applications or not, he understood why doctors wished to avoid smelling their patients, even if no odors could bother him. Pierre approached the fetid children and prodded them with his cane. The beaked mask nodded when there was no response.

"How long have they been like this?"

"I'm not sure. They were well when I spoke to their father about a month back, but between then and now, I can't say when they first became afflicted."

"Where is the father now?" Pierre asked while observing the children.

"He was the one being carted away when we arrived."

"Ah." Pierre moved the children's clothes with his cane to observe their armpits and bellies. Donadieu peered, curious about the doctor's methods. Daylight made the children's appearance more palatable. They looked ill, but not quite so unnatural.

"Well, without doubt, I can say they need nourishment," Pierre began, "but until we get the results from our experiment…" He trailed off.

"Of course! The experiment! How did that progress this morning?"

The doctor shuffled his feet and hung his head. "There was a slight hiccup with the experiment."

The priest raised an inquisitive brow. "A hiccup?"

"When the leech jar was being—I dropped it." Pierre's speech quickened, and his words overlapped as they came out in a garbled heap. "I get distracted when I work and when absentminded, I struggle. And well, things just go wrong. I ruin our work constantly, and—"

"Pierre." Donadieu raised his voice over the stuttering doctor in a calm but authoritative tone. "Everyone makes mistakes, such is the burden of free will. We need only remember that 'Blessed is the one who trusts in the Lord, whose confidence is in Him.' Even when you have no faith in yourself, know that God does. You will rise to your potential; it is the Lord's will. No one can oppose that, except yourself."

Pierre raised his head slightly. "Thank you, Father."

Donadieu placed his hand on the doctor's shoulder. "Now, about these children. What can we do while we wait for the results of your experiment?"

"Cool, clean water. It will help to reduce the heat of their humors and, judging by the cracking dryness of their skin, they could use the moisture as well."

Donadieu gently clapped. "That can be arranged. In fact, I'll go out and fetch some now. In the meantime, perhaps you can see if Louise, their mother, will require the same treatment. She's in the next room over, but her condition is certainly worse." He pointed Pierre toward the remaining room. "I'll leave you to that and return with the water, posthaste."

Just as the priest had reached the door to the street, Pierre called from behind. "Is there another room?"

Donadieu turned back. "No, why?"

"There's no one here. The bed is empty."

Befuddled, Donadieu retreated with a hasty step. He all but charged into the room which housed the ill woman the previous night. The bed was indeed empty. The imprint of her frame sunken into the mattress was the only clue she was ever there. Shock seized him, but the surprise faded when he realized what must have happened.

"Pascal," Donadieu said, his face drooping with disappointment. "He must have collected her, too."

"The groundskeeper? Why would he take her?"

Donadieu looked at the ground and replied in a disappointed tone. "When contracted to recover the bodies of the recently deceased, he has a habit of exploring their homes. Always on the lookout for any valuables that may not be missed: a spare coin, an unopened bottle of wine." Who was he kidding? Likely even an open one. "He probably wanted to save himself a second trip with Louise; she did look horrid, and if he wasn't paying attention, I suppose he may have missed her breathing."

"You go find the gravedigger," Pierre replied. "I'll find some water and give it to the children."

"You can find water at the spring where we met. Use that jug over there; that should be large enough, no?" He gestured to one of the potter's more elaborate work pieces sitting on a small table near the hearth.

"That will do nicely," Pierre said.

Donadieu smiled, patted the doorframe, and left for the street. Tracking down the groundskeeper shouldn't be too difficult; never one to linger with a rotting corpse in his care, Pascal would head directly to the cemetery. The priest followed the most likely path but did not have to walk far. When he rounded the same corner which had first produced Pascal, the groundskeeper appeared before the priest yet again. This time, the man sat by the side of the road, his cart skewed heavily to its side. One of its two wheels lay several feet away from the rest of the contraption.

Donadieu approached and a pang of worry struck him when he looked over the lumpy sheet that covered the back of the cart. He eyed the textile and then addressed the groundskeeper, "What all have you got in there, Pascal?" He did his best to sound calm, but previous misdeeds raised his suspicions. He would need to pray upon his prejudice.

"The potter, like I told ya," came the grumbly reply. "Although as ye can see, I barely moved 'im before my wheel fell off."

"I'm going to look in the back, alright Pascal?" Donadieu spoke with a much softer voice, an attempt to disguise his mistrust. "Just to make sure the potter hasn't been jostled too much in the accident."

The groundskeeper blew out his nose but did not object as Donadieu lifted up the sheet. Flopped on his side lay Thomas. Beside the man was a pair of wine bottles and some pristine ceramics. Nothing else. Donadieu tapped his foot as he thought. If not the gravedigger, then who? In that condition, Louise could not have walked away herself.

"Ya gonna help 'er what?" the gravedigger asked, cocking his head to the side; his eyes held coy hope that his supplementary reward would not be confiscated.

"Yes, of course." Donadieu lowered the sheet, too confused to scold about the theft. That would have to wait until confession. Pascal huffed and tilted the cart to its side, allowing Donadieu to slide the wheel back into place, his knees begrudging the effort.

When secure, Pascal allowed the cart to fall, and the wood groaned from the impact. Without so much as a thank you, the groundskeeper picked up the grips on his cart and continued to pull the body toward its waiting grave.

Satisfied that Louise was not with Pascal, Donadieu returned to the potter's house and found Pierre arriving as well, water in hand.

"No trouble finding the spring?" Donadieu asked, glancing toward the ceramic jug.

"None whatsoever," Pierre replied.

Together they reentered the sad home, careful to step around the bountiful red stains.

"I found Pascal," the priest continued. "He didn't take Louise."

Donadieu ducked as Pierre turned and nearly struck him with the mask's beak.

"Sorry!" the doctor said, leaning back to give the priest room. "You mentioned she was too ill to move. Would someone else have carried her away?"

Donadieu led them into the children's room. "No one that comes to mind."

"Strange."

The young doctor knelt at the children's bedside and dipped a gloved finger into the now full carafe. When removed, several droplets of water clung to the leather like morning dew. Drop by drop, he placed the water into the mouths of the children so that they would drink, even if only paltry amounts.

Donadieu fidgeted with the placement of his arms as he watched until he could remain silent no longer. "Pierre," he began, the doctor turning his beak to listen. "I wanted to apologize if you were upset by my question about your faith yesterday. I meant nothing by it. I understand it is an uncomfortable topic."

Pierre waved his hand dismissively at Donadieu and returned to his work. "No, it's quite alright. Think nothing of it."

The reaction did not please the priest, Pierre's response being too vague to satisfy. Knowing full well it was this same incessant need to push that created his trouble in the first place, Donadieu pressed on. "I don't mean to impose, but should you wish to discuss the matter further, please don't hesitate. My own history is not shy of conflicts with decisions made by the Church. Although those disagreements are quite minor in comparison, of course. We needn't even discuss faith; I just want to make myself open to you, and for you to feel welcome while you're helping us here. I can't assist much with the medicine, but providing counsel is my specialty."

Pierre now stood and turned to face the priest. With their proximity and the doctor's height, Donadieu found himself straining his neck to look up into the lens-covered eyes.

"I'm too young to know the conflict," Pierre said, his voice soft and forgiving, "only its results. I don't hold you accountable for the actions of others, Father Donadieu. I shouldn't have mentioned it. It was unfair. I apologize."

The priest tried to withhold a sigh of relief. "Thank you, Pierre. If you're all set with the children, perhaps we can step outside and get some fresh air?"

"All set here, yes. Some fresh air would be a good idea." Pierre motioned Donadieu to take the lead. "If there is miasma in Bastion, it certainly would be present in this home."

"I must admit," Donadieu said, "you are exceptionally knowledgeable for one so young. It's impressive. I'm only familiar with sparse whisperings on the subjects of the humors and of miasma, but there must be such intricacies of which the general populace is entirely unaware. Please educate an old man. Tell me of science's latest discoveries."

This request was at last the bridge Donadieu had been attempting to build. Whatever shyness Pierre had maintained now dissolved, and medical knowledge poured from his lips.

The pair exited the house midway into Pierre's lecture on the spreading of disease. They stopped a few steps into the street, the doctor waving his arms and pointing with his cane as they spoke. It was by far the most animated Donadieu had seen the man. Just as Pierre began bridging the talk to the four humors, a call from up the street grabbed their attention.

"Found you!"

Walking toward them strode a man Donadieu did not recognize. He was of average height and wore a dull brown woolen top with off-white linen pants; rather drab colors when compared to the fashion enjoyed by the locals. At his side was a large satchel nearly bursting with bundled herbs but, despite the medical bag, it was his well-fed stature that connected the dots for Donadieu.

"Guillaume," Pierre whispered. His muffled tone continued when they all stood together. "I'm sorry for leaving earlier. I don't know what came over me."

"You fret too much," Guillaume said. "Most of the leeches were unharmed by the fall. I attached them to their hosts and, when finished, placed them into an empty wine bottle and added some water from the bucket. Truth be told, I don't know if that will work for long, but it will keep them for now. While working with the water, I also took my time to examine it. No odor nor taste. It's clean."

Pierre too removed his mask and stuffed it into his satchel, its beak protruding as though it was not yet done sniffing the air.

"How long until the results of the experiment are known to us?" Donadieu asked, directly facing Guillaume. He had made headway with Pierre just now, but softening Guillaume's hard shell would be much more difficult.

To Donadieu's surprise, it was Pierre who responded. "The humors are quick to balance when properly adjusted. It's likely we'll see a response in the healthiest individuals by tomorrow morning."

Donadieu grinned, both from the news of the quickly expected results, and knowing Pierre felt comfortable enough to explain.

Guillaume nodded in agreement.

"Do you fellows have any plans for the rest of the afternoon?" Donadieu asked. "Why not sup with me in the church?"

Guillaume cut in quickly. "If there is miasma, it is thick in there. You're very lucky you have not been infected yourself. As such, I think we'll be fine to eat in our own wagon, or perhaps Pierre and I can find a suitable tavern around—"

Loud as a cannon, an ornate carriage pulled by white steeds thundered onto the street. The stomping hooves and the clacking wheels commanded the attention of the party, and the opulence maintained it. Painted a glossy midnight black, the carriage glistened with accents of inlaid gold leaf. Donadieu caught Pierre gaping at the luxury and rolled his eyes. *The Dubois.*

"Stop the horses!" came a shrill voice from within the buggy, and the driver commanding the carriage obliged. The momentum dipped the coachman forward before he snapped back to his proper upright posture. He was an aged gentleman adorned in well-tailored livery, white gloves included, but he also wore a heavy scarf uncharacteristic for the relatively mild day.

The curtain concealing the interior of the carriage screeched as it was pulled aside, and a pair of pasty white faces peered out into the street.

"Who might you two be?" the male asked, his voice an octave higher than one might have expected from his appearance. He wore a long, waxed mustache which he twirled as he spoke, and the hat he wore betrayed the balding head underneath. "We don't often get outsiders here, especially not now."

The elder doctor's posture straightened before he replied. "Guillaume Jourdain and Pierre Laflamme, traveling doctors, at your service." Guillaume bowed slightly. The courtesy paid toward these unknowns disgruntled Donadieu, and shame stung him when he noticed his displeasure.

The woman in the carriage peaked over her companion's shoulder with inquisitive eyes. Her face was lightly painted, a modest fashion which matched her pearl-colored dress. "My husband neglected to introduce us. We're the Dubois." She spoke quietly, but her voice carried gravitas. "He is Claude, and I—"

"You simply must join us for dinner," the man interrupted. "It has been so terribly long since we've had proper guests. These afternoon carriage rides have grown dull, and a pair of fresh faces are just what we need. Please, come so we may know you." Behind him, his wife sighed and leaned back.

"We would be delighted," Guillaume said, a smile upon his lips.

"And you must come as well, Father Donadieu," Claude said. "You've rejected so many invitations upon the excuse of caring for the sick but, with the doctors here to assist, you simply can't refuse."

Donadieu didn't exactly despise the Dubois, but their eccentricities and affluence left very little room for decency. Near as he could judge, they weren't innately malicious folk, but they certainly were rich. He swallowed hard and grimaced. "Very well."

"Wonderful!" Claude said. "We must hurry and prepare. We're going to have new guests tonight. Roland, take us home."

The servant sitting atop the carriage jostled the reins, and the horses started off.

"Come just before sunset," Claude called out from the carriage. "Donadieu can show you the way."

The priest watched the carriage ride off and sighed.

CHAPTER 6

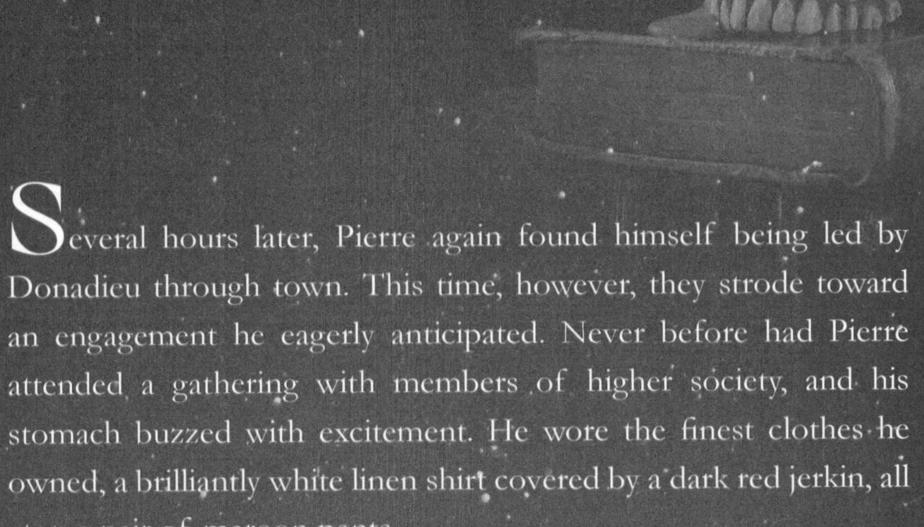

Several hours later, Pierre again found himself being led by Donadieu through town. This time, however, they strode toward an engagement he eagerly anticipated. Never before had Pierre attended a gathering with members of higher society, and his stomach buzzed with excitement. He wore the finest clothes he owned, a brilliantly white linen shirt covered by a dark red jerkin, all atop a pair of maroon pants.

He maintained no allusions that his attire was adequate for the status of the dinner, but the fact he'd woefully underdressed did not bother him as he'd speculated it might. Beside him, Guillaume had dressed similarly, only with darker and less vibrant colors. Together they were led by the priest, who had also changed; however, his best garments were also holy robes, only slightly darker and less worn.

"…nor would I consider Claude or Aliénor particularly pious," Donadieu continued his speech about their pending hosts. The priest spoke over his shoulder at the trailing doctors and Pierre only half listened; his attention was occupied imagining the evening's festivities.

"…heard someone had bought the old manor, sight unseen. Shortly after, they arrived. After some generous donations to improve local businesses and infrastructure, Claude quickly found himself the de facto lord of the town. And, I'll be honest, no one seems to mind. He leaves the townsfolk to their own devices, but more importantly, they leave him to do whatever he likes. I'll warn you both, that's what you are when you go and dine with them: *something to do.*"

Guillaume rubbed his stomach. "I think I'm alright being the entertainment as long as I'm compensated with some quality food."

"Just so long as you're both aware of what you're in for. Do doctors often have occasion to attend high societal meals? Are you well-versed in the etiquette?"

The questions cracked the looking glass in Pierre's mind, and the splendor became a distorted mess.

"Been to a few," Guillaume said. "Sometimes physicians are invited after curing the child of a well-to-do. Never cared to impress though, I don't stick around long enough for the potential of a follow-up invite based on good behavior."

Pierre's discomfort grew. Guillaume exuded indifference, but Pierre could not find it within himself to care so little; he wanted very badly to impress. The thought of being perceived a fool flustered the young man and his cheeks warmed despite the cooling afternoon.

"This will be new to me," he admitted. "I'd like any pointers you have to spare."

Donadieu slowed his pace momentarily so they could walk beside one another. "Gladly. A few simple tips and you'll be passing for a noble in no time. Here are three easy actions you can do to fool even the snobbiest of barons.

"First, when we arrive, they're sure to give us a tour of the house. Remark at least once per room that something is 'exquisite' or another complement of a similar nature. It shows you not only have good taste but affirms their own.

"Second, at dinner, you will find an alarming amount of cutlery. Always use the exterior set for each progressive dish. You can follow my lead there, if you wish.

"Third, after dinner, they will likely request that we join them in the parlor for drinks. Be prepared for *any* topic of conversation. Remember, you're the entertainment. They're going to want to get their evening's worth."

"Is it really so simple to be suave?" Guillaume asked sarcastically.

Donadieu continued, ignoring him. "One more thing. Try to have fun. It's not as intimidating when you realize they're trying just as hard to be proper. Believe me, they often fail. While it may not be difficult, it is occasionally uncomfortable. That I'll admit. You'll do fine." He smiled and patted Pierre's shoulder, and then quickened his pace to again lead the group.

Pierre memorized the advice as though it were one of his medical texts. When he looked at Guillaume and saw the man had not even bothered to comb his hair, he found he was comforted that Donadieu was coming too.

They strode in silence toward the setting sun until they reached the edge of town. There, a group of three men stumbled from the only tavern still in business and paused in the center of the street. Together, they shared a bottle of wine, passing it back and forth between them.

Pierre followed Donadieu's swerve to avoid the drinking men, many of whom had marched in Bastion's previous "welcome parade." One of the inebriated, the boldest of the three and a grizzly of a man, stepped forth when the two parties were closest.

Pierre recoiled from the advance, which cast a smirk upon the aggressor's face.

"Where are you going, Father?" he asked. "Have these birds convinced you Bastion is lost? Are you going to flee the quarantine? Didn't work so well for Guy."

Pierre's heart hammered, fearful of the man's aggressive tone and monstrous size. Donadieu replied without a hint of concern in his voice. "Wouldn't we all like to flee, Henri, but no. My place is here. I'm escorting our friends to the Dubois'. We've been invited to dinner."

Henri stepped back, his face draining of color. The men behind him lowered their heads to inspect their shoes and then looked behind them as though they had been called from within the tavern.

"You know better, Father. That is not a place for holy men."

"The Lord walks with me there, as He does in all places, Henri. There is nothing we can't overcome with him at our sides."

"He's yet to overcome the Withering," Henri spat. With that, the men behind Henri dispersed back into the tavern, leaving their leader to stand defiant and alone.

Pierre watched with concern as Donadieu walked up to the brute and placed a hand on his arm. "Follow your friends inside," the priest said. "In the morning, you will regret your harsh tongue, and God will be there to forgive you. We're going to continue on now, Henri. Have a good evening." He released the man's arm and continued on his way, Pierre following so close he nearly removed the priest's shoes.

"The hell was that?" Guillaume asked when they had passed earshot of the tavern.

"Old superstition regarding the land where we're heading; pagan remembrances from a millennium past, long overdue of being forgotten. Some beliefs refuse to die, even in the presence of a more enlightened faith."

Silence reigned as they digested the warning. Around them, it became clear they had reached the extent of Bastion proper. The landscape changed from a dilapidated town with cobbled streets to a dirt road that wound through a densely packed forest of leafless trees. Even the setting sun failed to mount much resistance against the darkness of the woods. Pierre looked around the scenery and found an uneasy anxiety growing within him. "How far away is this house?"

"The manor grounds are another ten-minute walk, and then a few more minutes to the house," Donadieu said. "I can assure you, when we get close, you won't miss it."

The priest did not lie. The rows of trees which bordered the road stopped abruptly when they reached the extent of the Dubois' property, replaced by an expansive wrought-iron fence which encircled the estate. Trees loomed over the fence line, but none dared to grow within the multi-acre property itself. A long gravel path swerved from the gate and through a vast field toward a house so grand it could have made a count blush.

The estate in its totality was one long, sloping hill that culminated with the mansion perched at the top. Three distinct wings comprised the manor; the main northern section was by far the largest. Flanking each side were the eastern and western wings, reaching toward them like lanky arms. Between the three sections of the home was an enormous and beautifully gardened courtyard.

Pierre was awestruck by the house and decided should he return, he must bring Hippo to enjoy the grandeur of the lawn and dine with the other horses upon what must only be the richest of hay.

"Looks like they left the gate open for us," Donadieu said as they walked onto the property. "Last chance to return and enjoy a nice bowl of soup in the church." The priest playfully bounced his eyebrows.

"How long has the house been here?" Guillaume asked.

Dismayed his jest was entirely ignored, the priest replied dryly. "There has been a building present for several centuries, but it was once a fortress. The Dubois have been repairing and updating it constantly since their arrival. The southernmost wall was completely removed while the others are being 'modernized.'"

"Must be costing a fortune," Pierre said, his eyes wide and mouth slightly agape at the scale of the building before him.

"The carpenters, masons, and the like have certainly filled their pockets. They've been in a near constant state of employment for years. The building's renovations were the largest draw in population to Bastion on record. Most are bedridden now, and no new folks can come due to the quarantine."

"Why remodel? What was wrong with it?" Pierre asked.

"According to the builders I've spoken to, Claude didn't find the aesthetic of a castle *suitable for modern tastes.*'"

"He certainly has enough space to expand," Guillaume added. He gestured at either side of the path and the vastness of the field it cut through.

Pierre's eyes sparkled at the opulence of the house, and its marvel only increased as they approached. The architecture resembled a royal palace, its scale small only when compared to the king's own. Distinct, the western wing retained its centuries old stonework, looking drab and worn beside the rest of the gleaming home. He reasoned it must be the last section to require remodeling.

When the party had trekked the majority of the house's walkway, the floral scents of quality tobacco began to perfume the air. Sitting on the grass in the center of the gardens were Claude and Aliénor, a book in Aliénor's hands and a pipe in that of her spouse. Their attire remained the fine garments they'd worn for their afternoon ride, but as they got closer Pierre realized it was not makeup that whitened Aliénor's face; it was naturally and astonishingly pale.

Beside the Dubois, still as a statue, stood Roland, their butler and coach driver. He dressed smartly but, despite the mild day, he still popped his collar and wore a scarf around most of his face. His hair was also too long and unkempt to be acceptable for a man in his position. Its greasy, long strands covered much of the remainder of his face. He watched the trio approach with an unflinching gaze. Claude's expression was much more welcoming.

Their host clamped his jaw upon the stem of his pipe and greeted his guests through clenched teeth. "How wonderful that you've all made it! We weren't convinced you would join us."

Aliénor gently closed her book and joined the conversation. "Especially not you, Martine, after you've refused—"

"None of that matters now that you've arrived," Claude interrupted. "Roland?"

"Sir?"

The servant's voice sent an icy shiver from Pierre's head to his hips; its hoarse inflection sounded as though Roland spoke and exhaled simultaneously.

"Go and check on the progress of our meal." Claude waved his hand around as though he directed an orchestra. "I'd like to eat in an hour, no more." A final flick of his wrist finished his command.

"Very good, sir." Roland bowed and retreated into the house.

Despite the slight at the hands of her husband, Aliénor did not express frustration and instead smiled at the trio. She eyed them one by one with a peculiar look on her face. Pierre couldn't decide if her features matched the excitement of a child with a new toy, or that of a cat who loomed above a cornered mouse.

"Would you all care for a tour of the manor?" Claude asked, rising from his seat. "It's something of a passion project of mine and I refuse to be modest when I get the chance to show it off."

"It would be our honor," Guillaume said with a slight bow.

His mentor's display of grace made Pierre smile. Perhaps the old man was capable of a show after all, even if he'd only dance for a meal.

Aliénor blinked when Claude made to move and suggested, "Perhaps they'd like a tour of my gardens before we head inside and lose the last of the sun."

"No one cares about your stupid plants," Claude snapped while glaring at his wife. As quickly as his rage came, it abated, and his pleasant composure returned. "Now, please, follow me." He smoothed his waistcoat and led them through the front door and into the foyer. Aliénor stood too and followed the group from the rear. Her demeanor remained pleasant despite the abuse, and Pierre mentally applauded her resilience.

When he entered, Pierre found the luxury palpable. The air itself tasted of the expensive Spanish oak decor which glistened from the thick layers of varnish. The vestibule was spacious enough to fit an entire medical ward, and a grand dual staircase stretched to the second floor.

"The foyer," Claude began. "I wanted something modest and functional to allow easier access to the more interesting rooms of my home. It was the first thing I redesigned when we acquired the property. It is the first room you see, after all, and should set the tone for what is to follow."

"I think it's exquisite," Pierre said. He saw Donadieu grin from the corner of his eye.

"I'm glad you find it so." Claude beamed with obvious pride. Behind Pierre, Aliénor released a gentle sigh, still loud enough that Claude could hear. A glare was exchanged between the spouses, and Pierre thanked God when no bickering followed. "Come, let me show you the rest."

The group marveled as they were led through the maze-like abode. Every rug, piece of furniture, and stretch of trim oozed the highest of quality and taste. Each piece hailed from the farthest reaches of known trade. Claude often requested on the tour that they step around the ornate rugs to avoid sullying the imported designs. Aliénor's occasionally muffled footsteps implied she was perfectly content to ignore the request.

Despite the size of the house, it struck Pierre just how empty it felt. Dozens of rooms sat entirely unused. When they did see a maid or groundskeeper scurrying about the property, it was only briefly and from a distance down the great halls. He wondered if the Dubois were ever lonely in their own home.

When they approached the westernmost wing, Pierre worried his legs may ache before they concluded the tour. It was clear through the innumerable windows the sun had nearly set, and visibility quickly diminished. The matter compounded when his stomach began to rumble, and he awkwardly covered his gut with both hands.

"…and this is the extent of the habitable rooms of our home. I hope you enjoyed its architectural display. I've put a great many months and years into its laborious restoration. If you'll all follow me, I'll guide you to the dining hall, where I'm sure by now our feast has been laid."

Behind Claude, tucked into the gaudy wallpaper, was a ratty door he neglected to mention. It hung loosely on its hinges and the rotting wood looked entirely out of place among the rest of the building's opulent motif. This mysterious portal piqued Pierre's interest, but dinner interested him more. He eagerly anticipated quieting his protesting stomach. It was clear Claude also had no intention of discussing it, but Guillaume did not let him get away so easily.

"What's through that door?" the doctor asked, pointing.

Surprising them all, it was Aliénor who spoke for the first time since the tour began. "That leads to the western wing of the house, the final stretch in need of restoration." Her voice carried a powerfully authoritative cadence. "During the summer, a particularly blusterous storm collapsed part of the roof. Due to the rather inconvenient quarantine, we haven't been able to summon the workers or supplies to have it repaired. The rooms have a terrible draft, and we worry the water may be rotting the floors. Currently, that section of the building isn't safe, main floor or second."

Pierre nodded along with the explanation. The thought of the cost and time required to maintain and improve such a large estate confounded him. Arithmetic started in his mind as he tried to estimate the potential costs but quickly gave up. It was beyond his reckoning.

Claude resumed his tour, eagerly pointing out this imported chandelier and that custom painted landscape missed on their first pass. Pierre's eyes greedily absorbed the scenery, resulting in a near collision with Father Donadieu, who had briefly slowed before the damaged door. After a pair of shared apologies, they quickened their stride to rejoin pace with their guide.

On their way, Pierre turned behind him to compliment Aliénor too on their wondrous home. The words stuck in his throat when he met her gaze. He attempted to smile, but her indifferent face swallowed the kindness like a deep well gobbled a coin. Shyness overcame him and he watched his feet instead.

After a few more minutes of following their guide, the party funneled into a grand dining room. The space could easily accommodate fifty guests and housed a mahogany table that spanned almost the entire length of the room, longer itself than any home in which Pierre had ever lived. An enormous stone hearth blazed heartily in the wall. The smell of the woodsmoke and platters of roasted meats caused saliva to pool in his mouth. At the head of the table lay four extravagant displays of silver cutlery, porcelain plates, and crested silk napkins, all waiting for the diners. Mountains of food sat between the settings and Pierre already began to plot his culinary course.

Far apart from the rest, a single place setting was arranged at the foot of the great table, a simple bowl of soup upon the plate.

"Come, let us sit and dine," Claude announced with a flourish, taking his seat at the head. Obeying their host, the guests sat, Pierre adjacent to Claude and across from Guillaume. Donadieu seated himself at Pierre's side. Meanwhile, Aliénor made the long walk to her own solitary setting.

Roland stood beside Claude, a napkin draped over his bent arm. Even though the blazing hearth drew sweat from Pierre, the butler still wore his scarf, and his collar remained at attention.

"Dinner is served," Roland said. Pierre's own throat burned in sympathy when he heard the butler's scratchy speech. "Tonight's menu consists of a hearty beef and barley pottage, roast pheasant, and a classic custard tart to round the courses. This will be accompanied by a near perfect Bordeaux during the meal and a glass of Champagne to conclude."

Being the first time physically near the butler, Pierre could not help but notice further oddities about the man. There was nothing specifically *wrong* that he could place, but Roland's eyes sunk so deeply into his head it struck Pierre as remarkable he could see at all. The possibility of strained breathing was also noted, but through the scarf and over the sounds of Claude and the roaring fire, it was impossible to be certain. The food also masked Pierre's senses, for at times he thought he detected a whiff of something feted before the scent was overpowered by the succulent dishes before him.

Pierre looked to Guillaume, expecting an equally curious eye, but his mentor was already distracted by his glass of wine. All the symptoms were there, all except the lapse into unconsciousness.

Pierre's head spun with anxiety at the thought, and his hands began to fidget in his lap. Wanting desperately to hide his nervous heart and terrified of being rude, he followed Guillaume's lead and began to drink.

"Roland is simply the most wonderful butler," Claude said. "I don't know what I'd do without him."

Pierre finished his gulp and turned away from Roland out of instinct. At the far end of the table, Aliénor slurped at her meal, but her eyes were glued toward them. Instead of the grand candelabra shared between the four, Aliénor's distant face was illuminated by a solitary candlestick. Pierre again attempted to send a smile in her direction. Again, she smiled back. Her pearly grin in the pale light caused the hair on the back of his neck to try to jump free of his skin.

A shudder rippled through him despite his attempt to restrain it and, not knowing what to do, he began to eat. He was the last to begin and when he looked at the staggering assortment of cutlery before him, Donadieu noticed and gestured with his pinkie finger which utensil to use.

The first bite of pottage exploded with flavor. A succulent and savory collection of seasonings tantalized his taste buds, herbs and spices complimenting the extravagant cuts of meat. For a moment, his worries evaporated. Now he understood why Guillaume had been so eager to feast at a high society table. After shoveling a few more bites into his mouth, his troubles had been all but forgotten, and only a gently placed hand on his forearm from the neighboring priest slowed his consumption. He looked at the priest with bulging cheeks and paused.

The older man had a sly smile on his face. "Chew," Donadieu whispered from the corner of his mouth. "It's not very polite to choke at the dinner table."

Pierre swallowed hard and the boulder of food stretched his throat as it rolled down. Having been reminded of his surroundings, he became aware of the conversation Guillaume and Claude had been sharing, and that Roland had departed from the room.

"…really is truly remarkable," Guillaume said.

"Thank you," Claude replied. "It has been a stimulating hobby working on this house. With an infinite amount of time, I'm not sure I'd ever be completely satisfied."

"Understandable. I imagine it must be highly rewarding to see such long-planned efforts come to fruition." Guillaume paused and turned to look at Aliénor.

"You wonder why my wife eats at the end of the table?" Claude asked with a knowing wink. "She's done so for years. It's her choice, just a quirk, I suppose." He shrugged. "If you want my honest opinion, I believe she fancies hers is the true head of the table and we all sit at the foot. She's vain like that. Believe me when I say she's not much for conversation anyway, never anything useful to say."

Guillaume stroked his chin knowingly. "Still playing pretend. Some people never grow up."

Pierre again cast a glance past Donadieu down the table. Aliénor had finished her meal and sat watching, swirling and sipping the last of her wine. She did not strike him as a person who lingered in idealized memories of childhood.

After their plates had been filled and emptied, as had the goblets many times, the guests set down their utensils and all patted their bulging stomachs.

"Shall we retire to the parlor?" Claude asked. "I'll have Roland fetch us a dessert wine from the cellar so that we may continue our evening with lubricated throats and minds." He reached to his side and rang a dainty bell, its chime echoing through the house. All fell silent after it rang, aside from the crackling fire.

Pierre jumped when the butler's voice croaked from behind him. "Sir?"

"Dessert wine, Roland, and bring it to the parlor." Claude waved his hand dismissively.

"Very good, sir." Roland turned and left, his footsteps quiet as a cat's.

"Now for the final room of the tour," Claude said while standing up. "Please, follow me."

Guillaume stood, massaging his belly as he rose. Beside Pierre, Donadieu stood and placed his napkin on the empty dessert plate before him. Pierre followed suit and, as a party, they left the room under Claude's direction.

When exiting the dining room into another grand hallway, Pierre cast a glance back. Aliénor too had risen, the distance between them closing rapidly thanks to the woman's meaningful stride. The young doctor quickly turned his attention back to the trail of the priest's robes and followed it unwaveringly until they reached the parlor.

CHAPTER 7

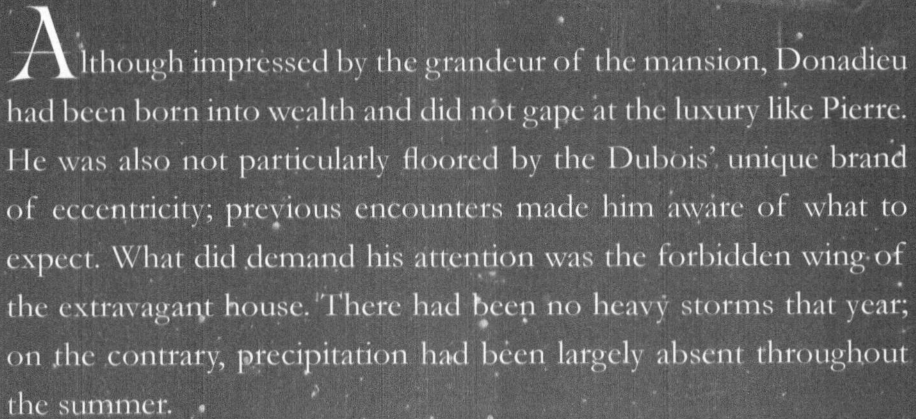

Although impressed by the grandeur of the mansion, Donadieu had been born into wealth and did not gape at the luxury like Pierre. He was also not particularly floored by the Dubois' unique brand of eccentricity; previous encounters made him aware of what to expect. What did demand his attention was the forbidden wing of the extravagant house. There had been no heavy storms that year; on the contrary, precipitation had been largely absent throughout the summer.

The unnecessary deception consumed his thoughts during the meal, that and the candle which taunted him from the center of the table, but by the time he and the others sat within the sprawling parlor, the oddity was forgotten.

Donadieu found himself more impressed by the social room than the rest of the home combined. An entire wall had been replaced with bookshelves that spanned floor-to-ceiling, each entirely filled with ornate and decorative volumes that begged to be read. Across from the shelves, yet another monstrous stone hearth blazed, its maw spewing embers as Roland tended the flame and jabbed at the coals with a poker. Donadieu did anything he could to avoid looking at the fire.

"This is one of the few rooms I would call complete," Claude said as he sank into a gargantuan chair, its features impressive enough to be a throne. "The literature and knowledge contained here would take a lifetime to consume."

"What I wouldn't give to spend my life trying," Pierre said, his mouth hanging open.

Several drinks of dessert wine later, the conversation took a spontaneous and sickening turn. Claude swigged the last of his glass, looked away from his books, and stared intently at Donadieu. "Tell me about your scars, Martine. I dare say I can't recall you've ever given us the tale."

A knot furled in the priest's stomach. There could be no pleasant end to this question. "They are the result of being caught in a fire," he said plainly, wishing that would be a sufficient explanation but knowing it would not.

"We can tell that by the nature of the scars," Claude persisted. "We want to know how you came to find yourself kissed by the flames' wicked tongue, as it were." Claude's attempt at elegance fell rather flat, a result of his wine-slurred speech. With a pleased look, he sank deeper into his chair.

Across the room, Aliénor sat up straight as a board and leaned into the conversation. Donadieu assumed she had only joined in the parlor at the request of her spouse, but the macabre question roused her attention fully.

He felt the eyes of all present groping the damaged skin on his face. An innocent curiosity from Pierre, something more morbid from the Dubois. Only Guillaume feigned indifference, but a subtle studious glance said they all desired a more conclusive answer. He breathed slowly from his nose and collected himself for the forced march into his past.

"Some years back, a lifetime now," Donadieu began, "there were a series of fires that plagued the area surrounding my old parish. Suspicious fires. That spring had been heavy with rain and the air itself tasted damp. Whispers of arson made their rounds; squints and glares worked over every unknown face that walked the commune grounds.

"Well, it wasn't a stranger's face that the populace should have been after. It was that of a young man; a teenager who attended church every Sunday with his family. The boy was well-liked. His golden hair and striking smile radiated piousness to all he met.

"Every Sunday, the boy came to my confessional. Truth be told, he never had any desire to repent, merely to gloat. He taunted me, knowing the seal of confession bound my tongue. This continued for five weeks, for eight fires. Many old buildings were lost, mostly abandoned farmsteads past the outskirts of town. With every blaze, the fires grew in size, and each week I attempted to return him to the path of righteousness and to God's light.

"Eventually, empty buildings became insufficient to fill his malevolent appetite, and he incinerated a chicken coop, roasting twelve birds alive.

"That Sunday he returned to the confessional, and I was prepared for his twisted pride, his domination of our conversation. Instead, his mood grew sullen. This was the first time I believed he realized the inevitable destination to where his actions led. He figured it was only a matter of time before he would be compelled to engulf human souls in his inferno. This, he knew, would damn him to Hell. At last, his heart opened before me, confiding he was scared of what he was becoming and the path he tread. He feared what the town would do to him if they found out. What his mother would say. How her soul would ache from his actions.

"Hope filled me, and I conveyed the grace and forgiveness of our Lord as best I was able. I spoke of redemption, and love, and the path back from sin; that it was never too late. When I finished, he began to chuckle. His laugh grew further to a full belly roar, and he mocked my attempt at saving his shattered soul. He swore to me nothing would stop his infernal crusade, and the following night he planned to burn his family home to the ground; the fire would consume his parents and sister until there was nothing left but cinders and ash.

"I arrived at their house on the foretold night knowing I must intervene, but I must do it alone lest I break my solemn vows. I waited across the empty street for the flickering light to draw me in so that I may render assistance before the blaze lost control. I waited hours for the flames, and to my eternal shame, I drifted to sleep while I watched.

"It was the bone chilling scream of a young girl that woke me from my slumber. I bounded to my feet and rushed toward the already engulfed building. The boy's younger sister, eight years old, ran out of the house glowing like a human torch, her hair entirely alight.

"I can't remember clearly what happened next, my memory fogged like the billowing black smoke, but in my attempt to help I ended up burned, as you see now. My next recollection is signing the cross above the girl, her parents still within the building.

"And I remember the boy's awful grin, watching from up the street. Ear-to-ear his lips stretched and his eyes danced in the light of his twisted flames."

Donadieu finally paused and his voice began to warble. "They eventually discovered it was he that had done it. He was hanged at fifteen-years-old." The priest wiped at a tear on his cheek and felt the ripples in his flesh from the long-healed burns. "That's how I got my scars."

The priest blinked hard and met the eyes of each attendee in the room. Pierre's face twisted into a portrait of pity and sorrow. Guillaume lost his expression of indifference and instead carried the curious look of bewilderment. Claude nodded along through the tale, as though it were no more interesting than talk of a cabbage harvest. Aliénor's eyes shone with an uncanny brightness and, when it was clear the story was done, leaned back into her chair, fully sated.

The ensuing silence grew so uncomfortable, it tickled him like ants beneath his robes. Pierre tried to speak, but he only managed a guttural stutter. Donadieu had known that in coming here his purpose would be to entertain, even warned about it, but he now felt more like a pheasant after a hunt rather than a court jester.

His eyes again darted around, only to meet unflinching expressions. "Where might I find the closet chamber pot?" he asked, already standing before he finished.

Claude pointed lazily at a door on the far side of the room and heavily jumbled the words that followed. "If you exit there, turn left—no, right. Walk up the hallway past five or ten doors or so, make a right, then a left when it's the right spot, and then it should be on your right. Shall I summon Roland to show you the way?"

"That's alright, thank you. I'll find it."

A few moments alone would do him good, even if those instructions would confuse a new world explorer. He thanked his host again and headed for hallway. By the time he was halfway out of the parlor, Claude had already moved on to grilling the doctors for insight into the grisliest aspects of their profession.

Darkness met Donadieu at the door. The sun was now long buried beneath the horizon and the stretch of mansion before him held no other source of illumination. The priest stalled and looked back. Claude sat listening intently to the doctors while twirling his mustache. No doubt the story shared involved some gruesome amputation, and the thought pushed him out into the hall. What little moonlight entered through the windows would suffice; he preferred natural light to a flame, anyway.

Despite the well-earned wrinkles around his eyes, Donadieu's eyesight was still as sharp as a hawk's, and he adjusted quickly. A few minutes in the shadows and his slow, cautious steps transformed into a steady stride.

His memory, however, was slightly rustier. Combining both a fuzzy recollection of his host's instructions and the dull lunar lighting, he found himself lost. Thinking back to their lengthy tour, he tried to discern his place in the manor but found the puzzle too complex to construct in his mind.

To confound matters further, an unwanted companion joined him on his explorations. A solitary fly looped around his head and buzzed incessantly. No number of swats could dissuade the insect; its presence remained constant.

Unable to conjure any other ideas, Donadieu wandered aimlessly, searching for any indication as to where in the building he was. Because of the sheer size of the construction, he decided luck would be a better guide than trying to remember every twisting passage.

For thirty minutes he blundered through the darkened halls, thinking by now the others must know he had lost his way; or perhaps they were so engulfed in conversation they hadn't noticed his absence at all. Regardless, he pressed on.

Underneath his feet, the stiff old boards moaned from his weight and every door creaked as he pressed it open to investigate the spaces within. Drafts from unknown origins ruffled his robes and, as he wound his way through the labyrinth, he thought he heard whispers in the gloom along with the buzzing fly.

Only when the pressure in his bladder threatened to rupture did he at last see the faint glow of light around a far hallway corner. Doubling his pace, he started after the source, but as he approached the turn which would lead him toward it, the light began to fade. By the time he rounded the bend, the light, too, had rounded one of its own.

Cramps stitched in his sides, and he called after the source to wait. Whether he was unheard or ignored did not matter, the light did not slow. Through the twisting corridors he pursued his quarry, and based on the growing luminosity, he was making ground. In the darkness, he quickened his pace again, stopping just short of a jog.

"I'm lost," Donadieu called again. "Please help, I can't find my way."

He followed the light through a door and into a cluttered room. There, he caught a glimpse of what he followed. The haunting image froze his pursuit.

The source of the glow was a candle, held by a twisted creature. It stood hunched in the corner, contorted as though in immense pain. Wild hair erupted from the skull of the being, and its skin looked dry as jerked meat. It turned to Donadieu, and he stared into its eyeless sockets, homes for a colony of flies which drunkenly buzzed around its head. With a gaping and toothless mouth, the ghoul strained to breathe, a terrible hissing passed through its gums. Turning away from the priest, the unholy thing left through a door on the far side of the room, the tails of its yellow nightgown gliding across the floor behind it.

Once again obscured by darkness, Donadieu regained control of his limbs, and his horror began to thaw. Despite himself, he called after the figure. "Louise?" He was horrified that he connected the poor mother with that creature from the pit, but her dress and bruises left little doubt.

Trepidation caused a quivering in his legs, but he found the strength to move them. He followed.

The target of his attention must have quickened its pace, for after Donadieu marched through the doorway, its light was again out of view and fading fast. Further lengthening his stride and the tempo of his steps, Donadieu strove ahead to catch the mysterious figure.

"Louise?" he called again. His mind argued with itself about the sensibility of chasing this thing. Truth be told, he did not know why he pursued, simply that he felt he must. It may have been an internalized sense of duty from his time walking the cloister grounds, or raw compassion for her suffering and that of her children. Whatever the motivation, he moved.

Continuing through the twisting home, Donadieu chased the trails of the candlelight, but he no longer seemed to gain any ground. Before long, his breathing hardened, and his lungs and legs began to burn. Just as he thought his heart may burst in his chest, he rounded yet another corner just in time to see a door slammed shut before him. From the gaps in the trim, the candle's glow dimmed, and he knew his quarry was escaping. For the first time since leaving the parlor, Donadieu recognized where he was. He knew the decrepit door set into the off-white wallpaper. It led to the condemned west wing.

The priest reached for the worn doorknob of the decaying door, but something repulsed him from grabbing it. The force was of his mind's construction, but the effect was the same and his courage faltered. As the traces of light diminished from under the cracks, a desperation forced his hand to clasp the old handle.

He turned the knob, its metal oddly warm, but before the mechanism had clicked, a new light began to grow—this time from behind him. Donadieu turned in a start.

"Sir?" Roland asked. In the gloom, what little skin he showed practically glowed it was so pale.

Donadieu's hand was still clasped around the handle to the battered door, and he sheepishly lowered his palm. "It seems I've gotten myself terribly lost looking for a lavatory. Perhaps you could help guide me somewhere I may relieve myself?"

Roland replied, monotone as ever. "Follow me, sir. I shall escort you personally." The only indication that Roland was not a mechanical construct came from the strained breathing from beneath his scarf.

"That would be ideal, thank you," Donadieu said, bowing slightly.

Roland led him back through the manor. As lost as Donadieu had become, it was around but a single corner where the two arrived at the closest privy. He could not help but laugh at having been so close. "I knew it was around here somewhere."

"I'll wait here for you, sir, to ensure your prompt return to the others."

Donadieu, not wanting to find himself wandering aimlessly yet again, heartily agreed to the butler's terms. He concluded his business and was shown back to the parlor.

When he returned, all but Aliénor were standing. By their swaying alone, he reasoned they had finished another bottle of sweet wine, and perhaps two more on top.

"Hope we didn't upset you with the question," Claude slurred. "Tell us you'll visit again, Martine. Your company this evening has been a delight. One of the few residents of Bastion with any culture or manners."

Guillaume swayed out of sync with Claude. "I concur it has been a wonderful evening; I hope you'll write us a letter every time you have a plague rip apart your town."

Donadieu feigned a smile as Guillaume and Claude erupted into laughter at the tasteless joke. Pierre was otherwise occupied, grasping the back of his chair to remain upright.

"Well," Guillaume said, observing his teetering apprentice, "it's been a pleasure, but we'd best be off. We've got work we need to do tomorrow." He lifted an imaginary hat from his head and bowed.

Claude patted the back of the departing doctor. "Of course. Of course. We will see you to the door. Come." He beckoned to Aliénor, then lowered his voice to feign discretion, but it was clear his wife was meant to hear. "She's stubborn as a mule, that one, impossible to please and always does only what she feels like. I fully understand why her dowry was so large; I think I'd pay heaps to be rid of her myself." Claude laughed obnoxiously, and Guillaume followed suit.

Meanwhile, Donadieu wrapped Pierre's arm around his neck to help steady the young man and they moved toward the door. Beside him, Aliénor's face displayed its first trace of color as she flushed with anger, but otherwise did not complain and stood to take her husband's hand.

Boisterously, Claude and Guillaume continued to jest until they reached the stairs out of the manor. At the bottom of the steps, Pierre turned one final time to address his hosts, mumbling, "Thank you for the wonderful evening. It was exquisite." The final word took several attempts from the overly intoxicated apprentice.

It was Aliénor who gave the final adieu. "You were all stimulating company. Thank you for coming. It's always wonderful to see how the other half live." Still standing beside her, Claude appeared to be falling asleep.

Donadieu led his inebriated companions through the Dubois' front gate. Along the way back to town, Pierre asked, "What did she mean about the other half?"

"The poor," Guillaume replied. "That's what we are to people like them. But hey, if they let us taste a slice of the pie, they can call me whatever they like."

The rest of the journey remained largely silent, Pierre and Guillaume having to focus more on foot placement than they could on conversation. Only when they were making their way through the confines of the silent town did Donadieu become aware of muffled footsteps following them from behind.

The priest swiveled his head to get a glimpse of their pursuer, but the street was empty. They'd progressed only a bit farther when he heard this noise again. This time, he slowly removed Pierre's arm from his shoulder and spun like a top. Again, nothing.

"Did you hear something behind us?" he asked.

"Hmmm?" Guillaume replied, one eye half-closed. Pierre did not look like he would be any more help.

Heart thumping in his chest, Donadieu resumed their march toward his church. Two possibilities swirled in his mind. Either Henri had waited for their return, wishing for another confrontation—or worse, the ghoulish creature followed them home.

After a few more steps, he twisted preemptively and caught their pursuer in the act. He breathed a hefty sigh of relief as Marianne giggled and shouted, "You caught me!"

Donadieu smiled and shook his head. "What are you still doing out, young lady? Your father wouldn't want you out this late. He must be worried sick."

She wiggled her foot on the ground. "Daddy's not feeling very well. He's been coughing all night. I couldn't sleep, so I went outside, and that's when I found you!"

Donadieu's heart grew heavy at the reply. "I did not know your father was unwell. I'm sorry, Marianne. You still need to hurry home. It's chilly tonight and you don't want to catch cold, too, do you?"

"No." Marianne dragged out the word.

"Good. Now I need to get the doctors home before—"

Pierre collapsed beside him.

Donadieu sighed. "… Well, before that happened. As soon as they figure out what ails this town, I promise I'll send one around to cure your father, and your mother, too. Deal?"

"Alright, deal." She nodded. The child turned her back and strolled home, humming all the way.

"Now, what's to be done about you?" Donadieu asked while shaking his head at Pierre. "Guillaume, can you give me a hand? We need to carry this sorry lad home."

CHAPTER 8

Across town, Claude sunk into the velvet cushioned chair in his study. He neglected the small room from his tour; it was his alone, and he shared it with no one. Comfortably secluded, he lit a pipe and took a few puffs to get the tobacco smoldering. The aromatic fragrance filled the air and, as the smoke worked its magic, the wealthy man melted into the upholstery.

Absentmindedly, he twirled his mustache. The bristly hair entwined and straightened as his soft hands played with the strands. He looked around his study and released a single burst of amused air through his nose. As much as he enjoyed designing new and grand stretches of his house, when it came time to unwind, nothing beat his tiny study.

A blaze crackled in the fireplace, lit in advance by Roland to ensure Claude remained toasty and warm. Books were haphazardly piled about the floor, always giving a wide berth to the fireplace lest a stray ember catch them alight. More texts adorned the walls, and a ladder further consumed floor space, offering access to the higher shelves. Claude rarely read the novels he collected, but he enjoyed knowing the option existed for him, should he so desire.

Paltry moonlight entered through the small round window across the room from his desk, adding a milky hue to the orange light cast by the fire.

Various quills adorned with peacock feathers lay scattered around his desk, as did a small vial of ink and parchment spread freely. More interesting was the assortment of scientific tools carefully arranged for display. He did not know how to use the gizmos, but they gave the room a certain enlightened distinction.

I'll bet the doctors would know what these are, he mused as he fiddled with an oddly shaped tool on his desk. He picked it up awkwardly and a small metal rod snapped from the contraption, the bulk of the item thumping back to his desk. He stared at the now broken device with indifference and set the rod next to the thing. He indulged another puff from his pipe and a sip of wine from his goblet as he delved even deeper into his chair. His back complained with a dull ache from his posture, but the wine helped to numb its protest.

His stomach ballooned from the meal and the buckets of wine, but his gut distended so with such regularity that it hardly complained. Above him, a fly circled around his head and occasionally landed on his desk next to an old and stale pastry. "These are my crumbs," he said to the fly. "Stay away." He attempted to swat the bug, but his arm responded sluggishly, and he missed by a considerable amount. "Next time."

It was fair that the pest should want a taste; the food prepared by his kitchen staff was always *"exquisite"*, as the young doctor seemed so keen to repeat during his stay. Claude truly did love his staff. Always out of sight, yet every task completed before even being asked. Arranging such adequate help was the best thing his drab and melancholic wife had ever done. Perhaps the *only* good thing she'd done. He wondered how she did it.

God, how awful she is, Claude thought. The dowry he received after agreeing to marry Aliénor had more than doubled his already considerable fortune. *I should have taken that as a hint. At least she keeps to herself most times, not that I'll ever have an heir that way.*

His mood now soured by reflection on matrimonial woes, Claude tapped his fingers on the desk and began to reevaluate his life. With clarity and assurance reserved exclusively for those past the point of acceptable inebriation, the wealthy husband decided he would relieve himself of his perceived burden.

"I'll kill her," he slurred aloud.

The fly, having successfully snuck onto the old pastry, took flight at his outburst and vacated his study with haste.

Town's quarantined, he continued to muse. *I could bury her out back and tell the family the Withering took her.* "Foolproof," he mumbled to himself, as drunks do.

His head nodded from the weight of the booze, but he jerked it back to alertness and began to plot. Suffocation? Poison? Dagger? He pondered over possible tools for the job but decided the exact method ought to be left to more sober reflection. For now, he painted the big picture. As long as she was buried quickly in the yard, nature would do the rest.

The chances that someone would discover a pile of loose earth on his grand estate did not seem likely. The peasantry of the surrounding area remained terrified of the grounds thanks to their childish superstitions. One of the main reasons he'd purchased the place was the assurance any transgressions from the poor would be kept to a minimum.

The only person who may raise concern would be Roland. True, it was Aliénor who had found and hired the man, but it was from

Claude's pocket the butler got paid. He doubted Roland would assist with anything so diabolical, but should the missus suddenly disappear, would he protest?

It was a troubling question, and his muddled mind struggled as it tried to reach a conclusion. The butler did not show outward loyalty to either of his masters, and he always did as Claude instructed, but Roland's stoic demeanor made it impossible to know his mind. It would be best to send him to town one day on some meaningless errand and accomplish the malicious deed without him lingering around.

As if on cue, rhythmic footsteps came from the hall outside his study. Roland's gravelly voice announced his presence, and the clacking of his dress shoes echoed through the small room. Without waiting for a cue from Claude, the butler paced to the desk and blotted up drops of spilt wine, the crimson pools staining his otherwise pristine white towel.

"Do you require anything, sir? Shall I take your goblet, or perhaps bring you another bottle?" Roland asked in his professional drawl.

"Goodness Roland, don't you ever rest? The glasses will still be there in the morning."

"There are tasks to be completed, so I will complete them. May I take your cup, or do you require it further?"

Claude eyed the half-full goblet to his side before downing it in a single gulp. He squinted as the fermented drink burned his throat and then released a satisfied sigh as he handed over the empty glass.

"Here you are, Roland."

His eyes lit when he remembered an already forgotten plan from mere moments ago.

"Say Roland, I have a—" Claude hiccupped. "—have a task for you tomorrow. I need you to travel to town and to get me," he paused, "how about some grapes? Yes, I'd like some fresh grapes.

Four bunches should do. No more." He smiled to himself at the progress of his coy plan.

Roland slightly bowed. "Anything else, sir?"

"No, that will be all." He blinked, one eye quicker than the other.

"Very good, sir." The butler turned and exited the room.

That makes tomorrow the day I'll be rid of that cawing bird. With Roland gone, there won't be a problem. He's not a horse I'd bet on.

Almost immediately after Roland's departure, Claude's sullied mind lost track of his plans and diverted to an entirely different train of thought: his house. The aristocrat always insisted his best architectural designs came after thoroughly exploring his nation's finest vintages. Tonight was no exception. Deeply absorbed by a hatching idea, he grabbed for his quill and began to jot notes for future renovations. It took great care to ensure the legibility of his drunken scrawls; it was not uncommon to lose his best ideas to a heavy hand.

He did not hear the now shoeless feet enter the room behind him.

When the rope looped around his neck, Claude could not shout for help nor muster a cry of pain; all he managed was a strangled gurgling after the cord had been pulled taut. Flailing wildly, he reached back in an attempt to claw at the hands of his assailant, but Claude's well-manicured nails did little to upset the skin under the assailant's gloved hands.

The wealthy man wriggled and squirmed as he attempted to escape the trap held firm against his throat, but the force restricting his breathing gripped tighter than a blacksmith's vice. Blobs of spit shot from his sputtering lips and snot began to run from his nose. Try as he might, he could not free himself from the iron grip of the rope.

Slowly, the edges of his vision began to darken and blur. Absolute black followed soon thereafter. The restraint held firm for several more minutes until his muscles began to twitch. When the convulsions reached their peak, his bladder released. One of the last sensations to which Claude Dubois was aware was a warm stream of urine sliding down his leg and onto the floor.

After all the spasming ceased, the rope went slack. Roland rewound the weapon and carried it away on his arm. He returned shortly after with mop in hand to clean the newly pooled mess.

Slumped like a poorly stuffed doll, Claude loafed in his chair. The previously bothersome fly returned to the room and began to crawl over the man's unflinching face before it scurried back to the stale pastry. Claude's chest slowly rose, and from his lips came a subtle wheezing.

CHAPTER 9

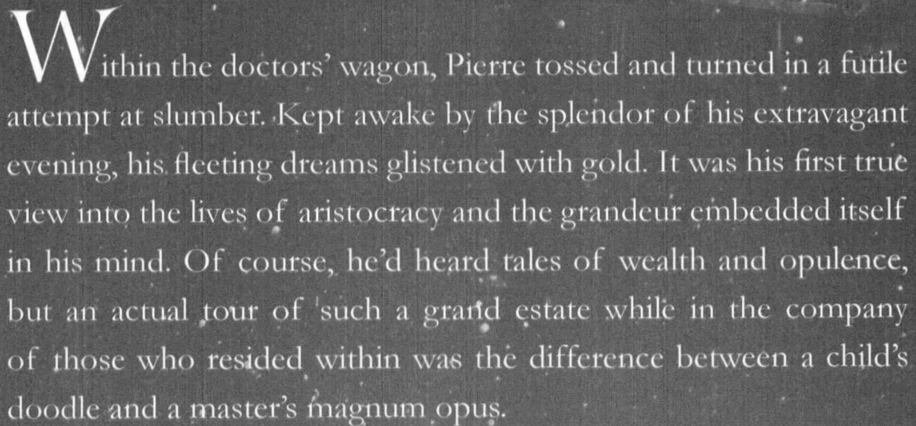

Within the doctors' wagon, Pierre tossed and turned in a futile attempt at slumber. Kept awake by the splendor of his extravagant evening, his fleeting dreams glistened with gold. It was his first true view into the lives of aristocracy and the grandeur embedded itself in his mind. Of course, he'd heard tales of wealth and opulence, but an actual tour of such a grand estate while in the company of those who resided within was the difference between a child's doodle and a master's magnum opus.

As all do after catching a glimpse of life free from hunger and worry, his mind constructed a world with himself as the owner of such a domain. He fantasized about expensive tastes for imported rugs and spices, and the great palaces to which he would travel for leisure and to dine with global elites.

Night progressed and Pierre fluttered in and out of sleep. His dreams promised him riches beyond imagination, but his mind desperately needed recovery from the stimulating day.

Hours later, still long before the sun's glow promised to crest the horizon, Pierre awoke and found his forehead drenched with cold sweat. All warmth supplied by the evening's wine had fled and a nose-nipping chill took its place. Guillaume bounced the wagon's suspension as he rolled on his side and continued to snore. An orange leaf riding the wind blew into their wagon and Pierre listened for unknown noises beyond the woolen walls. He heard only the frosty breeze.

Unable to calm himself, he kept watch out of the corner of his eyes, jerking his head at any flick of a shadow or stray beam of light from the thinning moon. Whatever summoned the apprentice away from his rest remained obscured, if there'd been anything at all. Gradually his attention faded, and Pierre returned to rest.

A wink of quality sleep graced the young man. His fantasies dulled and the warm embrace of his blankets hugged him tight. His fidgeting slowed and breathing relaxed.

"Let's go, we've work to do!"

The booming voice roused Pierre back to wakefulness with a start.

In what seemed like the timeframe of a single blink, the sky had jumped from twinkling stars to the rising sun, its rays blasting directly into his squinting eyes.

"If we don't get inside soon, we'll be deafened by that damn bell again."

Pierre's head throbbed and his stomach contorted into excruciating shapes. Worsened by the sun's radiant assault, his first glance of the morning world was one of incoherent spinning. He squeezed his eyes shut and only opened them again when he thought his vision would behave. Fumbling around the wagon, he began to collect his tools and outfit.

"Look at you," Guillaume said, laughing. "We'll take it a little slower this morning. You're stumbling as though you're a marionette and a six-year-old has control of the strings."

It was not often the pair indulged so. Coupled with the restless night, Pierre wished his limbs truly were being moved by another so he would not have to bother.

"How are you so lively?" he mumbled.

"I can out-drink you for the same reason I out-doctor you," Guillaume replied with a spreading grin. "Experience. In a short while, I'm sure you'll be beating me at both."

The two broke their fast on the usual salty bread and watered wine. Pierre ate much less than usual for fear his stomach would refuse the offering. Guillaume did not pester him as he sluggishly ate and dressed. Instead, the old doctor disembarked from the carriage to care for Hippo, a task usually reserved for the apprentice.

When sufficiently nourished and adorned, the young doctor clambered down the side of the wagon, trying not to fall. As his boot hit the ground, his spinning mind forced him to stop and acclimate to standing upright. Guillaume, who had just finished grooming their stallion, smacked him on the shoulder. The jostling was too much, and Pierre retched onto the earth.

"Ready to go?" Guillaume asked, a sly grin arching the corner of his mouth.

Pierre nodded slowly. "I may feel worse than those we aim to treat."

Guillaume's smile widened before it was obscured by the mask he strapped to the back of his head. Simultaneously, Pierre attached his own. The nearly overpowering fragrances erupting from the beak threatened the integrity of his stomach yet again. It was only the cool air wicking away the sweat on the back of his neck that allowed him to maintain his dubious composure.

Together they entered the church, and despite his hangover, anticipation blossomed within Pierre. Eagerness drove him forth to examine the results of the previous day's experiments, to see what the most efficacious treatment would be.

Donadieu was already up and tending to the needs of the ill when they entered. He knelt beside a barely conscious man, saying a prayer on his behalf. Pierre watched the priest count beads on his rosary; the unwavering dedication of this aging man to the care of those under his stewardship inspired the apprentice. Being a traveling doctor, he rarely forged such bonds with patients. Most commonly, they administered a remedy or salve and moved on to the next site in need of their aid.

Not wanting to disturb the praying man, Pierre followed Guillaume to the opposite side of the church. There, the old doctor began to dictate the patient's condition, and Pierre scribbled notes in his hastily retrieved notebook.

"First, we shall examine the section treated to relieve excessive dryness," Guillaume said, kneeling beside an unconscious young woman. "Patient maintains difficulty in breathing, a raspy wheezing noise accompanies struggling gasps. No new pustules, boils, or rashes present on skin. Temperature remains normal. Overall, no discernable change."

Pew-to-pew, the duo toured around the church visiting each row that housed their test subjects. Every patient yielded as concerning a result as the last. No matter the treatment, no medication affected a change in a single diseased villager who lay on the hard church benches.

Halfway through their rotation, Pierre noticed Donadieu had finished his prayer and was observing them make their rounds. His expression was neutral at first but soured into worry as he listened to Guillaume repeat "no change" with every parishioner they examined. Guilt welled within him. The priest's silver sat protected in their wagon, regardless of their dismal results.

Guillaume appeared to be wholly unbothered by the discoveries, or rather lack thereof, and his indifference to the setback relieved some of the burden the young doctor felt. If the master doctor remained undeterred, surely there must be a reason. Perhaps there was a new plan he was constructing in his mind.

"Well, I'm at a loss," Guillaume said as they examined the last patient on their list.

Pierre's well of guilt overflowed and cooled the excitement of his heart, leaving a cold melancholy in its place. He was thankful that his mask covered the reddening of his face. Upon delivery of this unsatisfactory diagnosis, Donadieu approached from the corner of his view. He dared not meet the priest's eyes, even while hidden behind the lenses of his medical mask.

Donadieu guided the doctors to a far corner of the church, away from the pews and the prying ears of the ill. "How are they?"

"Entirely unchanged," Guillaume replied with little care. Although facial expressions remained obscured from his costume, his tone relayed utter indifference.

Donadieu frowned. "Where do we go from here?"

"I'm not entirely sure." Guillaume shrugged. "In all my travels, I've never seen such a number of people remain entirely indifferent to all treatments, negative or positive. Whatever this is, it may not be something we can help with."

Donadieu's eyes briefly flashed with insult then drooped to despair, a reaction difficult for Pierre to watch and one that forced his own eyes to the floor.

"I don't accept that," the priest said. "There must be something you can do. These people need help and what they require is more than I can do. You *must* help them; you are the only ones who can."

"Look," Guillaume's tone now flared with confrontation, "we've done what we can. They don't respond to any treatment we've offered, so I don't know what you want us to do. We can't leave, thanks to our friends from the king, but as for the work we can do, it is done. All that's left is to continue the same tests until a positive result reveals itself. That will, of course, become quite costly as the requirement for our services extends. Now, shall we discuss the outstanding payment for our time and supplies thus far?"

Donadieu ignored the invoice and turned to Pierre, whose beak still pointed at the ground. "Please, Pierre. Can you think of anything else to try? No matter the difficulty, you must help me save these people."

A silence spread over them, broken only by the occasional cough from the diseased. Donadieu despondently waited for the young doctor to respond. Guillaume, too, was watching, casually swatting at a pair of flies circling his mask.

Pierre combed through the mountains of texts stored in his brain. Desperation pushed him; he felt compelled to heal these people, to prove that he was worth his pay.

"Well, suppositionally," Pierre said, trying to piece together his argument, "as there was no response to humoral remedies, it's possible there may also be a source of miasma at play. If we could locate and eradicate the source, it may help to relieve some of the strain on the unwell and then our remedies could do the rest. If we could do that, it would help the sufferers and likely prevent future cases."

Hope sparked within the priest's eyes and even this minor change of countenance raised Pierre's spirits as well. They both turned to Guillaume, waiting for the master's opinion.

Guillaume shook his head but, after a moment, he conceded. "Theoretically, Pierre's right. But it's a lot easier said than done. Locating a source of miasma powerful enough to contaminate an entire town, yet so mild that it is undetectable to human senses when strolling outside, will be extraordinarily difficult. We've already checked the water for any source of contamination and it's clean. We'd be looking for a needle in a haystack, especially if the source is not within city limits. This invisible and odorless fog could be spreading from anywhere. Besides, we're being paid to treat the ill, not hike the countryside."

"God brought you to this town because He knew you could help, and even when all appeared lost, He guided Pierre's tongue to another solution. Now it falls to us to execute that solution. We will succeed because we must."

Guillaume waved his hand dismissively. "We could be looking indefinitely. It's a hopeless search."

"Two days of searching, that's all I ask. Two more days and I'll pay upfront and in full for the rest of your stay. Extra even, if you so demand. We must try."

The old doctor's head perked at the promise of extra pay. Guillaume always changed his tune for a few extra coins.

"Two days. We'll search for two days."

A grin spread across the priest's face, and Pierre's own excitement matched. Being his first serious assignment, he yearned for it to be an undeniable success.

"Thank you from the bottom of my heart, Guillaume. Now, what exactly are we looking for?" Donadieu asked. "What would a source of miasma look like?"

Conviction surged within Pierre, the likes of which were unfamiliar to the usually timid man. His cadence accelerated to match his excitement. "That's the tricky part. There's no one confirmed source of disease, especially such a unique one as you have here." The words flowed from his mouth, eagerness expelling them faster than he could enunciate. "Generally, it would be a location rife with rot and decay. Miasma usually spreads with bad smells; obvious sources are things like bogs, but really, it could be anything."

Donadieu paused before he asked, "What about an old, decaying building?"

"It would need to be substantially decayed, but it's possible," Pierre replied.

"The west wing of the Dubois' estate, that's the only unrenovated part of the home and it has been left stagnant since before they moved in. Possibly for centuries. Who knows what's had time to fester in those old walls? That's the only place that jumps to mind. Could it be a potential source?"

Guillaume took a step back and leaned against the church wall while his apprentice continued the conversation.

"I would have imagined the miasma to be detectable last night when we passed by the entryway," Pierre replied, "but everything about this affliction is odd, so I suppose anything is possible. If that is the source, I find it peculiar that the Dubois aren't affected, but people do seem to be inflicted at random, so proximity may not be an important factor at here. I'm not sure how we'd investigate that, though. Claude and Aliénor don't strike me as the sort to be receptive to unsolicited guests patrolling through their home."

Donadieu's eyes looked to the sky, and he rocked his head from side-to-side before sighing in acquiescence. "Gentlemen, I'm going to share with you the events which transpired while I was absent from the parlor last night. I'm not sure you recall due to your consumption, but I was gone for quite some time." Pierre looked at Guillaume, who met his gaze before they prompted the priest to continue. "Were I in your shoes, I doubt I would believe what I'm about to say, but I must say it nonetheless in hopes it may advance our goal."

He began to narrate his explorations of the previous night. Years of rousing sermons honed Donadieu's oration, and Pierre hung off every word. The apprentice's mood jumped from curiosity to terror as Donadieu recounted chasing mysterious candlelight to the discovery of the wandering ghoul. It was as if Pierre himself had explored the darkened manor and by the story's end, his heart beat against his ribs with secondhand panic. Eyes wide beneath his mask, all traces of his hangover vanished.

Guillaume, ever the curmudgeon, scoffed when the priest finished. "You must have had more wine than even Pierre, and his temperament was quite bruised this morning, I can assure you."

"I don't blame your skepticism of my encounter," Donadieu replied. "I was there, and I hardly believe it myself. All the same, after hearing your apprentice relate the importance of discovering the disease's focal point, I see no harm in making sure it *was* only some bad wine last night."

Guillaume stood straight and folded his arms across his chest. "The harm is breaking into someone's house, our generous hosts of last night, no less. That sort of thing results in consequences. We know the local garrison isn't afraid to fire."

Having started to recover from the story and his heart still emboldened by his need to succeed, Pierre cut in with authoritative patience. "Guillaume, you always lecture on reputation and professionalism while practicing. This man is our employer. Do we not owe it to him, let alone the townspeople, to investigate every possible lead whilst we are here? And what if that which Father Donadieu implied is true? A mobile source of miasma now taking refuge in that fetid wing, the scientific implication is unprecedented.

I must confess, I had my own suspicions of Roland. The man looked on the verge of death beneath his heavy wrappings. We would be fools not to investigate, pariahs to our trade. There could be something groundbreaking locked within that home."

Donadieu nodded approvingly and they both turned to the master doctor for his response.

Guillaume sighed and raised his hands to the sky in submission. "It's your money, but if you want us in that house, you'll have to find us a way that doesn't involve trespassing. Do that, and we'll poke around for the source, and for that phantom woman of yours."

Pierre clenched a fist at his side in a personal celebration. He was glad for any direction, vague as it may be. Searching the west wing would be an easy enough feat, especially over the course of the two days Guillaume had allowed. The only obstacle was getting inside.

They retreated to the doctors' wagon and began passing ideas back-and-forth on how they may gain re-entry into the grand estate. Suggestions included bringing gifts as a thank you for their evening meal or returning to request more information about the stylistic architectural choices. They even considered sharing the truth, but that option was quickly dismissed.

As they debated, Pierre's excitement dissipated, replaced by growing dread. His leg bounced, and his mind began to twist. He'd been so eager to save the ailing town that he had volunteered himself, and the others, to explore a condemned home in search of some sort of hellish spawn. Perhaps the heroic path did not agree with him after all. Perhaps he much preferred the quiet and mundane.

The three did not plot long before the matter was decided for them. Pierre was the first to hear, instinctively tilting his ear to better capture the high-pitched noise rising to the west. Shortly after, the older ears also caught the sound, and they turned as well. In unison and without speech, they circled to the front of the church.

Several sickly heads poked from windows and through doorways as a woman in a billowing white dress came running down the street, wailing of sorrow and disease. Only when she slowed before the church did she stop screaming. Instead, she crumpled to her knees and panted feverishly for air.

Pierre watched the scene as though it were a play, entirely unsure how to react or whether he should intervene at all. When the frequency between the woman's exhausted gasps slowed, Aliénor looked up and began to weep before the assembled men.

CHAPTER 10

Donadieu had first met Aliénor shortly after she and Claude moved to Bastion. At least once a week, the Dubois and he had greeted each other in town and made pleasant but brief conversation. In all the time he'd known her, never would the priest have described Aliénor as anything other than restrained.

Having her before them now in a genuine frenzy rang every alarm bell in his head. Her usually pale face was stained pink from vigorous exercise, while her dress was torn from the run and drenched with sweat. Drying mud splattered up her legs, and both her bare feet were cracked raw and smeared with blood. Although the day now pressed well into mid-morning, the sun had yet to make an appearance; it hid behind a canopy of clouds and refused to check on the world below. The absence of warming light meant the street's cobbles retained the icy bite from the night before.

"Aliénor," Donadieu asked, calm and concerned, "what's the matter? Are you alright?"

"The doctors, I need the doctors," she panted, gasping between every other word. "It's Claude, he's unwell. He's succumbed to the Withering. I've shaken him and shaken him, and I can't wake him up. I need the doctors, I need you, I need anybody. Someone has to come and help. I'll pay whatever it takes."

"Fetch a blanket from the wagon," Guillaume barked.

Like an obedient dog, Pierre scampered away.

Donadieu looked at Guillame and raised an eyebrow. Their invitation back to the manor had just come screaming down the road. Guillaume gave a half-smile in reply. Donadieu knew the man was likely more interested in the extra pay than of finding the source of disease.

The priest then squatted beside the frantic woman and tried to hide a wince at the pain of lowering himself so. He placed a hand upon her back and offered words of comfort and divine grace. Aliénor's sobbing only grew in strength, and it scratched Donadieu's throat to speak louder than her wails.

Pierre returned and handed a coarse woolen blanket to Donadieu, who wasted no time in draping it around the shivering woman. He gently patted her shoulders, and at last her howling began to abate.

"Is your horse fit to tow?" Donadieu asked the doctors. "It's awfully cold this morning, and we couldn't force poor Aliénor to walk back with feet so torn. We should ride together and make haste. We must hurry and tend to Claude."

Neither Pierre nor Guillaume contested, and even before the priest finished his request, they were already heading toward the wagon. Surprised with the ease at which he got his way, especially with Guillaume's near constant abrasiveness, Donadieu helped Aliénor to her feet and gently pushed her after the doctors. By the time they'd reached the wagon, her tears had all but subsided and she sniveled quietly. Hippo shook his mane during their approach and stood still when the doctors attached his harness. A brief effort by the men helped Aliénor to mount the wagon and, before long, they were off and rumbling along the cobbled roads.

Aliénor sat in the passenger seat of the wagon while Guillaume took the reins. From Donadieu's place in the back, he could hear the physician attempting to console Aliénor by explaining about medicine and of his previous successes. The doctor spoke with great care and a gentle tone. His bedside manner surprised and impressed Donadieu.

Pierre, sitting across from Donadieu, removed his mask and clutched it tight in his lap. He stared intently at the priest, his eyes wide and his lips slightly tucked in. The apprentice did not look well. His face was pale, and his eyes carried bags.

"It seems we've had an opportunity fall into our lap. Lucky, is it not, Pierre?" Donadieu's stomach squirmed relentlessly from hope and anxiety, but he would not allow his face to frown, nor would he allow a crease across his forehead. Instead, he leaned toward Pierre and attempted to distract them both, speaking quietly so that Aliénor may not hear. "When we steal away to search the home, remind me again what it is we should be looking for? Anything specific?"

Pierre's unflinching gaze stared back at him. "Is it true?" he asked. "Does a creature stalk the halls of the Dubois' estate?"

Donadieu offered a weak smile to console him. Just as he opened his mouth, a wagon wheel hit a large hole in the road and violently jostled the interior. Pierre let out a yelp. Guillaume shouted apologies from the front.

When normality returned, the priest resumed. "I do believe so, yes. I thought it better to inform you and be mistaken than to not tell you and be right. I did not get a long look at the woman, nor did she respond to my calls, but from what I could see, I believe it was Louise, the potter's wife. She was the woman I wanted you to aid that went missing. She wore the same dress I'd seen her in the night before, and her flesh looked equally…*spoiled*."

Pierre grew frantic in his reply, raising his voice above what could remain solely between the two. "But why would she be there? *How* could she be there?"

Donadieu lowered his voice further to try to quiet Pierre. "I don't know. Perhaps she found the strength to walk all the way there. I'm not really sure that it matters. What does matter is she is there, and she may hold the key to all that afflicts this town. She was among the first infected, possibly the very first. That's what's important. If she isn't the source, maybe she can lead us to it."

"But what do we do if we find her?"

Donadieu shook his head. "I'm afraid that's where I'm going to have to defer to your expertise."

Pierre's brow dropped and he massaged his temples. "We get rid of the smell that's causing it. Best practice for direct exposure has always been to overpower it with stronger scents; that's how our masks work." He paused. "Depending on what we find, we must reduce its potency or find some way to secure it. I'm not sure what that means if Louise is the culprit." The apprentice looked up and Donadieu felt the glare pierce through his skull. "Do we bury her alive?"

The question singed the base of Donadieu's neck and he winced from thinking about it. He had been so emphatic about finding the creature that he hadn't considered what came after. "To be honest," he said, "I was hoping you two would take it from there. Perhaps run some tests, find out whatever it might be that you could learn from her."

"It might not work like that." Pierre's voice transitioned from worry to annoyance. "These are uncharted waters, Father. I think it's best we pray for guidance, because as of now, that's the only guidance we're going to get and more than I can give."

Donadieu took a moment to reflect and stared intensely at the empty space between himself and the apprentice. Pierre was right. He released a heavy sigh and recited some prayers of his own.

Only when the wagon turned off the dusty street and onto the gravel path of the Dubois' estate did the two stir. Together, they watched in silence as they approached the growing home. The centuries old architecture of the west wing juxtaposed with the modern stylized exterior of the rest of the house. Donadieu could not place why, but it appeared even more out of place in the midday sun.

A ray of green-tinted light reflected into his face and forced Donadieu to squint. He searched for the source through mostly closed eyes and spotted a small stained-glass window high on the second floor of the old west wing. The priest studied it curiously until it disappeared behind the wagon's woolen walls.

The Inertial sway rocked the wagon as it came to a stop before the grand estate. Even before all movement had ceased, Pierre jumped free from the wagon and disappeared from sight around the side of the carriage. Donadieu shambled to the edge of the interior and glanced down at the ground below; despite being only a few feet above, the descent taunted his ever-stiffening joints. Moments later, Pierre returned to offer assistance for which Donadieu profusely thanked him.

Between the wagon and the home, still as a statue, Roland waited on the lawn. His face remained mostly covered, and his long hair swayed in the cool afternoon breeze. Only when Aliénor made to dismount did he move to her side and offered an arm to escort her into the house.

Roland lamented to his master as they walked. "The house has gone mad looking for you, my lady. I do wish you'd let us know before you go running off."

Pierre took Hippo to the stables and Donadieu waited awkwardly with Guillaume for their young associate to return.

When all had ascended the stairs into the home, they found Aliénor already sitting in a foyer chair, her posture rigid. Roland stood beside her like a loyal dog awaiting command.

Donadieu jittered from purpose. He yearned to explore the west wing and craned his neck around the room as though looking for a shortcut there or for any indication of endemic disease. Beside him, the doctors donned their masks and dismay cooled his nerves; they were there to tend the master of the house, not solely to indulge his own curiosity.

When all appeared ready, Aliénor gave a frail wave of her hand and Roland stepped forward. "Follow me." He extended his hand and led the party up the double stairway without looking back.

The trio wasted no time following, eager to begin their investigation. Donadieu spent the better part of the trip mapping the estate in his mind and attempted to visualize the quickest path to the west wing. Being a group so few in number, it would be obvious if any went missing now. Instead, they must all find some more opportune time to steal away and trespass through the forbidden door.

Twice as they walked, Guillaume attempted to engage Roland in conversation. Twice he received no reply. Occasionally, they saw other servants and maids throughout the halls, but always at a distance and always scurrying away as though frightened of being seen. Had any of these same servants watched him from shadowed doorways? Did they know of Louise?

Roland stopped abruptly before a landscape painting that Claude had only briefly noted during their tour. The artwork stood some six feet tall and easily twelve feet long. It was a rather unremarkable forest scene and Donadieu had not minded when Claude had mostly neglected it, but now that Roland halted before it, his interest grew. Upon careful examination, small slits could be seen running along the height of the piece.

With a gentle push upon the center of the painting, Roland opened a hidden door that revealed Claude's private room. Relative to the rest of the home, the space was miniscule; objectively, it was more than large enough to fit all the present men.

Donadieu trailed the doctors into the room and admired the secluded and cozy place. Tendrils of smoke rose from the still smoldering fireplace. In the center of the room, with his back to the door, Claude slumped.

Wasting no time, Guillaume descended upon the unconscious man. Pierre followed, ready to note the results of his mentor's investigation and the experiments they performed. Despite having been the sole caretaker of the town's ill for many months, Donadieu now found himself obsolete and standing awkwardly to the side as the doctors performed.

He turned to eye the door, looking for a chance to break away. He'd expected Roland to disappear and wait on Aliénor after they began, but to his dismay, the butler stood unmoving in the doorway, presenting an obstacle between Donadieu and the rest of the home.

Not knowing what to do, Donadieu approached Claude, making sure to leave the doctors plenty of space to work. He quietly signed the cross and started to pray his rosary. Despite the ever-extending length of time they toiled, Roland remained steadfast in the doorway. An hour later, when Donadieu ran out of prayers both traditional and improvised, he began again in Latin.

Repeated glares from Guillaume made it known the physician did not approve of this distraction, and the indifference in the butler's face made Donadieu at last give up. It was clear the servant never planned to move. Donadieu's anxiety only grew as they further delayed, and his fingers increasingly fidgeted around his rosary. The fluttering of his chest compelled action.

"Excuse me, Roland," he said awkwardly and unable to contain himself anymore. "I'm afraid I need to relieve myself. After my failed attempt to navigate through this house last night, I'm hoping you can direct me to the closest commode."

Roland turned his head to the priest, his voice as droning as ever. "You'll find one just across the hall, sir." He stepped aside and extended an arm, pointing to an opposite door.

Donadieu thanked the butler and crossed the hall. How was it that the previous night when he required relief, the nearest chamber pot hid across the house? Now, when he wished to steal away, it was next door. Truth be told, Donadieu's aging and bloated bladder rejoiced greatly at the opportunity for release all the same, even if it did not further his goal.

When the priest concluded his business, he spent an extra minute nervously pacing the room. Like a rat in a cage, he felt trapped, unable to break away. Were he a younger man, a stealthy escape may have been an option, assuming he could sneak past their guard. Instead, he feared his old knees would never allow it, even if he did know the way through the sprawling home. No, he needed to return and wait for an opportunity to present itself, as monotonous as this day may turn out to be.

The next few hours passed excruciatingly slowly as the priest watched the doctors begin their experiments from scratch, yet again. With a singular subject for their combined efforts, the two slowly and methodically ran through a gambit of examinations, tests, experiments, and medicines. Multiple times they searched for spots, rashes, or pustules. They rubbed salves upon various joints and even applied their trusty leeches to see if an abundance of blood could be causing the malady but, as before, nothing they did yielded any results.

All the while, Donadieu absentmindedly fidgeted and watched them work. Having spent time around the doctors, he found he could follow the reasons for, and expected results from, the tests. Like the medical experts, he too was disappointed with every negative outcome.

To further agitate the mindless waiting, several flies joined them within the room. The incessant buzzing agonized the priest, making the day an eternity. He swatted at the insects but missed with every swipe.

Midday turned to afternoon, and afternoon passed to evening. The butler ever unmoving, the doctors entirely absorbed in their work trying desperately to earn their hosts extra pay, and Donadieu waiting for any opportunity to move. He rolled his eyes and internally screamed when Guillaume suggested they try just one final test, for the *fourth* time. It was remarkable how determined Guillaume could be when motivated by nobility's coin.

At last, the priest broke and decided he would ask Roland to accompany him to the exit. He could take no more. If he could not get to the west wing, he hoped the distraction would allow his companions the opportunity in his stead.

Before he could open his mouth to ask, Roland nodded at an unseen person in the hall and spoke. "Madame Dubois requests your combined company for the evening meal. Please follow me to the dining hall."

Guillaume snapped to attention. "Excellent! I don't think I've eaten since the morning," his voice still muffled by the mask. The elder doctor casually left his devices around the room and made for the door. Pierre, more deliberate with the placement of his notes, followed suit.

Halfway back through the house and with the ill man well behind them, the physicians removed their masks. Pierre remarked on the wondrous aromas of roasted meats and fresh baked bread which floated down the manor's halls; Donadieu sniffed in vain. A roaring fire again lit the dining room's grand hearth. Unlike the previous night, it was now Aliénor who sat at the head of the dining table, her old position abandoned to darkness. Other than their host, all took the same seats they'd used the night before.

Aliénor appeared fully recovered from her morning's trials. Her face returned to its usual ghastly white, and she had changed into a more appropriate dress for company. Slowly, she turned her head and surveyed each of the guests at her table.

Guillaume didn't seem to notice; his sight could not be torn from the food.

Pierre met her piercing stare, but he quickly broke and sheepishly looked down at the empty plate before him.

Turning her attention once more, her eyes passed over Donadieu's. The priest could not help but feel an accessory to the physicians, his presence not entirely wanted. Perhaps because she did not believe he could help her husband, or perhaps she already got what she wanted from him. Aliénor flicked him a miniscule smile from the corner of her mouth and addressed the table.

"How *is* Claude?" she asked in a slow and inquisitive cadence. With perfect posture straight and a steely glare, her commanding demeanor struck Donadieu. Previously meek and shy, she acclimatized quickly to heading the home.

Guillaume snapped to attention at the question, like a dog whose name had been called, yet he responded as bluntly as always. "Perplexing. As with the villagers who also suffer from the Withering, his breathing is impaired, and we can't wake him. Other than those two symptoms, he appears to be in perfect health."

Aliénor's expression turned solemn. "What's to be done for him?"

Guillaume replied quickly, and the priest thought he saw a small droplet of saliva pooling in the corner of the doctor's mouth. "It's a very complex and delicate situation; one we could perhaps discuss whilst we dine? The meal smells divine, and it would be a shame to let it grow cold."

Her face brightened and she grinned in response. "Of course, you all must be famished having attended to my spouse all afternoon. As for the meal, you'll have to thank Roland for that. He chose the courses and instructed the staff on its execution. Everything must always meet his exacting specifications."

"The rest of the staff," Donadieu said. "How many do you have working here? I've only seen one or two dart out of sight while we moved through the halls."

"They are excellent at remaining hidden, aren't they? Roland practically trained all the personnel himself. Look around. I'll bet you didn't even notice he left." All three of the guests scanned the room. Sure enough, the butler had skulked off without so much as a footstep to be heard. "We have between ten and twenty staff at any time assisting around the manor, depending on the season and the frequency of visitors. We're down to six now. The quarantine has greatly reduced the need for more, as well as the ability to hire.

"What a silly thing that quarantine is, is it not? Some bureaucrat heard a few peasants got sick and forced the shutdown of our entire town. No mind at all as to how it may hinder those living here." Aliénor released a long sigh. "A whole lot of excitement over some coughing. It seems a bit much to me. Near as I understand it, no one has even passed from the disease. Admittedly, it did give me quite the scare this morning, but knowing he'll surely wake up in no time has alleviated some of the panic. I'm not that lucky.

"Look at me going on. Without my husband here to nip at my heels, I find I actually enjoy conversation. Please, enjoy your meal. I intend to."

With that, Aliénor began to fill her plate, and Guillaume happily followed suit. He pulled at every platter within his reach.

Donadieu picked at the spread with less vigor. He ate only what others sampled first. The priest's suspicions were so vague that he himself wasn't entirely sure what he suspected. He thought it best not to chance anything before he got his answers.

After a few hardy bites had been eaten by all, Aliénor resumed the conversation. "Now, we were talking about my husband. What can we do for him?"

Donadieu nudged Pierre's side. He figured the proposition would seem more convincing from a medical professional, and the apprentice picked up on the implication. Neither of them had to worry about Guillaume responding. The master's mouth was crammed nearly beyond capacity.

"As Guillaume mentioned earlier," Pierre said, "we've hit a wall with what we can achieve in attempting to improve Claude's condition directly. There is another option, however, and that is to attempt to assist him *indirectly*."

Aliénor tilted her head and motioned Pierre to continue.

"Without getting too technical, disease is known to spread through bad air: miasma. If we can find and eliminate the source of the bad air, it may help improve the condition of those suffering. At the very least, it should prevent people from getting worse."

"How interesting." Aliénor's voice carried both hints of curiosity and annoyance in equal measure. "Where do you suggest we find this 'bad air'?"

Once more, Donadieu nudged the young doctor to continue.

"Miasma usually spreads from dark, damp, and rotting places. While being led around your exquisite estate last night, I recall a wing of your house has yet to be renovated. If there is significant damage to that part of the home and the wood is bountiful with mold and fungus, you could have a local source which is spreading from there. If you'd grant us permission to investigate, we can rule it out and ensure you are not at risk. If that is the source, everyone in the house would be affected in only a matter of time."

The guests all turned and awaited Aliénor's response. Even Guillaume had fed enough to regain interest in the conversation. A coarse voice replied from behind Donadieu, and all but Aliénor jumped in their seats at the unexpected response. Pierre jumped the highest and his knees smacked the table, causing the porcelain to clink as though even the dishes had been startled.

"That would be unwise," Roland said. "The west wing is unsafe."

"Precisely why it must be investigated," Guillaume interjected. "It could be more unsafe than you realize. Your health is at risk."

With great relief to the priest, Aliénor sided with the doctors. "Don't be such a worrywart, Roland. These men are professionals. They know what they're doing. If that old wing isn't safe for even them, how will the construction crew be able to enter and fix it? Claude needs help. If they have a chance of assisting him, then I say we let them."

"Very well," Roland replied, stoic as always.

Donadieu's eagerness sprung him to his feet. He intended to allow no time for further consideration when the next step of their plan dangled tantalizingly within his grasp. "Let's have a look now, then."

Pierre stood up shortly after, and Guillaume rose slowest of all, still eyeing the half-eaten tart on his plate.

"You'll forgive me if I don't join," the hostess said. "After this morning, I believe some rest would do me well."

"Of course, of course," Donadieu replied, eager to push the party along. "Roland, if you would be so kind, please lead the way."

Without pause, Roland spun and led the group into the hall.

During the course of their meal, the sun had retreated beneath the horizon and only the last echoes of daylight made it through the many windows. Roland carried a small oil lantern to light the way. Candlesticks were collected and handed back as they marched through the halls, each set alight by the previous and casting a dull glow around each person.

Donadieu suspiciously eyed every flame as he passed it along. The scars on his face burned in remembrance. Even still, his anticipation grew so intense he thought his lungs may burst. This mission to resolve the woes of the town was a gamble at best, but after being its caretaker for so long with no hope of improvement, he almost floated at the possibility of a resolution.

The walk felt an eternity to the priest, but at last they arrived. Roland had taken them to the second-floor access door and there, in the center of a hallway, stood the decrepit door. The wood looked darker than the rest of the house, as though it had been preserved in an early stage of rot. It hung ever so slightly ajar, enough to be noticeable but not so much to allow any helpful view into what lay beyond the wooden portal.

"We have arrived at the second story entrance to the western wing," Roland said. "Please, do be careful." With that, the butler opened the door and stepped aside.

CHAPTER 11

Aburst of humidity spilled from the rotten door and washed over those who stood before it. Pierre recoiled from the house's breath as the moisture worked its way up his robes from below. The muggy air forced an uncomfortable shiver from the apprentice.

Beyond the entryway waited a great void. Already, Guillaume and Donadieu had entered the cavernous hallway. Roland remained and stared at him expectantly. Rushing after those ahead, Pierre crossed the threshold and into the condemned west wing. Individually, their candles fought a losing battle against the darkness, but together their surroundings reluctantly accepted the light.

Pierre lamented his negligence as of late; he'd failed to polish the hazy glass eyes set within his mask. The lenses were fine for surgery, not nighttime exploration. Some spit and polish would have gone a long way to aiding his vision in the dark.

The antiquated stone walls dripped with condensation, food for the wallpaper of mildew. It did not take long for Pierre to all but forget the luxury and decadence of the halls in the mansion behind him. With one quick step, his imagination twisted his being. When roaming the renovated halls he pictured himself an opulent baron, now he was a rogue on a dastardly mission to pillage a deserted crypt.

His eyes darted with the flickering shadows, and his morning's fear came charging back. As Aliénor warned, a portion of the hallway ceiling had indeed opened and caved a great section of the roof into the cramped old hallway. Tiles and debris lay scattered around the floor. Whether this collapse happened recently or a decade ago was impossible to tell, but the pile of detritus nearly blocked the hall beyond. Had the night not been so cloudy, stars would have been visible through the roof's gaping hole.

A cursory glance around the place revealed more than enough rot to justify a mild miasma; some of the decaying doors even sprouted white and speckled mushrooms, but this hallway alone was not enough to destroy an entire town.

Pierre suspiciously eyed the floor for fear it may follow the roof's example and send them tumbling to the level below. Sections of the hall's burgundy carpet remained visible, but most of the rug was covered in fallen leaves and dust turned to mud. He inhaled deeply from an instinctual need to test the efficacy of his mask. Overpowering notes of cinnamon, sage, and various other herbs did their job and kept the bad odors at bay. He breathed deeply again, this time to calm his nerves.

Behind him, the light cast from Roland's candle began to dim and rusty hinges squealed. A jarring click sealed the way from which they'd entered. Pierre defeated an urge to lunge back and push against their exit. Neither Guillaume nor Donadieu seemed to care that the butler had sealed them in. *He was probably too afraid to follow,* Pierre told himself and continued after his elders in silence.

Despite the grandeur of the west wing, Pierre had to remind himself he was not trapped in an ancient prison. The hallway extended as far as he could see through his foggy mask, and equally spaced doors dotted either side of the corridor. None of them were open, and the thought of having to search every room caused his heart to beat in his throat.

Guillaume was the first to speak. The sound of his usually booming voice was quieted by his mask and further muted by the damp floor and walls. By the time the word reached Pierre's ears, they were no louder than a whisper. "We should each take a room and continue down the hall, searching everything along the way. The faster we check it all, the faster we can leave."

Pierre white-knuckled his candlestick at the suggestion of separation. With the potential of Donadieu's ghoul lurking about, abandoning the safety of numbers struck him as madness.

"I'm not convinced that's a good idea," Donadieu replied. The priest's trepidation released some of the guilt Pierre felt over his own fear. "I'm still not certain what I'm looking for, not to mention how much harder it will be without all three candles together."

Pierre sighed in relief. "Especially through our masks," he added to bolster the argument.

Guillaume placed a hand on his hip and bounced a finger upon his robes. "No, I think it's best we progress as quickly as possible. If the miasma does originate here, we should do whatever we can to avoid lingering. I agree some extra light would help. Keep your eyes out for spare candles. Martine, begin your search with these first few doors. Pierre and I will make our way around the collapsed roof and start at the far side of the hall. We'll work our way back and meet in the middle. At no point will we be out of earshot. If anything comes up, just yell."

Pierre's panicked mind could not piece together an argument as to why they should stick together, other than his own fear.

Defeated, he relented and adhered to the instructions. The authority of Guillaume's voice told the apprentice his mentor would not be receptive to opposition.

Donadieu shook his head but did not protest.

Guillaume proceeded down the hall and beckoned Pierre to follow. The young doctor trailed behind as though an invisible rope attached them at the waist; he even felt the tug. He bowed his head as they moved, finding it difficult to look up for fear of what he may see.

Even less graceful with his actions than with his tongue, Guillaume clambered over and around the pile of debris blocking most of the hallway. The trial was made even more difficult by the need to reserve a hand to keep his candle aloft.

When Guillaume had almost completed his feat, Pierre too began to climb. He cast a look back toward the priest. Donadieu's face looked somber and old, his wrinkles deepened by shadows cast from the light he held below his chin.

Summoning all the bravery he could muster, Pierre continued to scramble ahead. With his heavy costume, long beak, and medical satchel, the awkward jumble of tiles and beams proved a frustrating obstacle. As both the physicians moved around a particularly dense section of litter, Pierre's foot landed on a fragile wooden plank. The wood split under his weight with the crack of a falling tree. All at once, the uneven floor began to shift and the trash began to slide.

"Watch out!" Donadieu cried.

Through his foggy lenses Pierre caught the shadow of a collapsing joist and dove forward toward Guillaume, abandoning his candlestick in the process. A bone-vibrating crash reverberated through the hall as more of the roof collapsed around them. Together, they only narrowly avoided being crushed under a pile of rotting wood and tile.

When the rubble had settled, Pierre rolled from his stomach to his back and cautiously patted his limbs. No fractures, no wounds; a miracle. With his body audited and found to be complete, and Guillaume doing the same, Pierre turned to study the way they had come. Fortunately, Guillaume had saved his candle's flame in the commotion, and they still retained that single pittance of light. The collapse sealed the way back. What little space existed before was now thoroughly plugged.

"Are you alright?" Guillaume asked. "Perhaps we should have taken Roland's warning a little more seriously."

Pierre rose to his feet and dusted his clothes. "I think I'm alright. That was a little too close."

Guillaume grunted as Pierre helped pull him up. "I won't argue that."

From the other side of the sealed hall, a frantic but faint voice made its way through the pile of soggy wood and moldy leaves. It was certainly Donadieu screaming, but the words were too feeble to be decipherable.

"Father Donadieu, are you safe?" Pierre called, his hands cupped around his beak. "We are both unscathed!"

The muffled voice continued to shout, unclear whether its owner had heard them or not.

"I guess we should try to move some of this spoiled wood and create a path back," Guillaume said. "So much for the priest's hunt. We'll have to make sure he still pays us for all the trouble."

Pierre swiveled his gaze between their solitary candle, the sealed path before them, and the hallway's gloom behind. A war between his fears raged within him. The apprentice quaked at the thought of Donadieu's stalking ghoul, but it was not this terror that dominated the battle for his mind; it was the crushing anxiety of failing those who counted on him. When he spoke, he could hardly believe what he heard himself say.

"Guillaume, we came here to look for the source of the miasma at the request of our payer. How has this accident changed that? The debris isn't stopping us from searching the halls and rooms of the house. We may as well do that now and look for another exit in the process. It would save us having to move all this wood."

Guillaume would avoid the option to do the Priest's bidding if at all convenient, but Pierre gambled correctly on the assumption his teacher detested the idea of physical labor even more.

"I suppose you have a point. Best not to do so much work in case there's a more convenient exit up the hall. We should probably earn that bonus pay as well, from both the priest and Aliénor. Come, follow me. We'll search the rooms together until we find you another candle. After that, we can search twice as quickly. I don't want to stay in this death trap any longer than required. Let's check this door on the left."

"Are you sure we shouldn't stick together?" A tremble in Pierre's voice gave away his distaste for the notion. "The house nearly just crushed us. Should we not remain close for safety?"

Impatience soured Guillaume's tone. "Pierre, make up your mind! Are we helping this priest or not? We're potentially trapped in an abandoned section of a centuries old building, no sure sign of escape. You've just convinced me to keep looking for the miasma, but now you insist on doing it in the most inefficient way?"

Pierre's voice warbled as he replied. "It could be dangerous."

"Everything we do is dangerous. It's our job. We enter places no one is allowed to leave. If it's that holy man's story that's got you spooked, you'd best just forget it. The wine was playing tricks on the old man's sight, or memory, or both." Guillaume turned and entered the door closest to him. "Whatever he thought he saw, it wasn't real, and it isn't here."

Pierre reluctantly followed, and almost immediately upon entering the room, Guillaume found a new candlestick by the door.

"See? Our fortunes have turned. Ask and ye shall receive." He held the blackened wick to his own. The damp flax sputtered and smoked defiantly before it relented and took the flame.

The pair of candles illuminated the room and the two got a good survey of the space. Covered in dust and cobwebs, this antiquated part of the building remembered its original purpose: a fortress. Scattered about the room and resting upon rows of racks lay dozens of steel-tipped spears, all rusted to a coppery orange. Crossbows sat neatly upon tables, the wood of the bows so covered in mildew they looked green, and the bowstrings had long since rotted away. Should the English suddenly descend upon this isolated town, the remnants of this armory would do the locals little good.

Guillaume kicked at the weapons on the floor and pushed around some bolts with his boot. "Doesn't look like this room was ever used. Probably one of those 'better safe than sorry' stockpiles. Here, take the light." The newly lit candlestick traded hands, and Pierre backed out of the room. "If you find another stick," Guillaume continued, "or a candelabra, or lamp, best set them alight and leave them in place. It would be useful to have a source to return to in case a draft comes and steals our flames."

Pierre nodded earnestly. While leaving lit candles haphazardly around an abandoned house seemed a terrible idea, the dampness of the space reduced his worry. The idea of illuminated progress markers gave Pierre a feeling of security he desperately needed.

"You poke in that room; I'll poke in this one." Guillaume pointed to adjacent rooms farther up the hall.

Pierre swallowed hard and obeyed. He approached his assigned door and stared at the handle. It was a standard brass affair, not ornate or special in any way. His skin turned to gooseflesh underneath his robes when he reached for the knob. An imagined monster sat ready to pounce across the thin wooden barrier, but he pushed the door open, nonetheless.

Rat claws skittered in response to the unexpected intrusion. The sole candle caught only fleeting glimpses of their retreating tails. Tattered and gnawed sheets adorned the rows of bunk beds filling the room, mold covered all visible fabrics. In the corner sat an unoccupied chair, and around the walls stood several plain and beaten dressers. An empty hearth indented the wall across from the beds, and another candlestick sat on a table directly to his right. Pierre readily shared his flame with this forgotten wax, and although it again took a few moments for the wick to light, the second candle bolstered his vision significantly.

He swept his beak from side-to-side and observed what must have been the soldiers' bunkhouse. Creeping inside, he began to poke at the beds and nudge the chair; everything was perfectly mundane. A few moldy sheets were not enough to be the source of the Withering, and after a quick circle through the room, Pierre was satisfied this was not the home of some disease-spreading horror.

When he exited, he met Guillaume in the hall.

"Nothing?" Guillaume asked.

"Nothing."

"Then we continue to the next ones."

Together they walked down the hall before separating to explore once more. Pierre again delayed before grabbing the next handle, his imagination continuing to convince him unknown evils lay just beyond. The doorknob whined as it twirled, its mechanisms having rusted long ago. He released it when the door unlatched and marched inside before even peeking within, fearful any further delay would tip the balance of his psyche toward his animal need to flee.

More beds filled the space, although there were fewer and with greater room between them than before. Other than the shadows, nothing stirred. Pierre found another candle by the entrance of the room and the wax took light with no hesitation. With the second source, the room began to reveal secrets otherwise hidden in the dark. This was not another dormitory; this room had been an infirmary, as evidenced by a collection of blood-soiled rags and sheets piled in the corner. Medical relics lay scattered upon the bedside tables, a great many corroded knives and saws.

This development intrigued Pierre. It was rare to get such a clear look into the practices of doctors past and the glimpse ignited his scholar's heart. There was always much to learn from antiquated practices, even if they were no longer used. And what of the patients? What could he have learned from those who suffered here?

Pierre shook his head. He was not here to mourn the long dead or to research their woes. For the purposes of his search, this room, too, was void of any great rot.

Just as he was about to leave, a peculiarity caught his eye. Many of the bedframes were adorned with deep gouges. At first he dismissed them as accidental scratches, but when he caught them at the correct angle, it was clear the markings were more intentional. Someone had carved a series of bizarre symbols into the wooden frames. He did not recognize the text but, as he strained to make sense in the fickle light, it became clear that the bloodier the sheets, the greater the quantity of writing.

Warnings from the locals crossed his mind and he tried to recall the specifics of their distaste for the place. What had happened here? To the extent of his knowledge, no force had ever besieged Bastion. Why should the beds and floor carry blood at all?

In the end, he supposed it didn't matter. Carved wood could not cause miasma, and whatever had happened here happened long ago. A question for Donadieu later, perhaps, but for now he would leave the mystery alone.

Pierre exited the infirmary and cast a look farther down the hallway. He tried to count the remaining doors, but the hall stretched away from him farther than his light could travel. There was still much more work to do.

As he stared into the dark, whether a manifestation of his anxiety or a trick of the light, he thought he caught a glimpse of a lightly colored dress entering a room farther up the corridor.

A grumble beside him snapped his attention back. Guillaume stood across the hall, closing the door to the room he'd just searched.

"Nothing in there, I take it?" Pierre asked.

Guillaume turned to his apprentice and then froze.

"Guillaume?"

The master slowly raised his hand, which quivered as it moved. The gloved index finger rose accusingly and pointed at Pierre. To the apprentice's horror, he realized Guillaume was not pointing at him, but *behind* him. As slowly as the pointing finger was raised, Pierre turned, entirely convinced what lay behind him would surely be his demise. Behind the lenses, his eyes bulged, and a nervous twitch shook his hand. Panicked, Pierre scanned the infirmary yet again, snapping his head to any new shadow cast by candle's flame. The ward was still a ward, and the room remained empty.

Guillaume burst into laughter. Pierre clutched his chest and rolled his eyes so hard they hurt.

"You scared me half to death," he groaned. "Why don't you audition to be a fool for the king, or a playwright, or anything where I needn't suffer from your dark comedy?"

"And deprive you of all my wit? Never."

"I will admit, the rouse was impressive. How did you do that trick with the fabric down the hall?" Pierre pointed into the dark.

Guillaume's beak followed his finger. "The what?"

"Don't play dumb. You've already had your laugh. When I came out, I saw someone in a dress down the hall entering that room. How did you do that?"

A muffled chuckle seeped from Guillaume's mask. "Now you're the one playing jokes. You can't beat a master at his trade, Pierre."

"…I'm not joking, Guillaume."

A lingering silence grew between the two. Pierre's heart again began to thump in his chest, and the pair of beaks turned to look down the empty corridor.

"Shall we go have a look? Put your mind at ease?" All the joyfulness had left the master's voice. Had it been anyone else, Pierre would think his companion was afraid. Guillaume did not get afraid. Knowing his mentor, it was far more likely the old man worried he'd pushed his apprentice too far and was trying to atone.

"Yes, please, just to be sure."

Guillaume's stalwart courage eased Pierre's troubled mind, and they moved together into the darkness.

CHAPTER 12

"Pierre? Guillaume?" Donadieu screamed at the rubble. "Can you hear me? Are you alright?" In between shouts, he thought he heard an unintelligible reply. Fearing the worst, he continued to yell until his throat grew hoarse, praying the doctor's clear voices would carry through and that they be unharmed.

Further attempts to coax sound from the far side of the hallway yielded no result. His worry swelled, its pressure threatening to squeeze his throat shut. Urgency coursed through the old priest's veins and worry hazed his thoughts. He briefly paced in a circle, debating with himself what to do next. Try as he might, he could decide on no plan.

Helpless and alone, Donadieu scurried back to the healthy section of the house. He ripped open the door and screamed for assistance. He expected Roland to be standing nearby, again guarding the visitors as he had done throughout the day. Save for himself and his candle, the hallway was empty and dark. He continued to shout into the twisting halls, his voice sore and strained, but no one answered. A clock began to tick in his head, counting down the moments left for young Pierre and crotchety Guillaume before they were smothered beneath the debris. This thought dragged Donadieu back to the scene and the imposing mountain of rotting house.

Only two doorways remained this side of the rubble, one to the rest of the home, and one closed beside him. With nothing on hand to assist with an excavation, Donadieu reluctantly diverted his attention to the search of the abandoned room.

With care, he opened the door and studied the frame before advancing. He pressed his hand into the trim; the wood was damp but not spongy and pushed back with force equal to his own. Satisfied this passage would not trap him too, he allowed his focus to shift into the vacant space before him.

The chamber was more spacious than Donadieu would have presumed. It contained a large hearth and an even larger dining table that stretched the entirety of the room. Over two dozen chairs surrounded it, cracked plates and rusty utensils lay scattered across.

Small piles of bones also lay upon the table, all picked clean by insects and time. The quantity of the bones implied a grand feast, yet such luxury would have been too extravagant for any of the men who'd dined within this former fortress. Donadieu studied the scene and then gasped.

Within the piles, he recognized a human jawbone. Following that, half of a skull. Revulsion swept through him, and he turned from the table in disgust. He'd heard no tales of cannibalism here. In fact, he'd heard no tales *at all.* No one discussed Bastion's history, and from what lay before him, he understood why. Pushing the macabre thoughts aside, he allowed himself no more delay. If the doctors were buried beneath that pile, any tool he could find to move that lumber would help.

From his cursory survey, the mess hall only contained objects capable of adding to the pile of debris, not subtracting from it. Donadieu gave the place a second look, desperately hoping some of the chairs would prove sturdy enough to brace the pile as he worked.

While peering into the gloom, he caught a shimmer of metal on the center of the table. A three-pronged pewter candelabra, still holding three healthy candles just waiting for his flame to bring it to life. If the chairs were too rotten to use, the extra light would have to do. Without caution, he rushed to recover the centerpiece. The priest did not mind his surroundings, and the gloom took full advantage; it obstructed a small wrinkle in an old carpet unobserved by the man. Careless placement of feet caught the fold mid-stride and the unexpected obstacle tumbled the elderly priest.

Donadieu squeezed his eyes shut to counter the pain of a skull shattering headache. Even behind the shadows of his pressed eyelids, the room spun. Sprawled across the floor, he pressed his forehead into the damp carpet. Instead of relief, the pressure tormented the priest. Aching pain from a swelling bruise spread to the base of his neck.

Whether he'd fallen only a moment ago or had been lying undiscovered for hours, he did not know. If it were the latter, that did not bode well for the fate of the doctors.

His eyelids cautiously opened, and his vision darted about as he searched for any sign of light. When he found none, he prayed.

"God, give this frame the strength needed to see the completion of my task. I seek with all my heart to drive away the evil beset upon this town. To repel a grotesque manifestation of the original sin. To help those who had come to help us.

"I know You are with us, for the Lord gives strength to His people; the Lord blesses His people with peace. Guide my hands to do these feats. This I pray in the name of the Father, the Son, and the Holy Spirit. Amen."

When finished, he tested his joints for injury. Pleasant surprise cut through his mental fog when it seemed the sole damage to his person was the tender lump on his head. He brought himself to his knees, and then slowly to his feet. The darkness swirled again, and after a moment of weakness, his senses returned. Now upright, he moaned to himself; he had not the faintest idea in which direction to go.

Arms waving in the darkness, Donadieu fumbled about the room. He shuffled like a toddler in fear that another obstacle would bring him low. His senses strained to paint even a vague picture of the abyss he wandered, but they gathered nothing. The air in the room was dead calm, and even the finest of hairs on his hands and face could not detect even a whisper of a breeze. He inhaled through his nose, and the humidity coated the back of his throat. Besides the shuffling of his feet on the floor and the air through his nostrils, he heard nothing.

His stomach dropped like a boulder, and a cold sweat broke across his arms and forehead. Had he come down harder than he first thought? A word floated around his mind; its implication pierced him as an arrow rips through game.

Purgatory.

He tried to push the thought aside, but it returned moments after each eviction. Here he stood, devoid of all substance, in an inky expanse. He saw no brilliant light above nor inferno below. There were no songs of angels nor screams of the damned. He tried to convince himself the drumbeat of his heart was proof enough he still lived but could not fully believe it.

At last, his fingers found the back of a wooden chair and an avalanche of relief cascaded over him. In triumph, the priest grasped the chair. Its rigid presence assured Donadieu he was not yet lost, and he breathed a long sigh of relief.

With hungry hands, he reached to discover more pieces of furniture. His knuckles grazed a second chair to his left but could feel no more to the right. After that, he found the table ahead. From there, he deduced where he stood and where the exit must be. More carefully than before, he slid his feet across the damp ground and headed for the door. After his injury, he feared he would be too weak to assist the doctors alone. He needed to find Roland or other members of staff to help him clear the way.

His fingers pressed upon a surface, cold and rough. Stepping closer, he planted his feet and stretched his arms to follow the stone wall. The doorframe was less than one pace to his left and this little success charged his soul. On tactile feedback alone, he passed through the frame into the hall, gliding his fingers along the walls as a guide.

The main hallway glowed faintly from what little light made it through the heavy clouds, but it was not enough to walk freely. Donadieu saw edges of shapes and suggestions of forms, but to break from the safety of the wall would be madness.

He traveled toward his escape and before long, his hands discovered the frame back to the habitable section of the house. He clasped his hands around the doorknob and pushed while he turned. Preemptively, he stepped to move through the door and instead collided into it with a thud. His recovering head again throbbed, now with vengeance.

Donadieu's free hand raised to massage his aching lump. After the momentary daze had passed, he more deliberately attempted to open the door, but it would not yield. He twisted the handle and pushed on the wood, but it refused to budge. Donadieu released his grip and stood staring ahead. Somehow, his escape had been sealed. The door was no more than a foot from his face, but in the unrelenting darkness it may as well have been a life's journey away.

Locked into a hallway of oppressive humidity, omnipresent obscurity, a collapsed roof and missing colleagues, Donadieu needed a new plan. He racked his throbbing brain by pouring over every detail he could remember of his surroundings, hoping he could recall anything that may aid him in the dark. It then occurred to him: the dining hall contained a fireplace.

Retracing his steps, he found his way back to the oppressive darkness of the other room. While sliding his feet to avoid another collapse, Donadieu kicked a piece of metal debris. The object bounced, clanking across the floor, and he raised his foot in pain from the collision. He moaned while his toe ached, but he stopped abruptly upon realizing what his foot had discovered. His candlestick. The freshly burnt wick would take a new light more easily than the old candelabra. He needed to find it.

His knees lamented as he lowered himself to the ground, and the priest began to crawl. He followed the clamor of rolling pewter by patting his hands along the floor toward its raucous vibrations. He weaved under the table and around the chairs, bumping his head again and again, the impacts extra painful because of his earlier fall.

When he reached the spot where the candle ought to have rolled, he pawed his hands around the floor. Only damp carpet and stone. In a growing circle, he expanded outward in search of his extinguished light.

A new sound broke the silence, and in reflection, he was surprised he had not heard it earlier, given the ghostly silence of the home. It was the buzzing of a fly. Donadieu pitied the creature as it attempted to navigate as blindly as he himself did. The company of the innocent animal was unexpectedly soothing to the priest, happy to no longer be alone. With his animal companion above, he continued to grope around for the missing light source below.

Frustratingly, said light source refused to materialize, despite his extensive search. Just before he was about to begin his circles anew, the candlestick stirred anew from across the room. Still on his knees, he crawled toward it once again.

As he approached, a second fly joined the first. The droning from their aerial dance weaved and swerved overhead. Bewildered by the sudden appearance of the second bug, he stopped to listen to their hum. As he did, he heard the candlestick again. The noise now propagated from a new location within the room.

Not wanting to lose the trail, he moved more quickly toward the source, failing to arrive before the clamor of the candlestick ceased and finding only the cold wall when he arrived. The ever-increasing buzz overhead suggested the flies were growing in number.

Something was wrong. Panic quickened his heart, beating hard in his swollen lump. The priest waited for the candlestick to summon him again, listening astutely in the darkness. What he heard instead was the coalescence of dozens of buzzing insects overlapping in unison in a way which mimicked a human voice.

Martine, the swarm sounded.

Disbelief overruled the input of his ears. Donadieu refused to accept what he thought he heard, attributing it to a mild delusion of his stressful circumstances.

Martine, the swarm buzzed again. It was clearer this time.

"God?" Donadieu asked, now allowing belief to edge its way in.

A furious cacophony from the bugs erupted above him; a few of the insects lowered and tickled the skin on his face.

Overtaken by terror, Donadieu scurried around the floor like a blinded rat.

Above him, the swarm pursued. *Martine,* it hummed again and again. Individual flies bombed the priest's face in search of weakness. Donadieu responded by keeping his eyes and mouth firmly shut and breathing only through half-closed nostrils. Frantically, he grasped at the empty air, searching for anything. He crawled as fast as his limbs would move until at last his shoulder bumped heavily into the leg of the center table. The collision was enough to cause a heavy thump from above. He pictured the room as though he was again standing in the doorway, casting his candlelight. The weight was no doubt from the toppled candelabra he had seen before. Given his circumstances, the old wicks would have to do.

Using the table leg as an improvised cane, he followed it up to a standing position and, by touch, made his way down the surface of the table. The swarm now encompassed his head. He hardly dared to breathe at all. A jolt of success surged through him when his fingers discovered the fallen metal, and by luck, two of the three candles remained in their holder. He clasped the pewter like a weapon, his only defense against the dark.

Upon discovery of his prize, the flies doubled their assaults. Dozens landed on his body and began to crawl down his robes and across his face. With his free hand, Donadieu frantically swatted at the insects, attempting to keep them out of his nostrils and ears. Stumbling forth with only a guess at his location, he made for the hearth. The swarm shrieked his name, increasing both volume and frequency as he moved. The assault troops amongst the ranks of flies crawled upon the old man's flesh, looking for any opening in which to delve.

Four large steps brought Donadieu to the wall. With his free hand following the stone, he kicked with his feet he found the opening for the fireplace. Again, dropping to his knees, he used his free hand to pat the cold ground by the corners of the hearth. He flopped his head from shoulder to shoulder in an attempt to crush the insects which closed in on his ears, and he breathed out his nose in short bursts to blast away the bugs which tried to enter there.

In a short time, he located the second piece of his puzzle—the tinderbox used to light the fireplace logs. He ripped the pouch open and by feel alone, he collected a pile of char cloth, a piece of flint, and another of iron. Donadieu stole a sip of air from the corner of his mouth and struck the flint. To his immense delight, the iron sparked. Almost immediately, the tinder began to glow. He ripped a candle from its holder and held the wick to the smoldering pile. It lit. A gentle light returned to the room as the candle danced and the priest waved the flame wildly around in an attempt to repulse the insectoid assault.

When his eyes adjusted, his motion stopped. The air was still, and his own was the sole beating heart within the room. He lit the second candle in the mount and replaced the one he had taken. Twice the light yielded the same result. He was alone, and any trace of the flies had disappeared with the coming of the light.

Distressed was too gentle a word to describe the turmoil within the priest. Visions were new to him and, based on his first experience, he did not desire more. Nor did he have time to decipher the meanings of what he had seen and heard and felt. He stood and made his way to the table to reclaim the third candle knocked from its holder. That too he lit, and with the three candles in his holder burning bright, he saw the gleam of the single candlestick he had brought with him into the room. It lay by a folded piece of rug, no more than an arm's length from where he had fallen. He lit it too and brought them both as he moved.

He did his best to banish the experience from his mind and returned to the site of the roof's collapse. No longer could he delay. Piece-by-piece he began to remove the rubble, piling it further back within the hall. He also piled some by the door to the dining hall, lest anything unwanted try to follow him out. As he worked, Donadieu repeatedly eyed the candles. He could not recall a time where he was so glad to have fires burning close while he worked. It was a strenuous task, and progress was slow, but gradually the stacks he made grew larger. Grunts escaped his throat as he hauled large beams and chunks of stone. After much effort, a trickle of light began to make it through the holes between heaps of rubble. Someone had lit candles on the other side.

CHAPTER 13

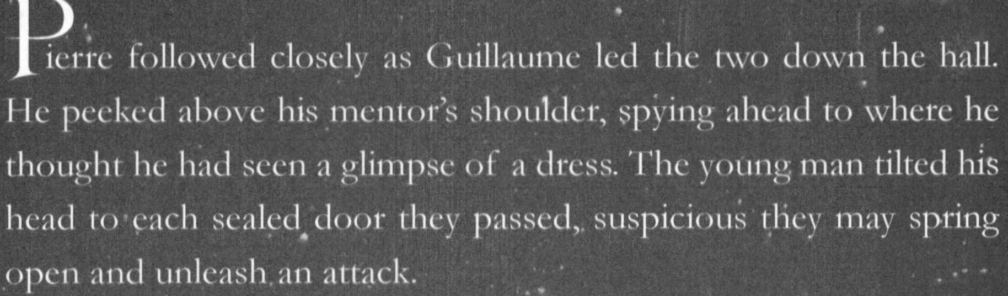

Pierre followed closely as Guillaume led the two down the hall. He peeked above his mentor's shoulder, spying ahead to where he thought he had seen a glimpse of a dress. The young man tilted his head to each sealed door they passed, suspicious they may spring open and unleash an attack.

When they reached the room housing Pierre's worries, Guillaume tried the handle. The hinges whined as the door opened, but after an inch, it would budge no more. "Something's blocking it," Guillaume said. "Nothing could have gone through here. It won't move."

"Maybe whoever went through sealed the door from the other side? Does it have a chain lock?"

Guillaume held his candle up to the open crack of the door and, sure enough, a rusty chain locked its full opening.

"Well, let's see if we can't get in then," he said, "to put your mind at ease." He handed back his candlestick and, with both hands, began to push on the door. When no progress was made, he motioned Pierre to give him space. "Stand back. This one is going to take a little extra." Guillaume took a few steps, then threw his shoulder into the door. The sudden force burst the old chain free, and the master tumbled through the opening and straight to the ground. The crisp noise of broken glass accompanied his fall.

"Guillaume!" Pierre called. He set both candlesticks carefully upon the floor and ran to triage his mentor. When he got close, the darkness all but swallowed him. Frustrated, he relayed back to gather the light, knowing he could do no good without it. When the candles were placed nearer his injured mentor, he set to survey any wounds.

The elder physician groaned on the ground and rolled himself over. When Pierre saw the condition of Guillaume's face, he froze. The shattering glass he'd heard was the left eyepiece in Guillaume's mask. Even in the dim light, Pierre could see the injury looked severe, as did the growing flow of blood.

"How bad is the pain?" he asked while he knelt, already searching through his bag for gauze while throwing other tools about the floor.

Guillaume's reply came as frenzied coughing, all the while a stream of blood ran from the bottom of his mask. The hacking of his cough became so intense Pierre feared his mentor may tear a lung.

"Guillaume?" he asked again. He tried to sound commanding, but a quiver in his voice exposed his frayed nerves.

"I can hear you," Guillaume wheezed when his fit abated. "It smells of death in here, thick miasma without a doubt. I can hardly breathe. Take my mask off. With the broken lens, it can't keep the stench out now, anyway."

Pierre helped him to sit upright and, when requested, he pulled back his mentor's hood to undo the leather straps. Gently, as he pulled it off, he drew the candles closer. The flames glinted on the shrapnel. The shards had sliced several gouges across his face, and one of the pieces had impaled itself through Guillaume's eyelid and deep into the eye itself. Blood seeped from the wounds, looking black in the pale light.

"Your face is… It's bleeding badly. Don't try to open your eye. It could make things much worse."

"Get the thing out and slap some bandages on me, then let's find a way out of this cursed place. I've had just about enough of this town, the priest and his money be damned." One of the cuts had pierced Guillaume's cheek, and a pause followed every other word when he needed to spit the pooling blood.

Pierre winced at the curse toward the priest, but now was not the time to criticize.

"Maybe we should wait until someplace safer for me to work on you. Your forehead has a nasty gash, and I don't feel good about treating your eye without much light. If I can't get the bleeding to stop, this could become very serious, very quickly."

Guillaume waved off the concern and replied coarsely, "Get it out and wrap me up. I don't want to be carrying this glass around with me. It's best if it comes out now. The gauze will do its job. Do it quick; I don't want nervous hands poking it around."

Worried as he was, Pierre's hands remained steady. He grasped the back of Guillaume's head and readied three fingers for the glass. "Should I count down?"

"Not on your life."

With that, Pierre pulled the shard. The glass withdrew with a sickening slurp and Guillaume roared in pain, rolling on the floor, cursing and holding his bleeding face. The piece was as big as Pierre's thumb. Guillaume would never see with both eyes again. A slurry of blood and tears covered the glass and Pierre's stomach quivered at the sight. He tossed the shrapnel aside and reached for the gauze.

Wasting no time, he steadied Guillaume and wrapped the mutilated side of his face. The thirsty material fully saturated itself with blood before the bandages came round for their second wrap. When he had finished, Guillaume resembled half of an Egyptian mummy.

Slinging one of his mentor's arms around his neck, Pierre huffed and helped Guillaume to his feet. The wounded man hung off him like a satchel, his usually stoic demeanor gone and replaced with a weakening grasp on consciousness. This worried Pierre; Guillaume had always been a fortress of calm and logic; these wounds and the bad air diminished him with worrying rapidity.

"We need to get you out of here," Pierre said while he looked around. The light from the candles did not extend far.

Guillaume retrieved his arm and stumbled forward. "There must be a way out ahead. I'll go first; even with one eye, I'll see better than you will through your mask. If you did see someone enter through here, they must have found another way out."

Pierre lamented that he again required Guillaume to lead, especially with the injuries, but his failing courage did not allow him to rebut the plan. He picked up the candlesticks, handed one back to Guillaume, and they began to search. Crates, barrels, and mountains of half-rotten fabrics lay piled about. The stacks of old supplies formed new walls, turning the room into a cluttered maze.

"Some kind of storehouse for the soldiers?" Pierre asked.

Guillaume did not reply. Instead, he continued to lumber around the room and braced his gait by leaning a heavy hand upon the boxes. Chips of paint from the crates' labels had peeled off the wood. Most of their meanings were now too faint to read, but Pierre could still make out a few. They contained foods and furs, at least they had at some point. He feared to see what sludge may remain after centuries of abandonment.

"Guillaume?" he asked again as the master stumbled into an adjoining storeroom and then back into the hallway through a newly opened door. Pierre quickened his pace to chase the fleeing light of his mentor's candle and accosted him in short fashion. "We need to stick together, Guillaume. It would not suit us well to become separated and lost in a place such as this. How are you feeling?"

"I'm fine," came the short reply. "Just a bit dizzy. We must be close."

"Perhaps I should lead for a spell," Pierre said. He loathed the idea, but if the alternative was to follow Guillaume blindly through the dark while the man deteriorated, he had no choice. "Hold back a moment. You can follow me."

Guillaume did not slow.

The hall opened into a grand and empty room, in which their meager light could not even reach the far walls. The flames caught several sets of glowing eyes, and Pierre's heart skipped a beat. His panic was short-lived. When confronted by fire, the swarm of rats skittered in retreat toward their homes in the walls.

Refusing to flee like the rodents, a squadron of flies hung in the air. They hovered above a series of faded symbols that had been painted upon the ground. The script looked to be the same as that which Pierre found on the beds in the medical room. Also, upon the floor stood ten erect candles, all cemented in place by puddles of old wax. Their orientation did not construct any known shape to Pierre, yet he knew their locations must have meaning.

"What do you suppose this was about?" he asked.

"Perhaps if we light the candles, it will give us a better idea." Guillaume stooped down with his new flame, reaching to light the old.

With a firm grasp on his shoulder, Pierre pulled him back. "This is a mystery for another time, Guillaume. We can come back later. Right now, we need to get you safe."

"Hmm? Yes, right. Somewhere safe." Guillaume sounded disoriented, but had stopped his groans of pain. That may have been worse.

"Follow me." Pierre grabbed his hand and led them farther into the open space. Moments after they resumed their escape, Pierre heard a door open and close deeper within the room, and then he heard another.

"Hello?" Only the rats and flies responded in their native tongues. Pierre turned to Guillaume. "Did you hear that door?"

His mentor nodded. "Maybe it's someone trying to find us. The priest must have summoned help by now. That means there's a way out ahead. Let's go." Even in the candlelight Pierre could see Guillaume's face had grown pale while the red on his bandages crept ever outward. For both their sakes, Pierre hoped he was right.

They continued through the room, occasionally calling out in hopes of a response but never receiving a reply.

"My head is swimming," Guillaume mumbled. "What are we doing here?"

The hair on the back of Pierre's neck jumped to attention. Guillaume was slurring his words, and his memory was failing. He needed to be extracted fast. "We're trying to leave here. Follow me, we're almost out."

"Maybe I'll just have a sit for a minute, catch my breath." Guillaume began to seat himself, but Pierre forced him to remain on his feet with a powerful grip on his robes.

"The air is bad here, Guillaume. You're breathing it deeply and you've lost a lot of blood. Think clearly. We need to be careful. You must follow me." Pierre again threw Guillaume's arm around his shoulder, and this time there was no objection.

At last, they reached the end of the expanse and found two doors awaiting them. One on the wall to their left, and another to their right.

Pierre pointed his beak at each as he surveyed his options. "Stay here. I'm going to see if we've found our way out."

He left Guillaume standing and moved to the door on the right. He swung it open, and his greatest hopes materialized. An exit. He looked down a spiral stone staircase and a faint breeze wafted up. The wind blew away his anxiety as though it were a dry fall leaf.

"I've found it!" he said with boyish joy. "The exit. If we follow these stairs down, we'll be free and clear of this place." He turned to summon his bleeding partner. Guillaume did not look back. Instead, the wounded man stared at the remaining door. "Guillaume, let's go," Pierre urged again, louder this time to cut through the fog of his mentor's brain.

"Look at the light, Pierre," came a dry reply.

"There is no light, Guillaume. The miasma is making you unwell. We need to go, just down these stairs. *Please.*" His final word escaped as a pleading whisper.

"But do you see the light?" Guillaume's voice had changed. It became grating, coarse.

Only then did Pierre realize there was, in fact, a dim and pulsating light. It strobed with a crimson hue and seeped from under the remaining door. It throbbed rhythmically like the beating of a heart. It did not come from a flame; it was too orderly, too red. Whatever lay beyond the wooden seal repulsed Pierre, but Guillaume remained transfixed by the light.

Pierre practically begged. "I see it now, but you need pay it no mind. We must leave that light. Let's go down these stairs, we'll get you all fixed up. Please Guillaume, let's go."

In a display of indifference, or perhaps defiance, Guillaume and his bloody face walked away from the stairwell and stopped directly in front of the second door.

"Guillaume!" Pierre screamed through his mask, unable to force himself to move. "Go no farther! We're so close. We can leave!"

His pleas fell on deaf ears. Guillaume swung the door open. The light washed the man with each radiant strobe. Pierre's limbs grew weak as he watched his mentor cross the threshold, helpless to stop him, his fearful limbs not responding to his mind's commands.

Pierre looked back at the staircase. He yearned for the safety mere steps away. He took a pace towards the escape but stopped himself and looked back at the gaping doorway and the light which spilled from within. Shame twisted his heart, and with a deep breath, he made his way after Guillaume.

Pierre approached from an angle and stopped just short of the opening. With immense trepidation, he leaned forward and peered inside.

This final room at the end of the west wing was a chapel. At least it used to be. Three short rows of pews sat on either side of a central aisle; the maximum occupancy would have been no more than eighteen parishioners. Several wooden crosses lay scattered across the floor. Most were broken in half, some reduced to splinters; those which still hung on the walls had been inverted.

Long-dried blood stained the surfaces of the space—the floor, the pews, even the roof. A chaotic swarm of flies patrolled the air, each darting haphazardly in the sullen room. At the back of the chapel was a stained-glass window with a fractal pattern that allowed in a pathetic trickle of colored moonlight.

Between the pews and the far wall of the chapel stood two supporting pillars. Expertly carved scenes decorated the support structures, depicting both human debauchery and sacrifice. And between those pillars strobed the light, though his mentor's silhouette obstructed its source.

"Guillaume," Pierre whispered. "Please come."

"Come," Guillaume said, his voice distorted and grotesque. "Stare into the light."

"We need to leave!"

"Come."

Neither moved. Pierre waited, too timid to enter the room, too afraid of what lay beyond, of what possessed his mentor, his *friend*.

"Come!" Guillaume screamed, his voice barbaric and no longer his own.

It was clear there would be no reasoning with him. Pierre would have to remove Guillaume, by force if need be. Should his mentor put up a fight, Pierre would lose against the stout man, but he hoped a light tug was all that would be required. He inched towards Guillaume's turned back. The beating of his heart hammered against his chest, and he breathed deeply through his scented mask.

Even through his protective suit, Pierre felt a change when he crossed the threshold into the chapel. The air was denser. His movements slowed and his perception blurred briefly before it returned. Even though the air hung still and his mask remained perfectly sealed, he heard a breeze blowing around his ears. As he trekked further, the noise grew louder, and the sounds became clearer. They were whispers. He could find no source for the words. He and Guillaume were alone.

The young doctor's spotty grasp of alternate languages allowed him to know the voices spoke in a variety of tongues, but he could not discern the specifics of what they said. *Donadieu would know the Latin*, Pierre thought. He allowed himself a moment of self-pity that he braved this rescue alone. What he wouldn't have given to still have Donadieu with them.

When Pierre crept close enough to reach Guillaume, he gave his mentor's robes a tug. It failed to sway the man from his cemented pose. The red glow commanded Guillaume's attention like a moth drawn to a flame.

The light continued to pulse, and Pierre's curiosity grew until he could no longer resist. How could he save Guillaume if he did not know what to save him from? Against his better judgment, he shuffled a few inches closer to peer over his mentor's shoulder. He reasoned the best way to break the magnetism was to understand the source of Guillaume's corruption.

Through the cloudy glasses in his mask, Pierre discovered it was a book that sat upon the once holy pulpit. The tome lay open to its central page. While the binding and cover of the book looked mundane, the script on the pages did not.

Black ink danced and swirled upon the paper, refusing to conform to the confines of human words. It formed new symbols and text as it desired, and the light which enveloped the entire pulpit changed in rhythm with the twisting ink. The shapes created and abandoned by the book resembled those found all throughout the west wing. They did not look like any language he knew, yet some long dormant part of his brain was able to decipher sections of this infernal text. The words he understood were the same as those which floated on the nonexistent wind and whispered in his ear. Phrases describing rot, ruin, and *disease*. Pierre strained hard to stop vomit from filling his mask.

A strong waft of cinnamon and spice reset his attention and allowed him to break his fixation on the tome. Pierre stepped back and shuddered. This was something new. Something unholy. Leeches could not fix this disease. His urgency to remove Guillaume grew, but he knew not how. A confrontation could result in damage to his own mask…not something he could afford.

While he debated how best to proceed, there arose a new source of noise. A strained breathing from behind. Unlike the whispers through his mask, he knew this sound to be real.

Turning slowly, he found Louise standing at the door. She looked exactly as Donadieu had described: an embodiment of famine and waste. The frail-looking creature stood in the empty room and blocked any hope of an easy retreat.

Her yellow dress was stained with sweat—and worse. It hung off her wiry frame like a toddler wearing their parent's nightgown. Pierre recoiled at the sight of her empty eye sockets and wild hair. When he'd first heard the priest's description, he could not fully accept what was so vividly recounted to him. Standing here face-to-face, the reality was undeniable.

As if drawn by the book and its unholy glow, Louise lurched across the threshold and into the chapel. When she crossed, a transformation took place; each pulse of the tome's light reformed her appearance, adding layers in the same translucent crimson. The light filled her empty sockets and replaced the void with a fiery gleam, and all the while it danced throughout her hair like ribbons made of fireflies. Buboes and lesions appeared upon her withered flesh, each seeping blood and pus across her stale skin.

Horrified as the ghoul before him worsened with each passing step, Pierre retreated into the pews until his back touched a wall in the desecrated space. His heart raced like a horse, and he held his breath, fearing to make even the most subtle of noises. The weight of the room bludgeoned at his consciousness, and the oxygen deprivation joined the assault.

When halfway through the chapel, Louise turned to look at the cowering apprentice. She glared at him with her smoldering eyes, and his knees began to shake. The world spun. He dared not move. Still staring, Louise opened her mouth. A cross between a growl and a croak erupted from her throat.

The fear, the creature, the air—it was too much. Black crept inward from the corners of his vision and he refused to flinch or breathe until his senses endured no more. Pierre collapsed unconscious upon the floor.

CHAPTER 14

Donadieu removed a final piece of scaffolding, dragged it across the hall, and heaved it onto the new pile of his own creation. Exhausted, he rested his hands upon his knees and breathed deeply. A sinful moment of pride tempered his resolve as he beheld the mountain of debris and the path he had created. It was only a narrow gap carved through the collapsed hall, but it would be enough.

While excavating, he'd found no trace of buried doctors. The initial relief of their absence soured when he realized they must still be within the wing ahead, else they would have come for him while he worked or when he lay unconscious. Something must be wrong.

Rising again to his full height, Donadieu trudged deeper into the black in search of his missing allies. The priest pivoted his torso to slide into the claustrophobic gap and inched through the passage, his back pressed to the wall. Stray pieces of lumber jabbed at his ribs and ankles as he squeezed himself through. Fortunately, his robes were thick, and he emerged unscathed.

Reaching back, he pulled his hard-won candelabra through the passage and held it close as he surveyed the hall. Donadieu did not like having the flames so near to his person, but as much as the fire made him nervous, the fear of what may happen should he again lose the light dominated all other terror.

Along the hall ahead, several open doors cast their own flickering glow from within.

"Pierre? Guillaume?"

After waiting in vain for a reply, Donadieu moved. For comfort, his free hand fondled the cross around his neck. Slowly, he approached the closest open door to his right. When he peeked inside, a candle flickered by the door and assisted his own three in brightening the space. The room appeared to be a soldier's dormitory, vacant of the doctors.

Like following flaming breadcrumbs, Donadieu bounced back and forth across the hall, tracing the steps of those that had gone before by the candles they left in behind. After each empty room and unanswered call, his pace quickened. He feared they may be lost in the sprawling mansion—or worse, injured at the hand of some other structural catastrophe and unable to call back.

It was not long before the trail ran cold. Donadieu visited every room with a lit candle, and none gave a clue to their whereabouts. The next several doors along the hall remained firmly closed and, when he poked his head inside, none contained any trace of a recent visit. Irritated by his lack of discovery, he continued until he at last found one showing signs of recent traversal. The door in question hung drunkenly on a single hinge and swayed as if to beckon the priest to enter. With no other course of action, he accepted the invitation.

Upon stepping inside, he heard a brittle crunch, and a stinging pain shot through Donadieu's sole and into his calf. He recoiled his injured foot from the ground and hopped back upon the other.

Teetering unevenly on his uninjured foot, he retreated into the hallway and sank to the ground. He set his lights beside him and held up his foot to inspect the damage. A small piece of broken glass jutted from the bottom of his thin shoe. Wincing, he removed the shard and clenched his teeth to stop himself from hissing at the pain.

Fortunately, the shard was small, and the pain implied an injury far more dire than the wound justified. The priest regained his footing and tested the injury by applying increasing amounts of weight, relieved to find little resistance. He would have to be more careful, but he would manage.

Only when Donadieu stooped to pick up his light did he notice the other puddles of blood on the floor. These pools contained substantially more than what had been leaked by his own foot. Upon closer examination, he noticed this blood too was fresh.

Concern wrinkled his forehead and caused the remnants of his own pain to be forgotten. The breadcrumbs he'd followed had morphed, first glowing beacons of light, and now a trail of cooling blood. How long had he spent on the floor of the dining hall?

Donadieu doubled back to the corridor and waved his candles above the ground. The still liquid blood caught glimmers of light and reflected it back in crimson-tinted flashes. He marched on after the physicians. Again, for better or for worse, he had a trail to follow.

Donadieu followed the blood until he believed his mind had begun to play tricks. It was not possible he could walk for so long without interruption, even in a house as large as this. Determination and grit pushed him on, and eventually, the hallway relinquished its hold on the priest. The constricting tunnel opened to a room so large his light would not carry to the distant side.

Droplets of red continued across the space, and thus so too did Donadieu. He passed a bizarre occult symbol on the floor, its extremities concluded by standing black candles. What unholy rites had been performed here?

Averting his gaze from the markings, he marched on through the void until the light from his flame at last found a distant wall, along with two doors. One on the wall to his right, and the other ahead and to his left.

The door on the right was open. It led to a spiral stone staircase, an obvious exit. Much to the confusion of the priest, the trail did not lead to the exit. Instead, it led to the second door, the contents of which were obstructed by unfavorable angles. A bizarre strobing light protruded from within the space, but he could see no more.

He could, however, hear what came from it. The noise was a grotesque gurgling sound, a combination of choking and retching. As he followed the blood closer, he thought he heard something else. Whimpering.

The priest breathed deeply through his nose, his scarred tissue protecting him from the stench which fogged the air. When within two strides of the door, he bent low and placed his candelabra on the floor, set to be ready for whatever lay ahead. One carefully placed step at a time, he crept forward, his heart beating even more violently than the flashing red light within.

For the third time in his life, a powerful force bade him to plant his feet and tread no further. It was the same malevolent repulsion—this time coupled with spasms of his own fear—he had experienced in his church and before the potter's home.

As before, Donadieu would not stop. He gripped his cross until his knuckles turned white and pressed on.

At the edge of the doorframe, the priest craned his head past its boundaries and peered into the room. The blood drained from his face and his skin turned cold. Beads of sweat appeared on his forehead and his head began to swim.

Unmistakably, there was Louise, crouched atop the desecrated pulpit like a plague-ridden gargoyle. Her features were distorted and malevolent, altered by the flashing light. Beneath her lay a book, the mysterious light escaping from its open pages. Guillaume stood beside her, his mask discarded and face bound by yards of blood-soaked bandages. Her right hand grasped the back of Guillaume's head, his hair poking out between her fingers. Her left arm snaked around the elder doctor's throat. It was he who sputtered and gagged from the limb, restricting his breath.

"Dear God," Donadieu whispered before he could claw the words back. His eyes widened when he realized what he had done. Louise turned to him and smiled a toothless grin. White foam frothed at the sides of her mouth, no different from a rabid dog. The glow within her vacant sockets pointed at the doorway, central dots of darker burgundy aimed directly at the priest.

She addressed him, her voice croaking, spittle and froth spewing from her mouth into the face of Guillaume.

"Hello, Father."

Donadieu unwrapped his hand from the cross and thrust the symbol out before him as he brought his full body into view of the doorway. From this new angle, he could see Pierre. The young doctor cowered in the corner of the desecrated space, weeping behind his mask.

Louise's address caused the apprentice to raise his head and he met the priest's eyes. "Father Donadieu," Pierre said, his voice stifled by a clogged nose but otherwise free of distortion.

"Quiet!" Louise shrieked, spittle flying halfway across the room from her outburst. Pierre flinched from the scream and again buried his head into his hands.

"Louise," Donadieu began, his voice weak and sorrowful. "What has become of you? What have you done? Think of your children. They are sick, but they are safe. I am caring for them in the church."

"I am no longer burdened by such temporary concerns." Her voice was like the crunching of gravel. "I serve a greater purpose now. You will see soon enough." A gut-twisting crack followed as Louise wrenched Guillaume's head almost entirely around. The elder doctor collapsed to the floor and shuddered like a clubbed fish, giving its final spasms on the shore. When his twitching ceased, only a harsh, shallow breathing remained.

Donadieu paced back, abhorred by the casual discard of life. "Pierre," he called, "we must go. Now!"

Louise remained perched on her pedestal, smiling. Slowly, she turned her neck to the corner of the room and switched her gaze to Pierre. "He's next," she said, taunting the priest.

Desperation swelled within Donadieu, and he walked through the wooden arch. When he entered the corrupted room, he knew the space was *wrong*. The air beat him down with unrelenting weight, only through great effort could his straining legs keep him upright. He gripped his outstretched cross so tightly that it began to bend, threatening to snap from the strain.

"This place was holy once. You have no right to be here!"

Donadieu removed the cross's string from around his neck and thrust it forth with the full length of his arm towards the beast, who scowled at its presence. "Now Pierre, run!"

The broken young man remained sobbing in the corner, shaking his head.

"*In nómine Pátris, et Fílii, et Spíritus Sancti,*" Donadieu began to chant. His adversary displayed both confusion and repulsion. Keeping his crucifix threateningly pointed, he slowly circled around the room, maintaining the Latin prayer as he moved.

Although Louise attempted to conceal her discomfort, it was clear the prayer was having an effect.

When he reached Pierre, Donadieu attempted to yank the apprentice to his feet. The doctor was too heavy, too defeated. He broke his chant but refused to remove his eyes from the watching creature. "Pierre, please, stand up. You need to leave here. Don't succumb to this disease before you've even been inflicted by it. We'll come back for Guillaume," the lie pained him, "but I need you to stand up now. The town needs you. Think of those like little Marianne. They are hopeless without you." Donadieu had gambled with his verbal slap, but when he heard the young man stir, he knew he'd won. "Good, Pierre. Stand up!"

Louise cawed back, "Don't you leave, boy! Did you see how your master twitched on the ground? He needs you. He'll die if you don't stay."

Donadieu shouted louder, trying now to persuade with volume alone. "We'll come back, Pierre, but we need to go. We need to go *now*." Still facing Louise with his extended cross, Donadieu heard the ruffling of robes as Pierre rose to his feet. "Now out the door. I'll be right behind you."

Pierre's voice came as a muffled whisper from behind his beaked mask. "Guillaume—"

"He'll be okay, he will. We'll come back for him." It hurt equally every time he lied. "We need to get ourselves to safety first."

Pierre moved. First behind Donadieu, then around him, then toward Guillaume, who still lay wheezing on the floor.

Frustration and desperation surged through the priest, and he grabbed the back of Pierre's robes. Pulling with all his might, he backpedaled toward the exit of the desecrated chapel, Pierre in one hand, his weaponized crucifix in the other.

Surprised by the tug, Pierre stumbled backward and in a few brief steps, they had crossed the threshold out of the room. Exiting the chapel removed a heavy weight from Donadieu's weary shoulders, and again he could breathe and stand without strain. Pierre, too, found his footing, and Donadieu cautiously released his grip.

"We must fly," Donadieu urged. To his relief, Pierre made for the staircase without looking back.

Upon her pedestal, Louise roared. The priest caught only a glimpse of her descending the podium. Her movements were bestial, and her joints contorted beyond possibility as she crawled to the floor.

Donadieu sprinted for the staircase after Pierre and toward the promise of safety. Not wanting to stop for even a moment, he refrained from retrieving his candelabra. Instead, he kicked it back toward the chapel, hoping it would create a small fire to block their retreat. Or perhaps, a larger blaze to immolate that accursed space. Instead, the flames snuffed out upon contact with the damp floor. Gutted, he progressed by memory through the darkness and threw his cross back around his neck on his way to the door.

One final time, he cast a look over his shoulder as Louise emerged from the pulsating room. As soon as she exited the chapel, all signs of disease vanished, as did her glowing eyes. Only her leathery, hollow skin remained. In that fleeting glimpse, she turned to the staircase, and then she was out of sight.

He bounded down the spiral stairs two at a time, and very nearly tripped on his robe along the way. As he hurried, he listened for footsteps behind him. Nothing. Given what he had witnessed, the silence terrified him more than the pattering footsteps ever could. He fretted that Louise might manifest before them in some new and ungodly way.

A tremendous crash echoed as Pierre forced his way through a door below. Closely behind, Donadieu emerged into a darkened hallway beside him. They now stood on the first floor of the west wing, though which way to proceed remained unclear. Delicate moonbeams entered through tears in the drapes of the hallway windows. Yet to be renovated, the space remained built of cold and indifferent stone.

As the pair scanned left and right to find an exit, a door swung open at one end of the hall and firelight escaped from within. A silhouette stood in the space, the light at its back. Initial panic subsided when they heard the man speak.

"Father Donadieu? Mister Pierre? Is everything alright? I heard quite a ruckus." Roland's voice remained calm as ever, despite the frantic state of the two before him.

"You need to leave this house," Donadieu replied, his voice strained and uneven. "Find Aliénor, meet us at the church, this place is not safe."

The butler remained unphased. "I did try to warn you, sir. The building is old; its construction is not sound."

"Remain or do not. The peril is yours!" With no inclination to stay and argue, Donadieu grabbed Pierre by the shoulder and pushed him along, away from Roland. They did not slow even after they burst from a final door and into the mansion's vacant courtyard.

Out in the chilling air, the moon supplied only a trifling sum of light. Each night, its radiance reduced as it waned, the new moon less than a week away. Sparse clouds further obstructed the light as they made their way across the open space.

Young legs made it so Pierre reached the stable first. By the time Donadieu arrived, Hippo had been hitched to the wagon. Pierre scrambled aboard and Donadieu mounted soon after. Half a moment later, they were off. Pierre strained the reins and coaxed his horse to run as fast as it was able. They tore past the gate, still open from their midday arrival.

Inadequate suspension bounced the pair wildly during their retreat and forced Donadieu to grasp his seat with both arms to prevent himself from joining the bats flying above. A jarring cacophony of shattering glass came from the back as their hasty speed threw jars and vials from the rudimentarily sorted shelves of the wagon's interior.

Only when the town was in sight in front, and the Dubois' far from view behind with no evidence of pursuit, did Pierre allow Hippo to slow. Donadieu calmed, and his own galloping heart began to ease. He turned to look at the young man sitting next to him. A pair of glass lenses and a protruding beak met his gaze.

"Are you hurt?" Donadieu asked.

Pierre removed his hood and then his mask. His hair glistened in the moonlight and his glare pierced through Donadieu and continued beyond. Pierre turned back and continued to pilot the wagon ahead.

The starving moon appeared temporarily free from cloud cover. The streets sat empty. Remembering happier days, Donadieu supposed he should be in his church, ringing the midnight bell around now. As it stood, the only noises for the retreat were the clomping of Hippo's hooves, the clacking of the wagon wheels on the cobbled street, and the chirping of insects scattered about the town.

A chill settled upon the village, and the priest pulled a hefty wool blanket onto his lap. His head turned to follow the houses and he tried to recall which of his parishioners lived where. Many of the occupants had not been to mass in some time. What quantity of the homes contained people mummified by the Withering? Were there more like Louise, or any who may yet become like her? A seed of dread grew within his stomach, a void threatening to consume the rest of his hope.

Pierre stirred. "We left him to die."

"Pardon?"

Without turning, the apprentice continued. "We left him to die up there, alone, with that creature. I could have helped him."

A tear rolled down the cheek of the distraught man. Seeing the sorrow on Pierre's face transferred it in equal measure to his own. Although Donadieu and Guillaume had never connected as much as he would have liked, it was clear the master meant everything to Pierre.

"There's nothing you could have done. He was already gone."

Staring straight ahead, tears flowing freely down his face, Pierre snapped. "You don't know that. How could you know? He was still breathing when we left. *We left*. Left him there to die."

After the trauma they had just endured, Donadieu needed to tread carefully, but he could not deny the reality they had seen. Turning back to watch the houses, he replied. "You heard the cracking of his neck, as did I. I'm sorry, Pierre. Louise turned his head right around. There's no surviving that. Nothing you could have done would have fixed it. Had you remained, you would have suffered the same fate." Donadieu sighed. Finding words to try to soothe another while his own mind spiraled was a daunting task. He turned back, startled to find the young man glaring. Pierre's cheeks sparkled from trails of tears, and the whites of his eyes were now stained red from the same.

"Why weren't *you* affected?"

"Affected?"

"Why didn't you go mad? You didn't have a mask." Pierre shifted in his seat to further face the priest. "Guillaume got one whiff of that air and he retched. His mind fled shortly after. Why were you able to so freely breathe the miasma and escape with your senses intact? What makes you different from him?"

The inquisition caught Donadieu entirely by surprise. With no time to think or produce a more satisfactory answer, he defaulted. "God must have protected me."

"And where was *He* for Guillaume?"

"I don't know." Donadieu was not satisfied with his response any more than he knew Pierre would be, but it was the only answer he had.

The church was still two blocks away, but they did not speak for the remainder of the ride, preferring tense silence. When they arrived, Pierre stopped the wagon and stared expectantly at Donadieu. Understanding his presence was no longer wanted nor welcome, Donadieu dismounted and walked to his steepled home. When he opened the door, he twisted back to look at Pierre. The young man was shuddering from the tears about to burst free.

The priest entered the church with his head hung low and the wheezing from the pews assaulted his ears. This day had not resolved as hoped. He paused beside a sleeping man and listened to him gasp. For all his efforts, they had accomplished nothing. This parishioner remained unchanged, and a doctor was dead.

God was surely here in this place devoted to His worship, but the lasting effects of that original sin blanketed thick over this small town. Pacing around the church, Donadieu stared into the baptismal font and hardly recognized the aged visage which stared back. The hair of this face was gray and the wrinkles deep. The past year felt like a decade and had aged him just as much. His eyes lowered to the reflection of his clerical collar. Today it seemed like a burden more than a badge.

He left the font and found himself before the hearth. Embers glowed within, and a weak soup simmered in a half-empty pot. He had not made this meal nor lit this fire. It could only have been the work of Pascal.

The groundskeeper was as gritty as the earth upon which he labored, but beneath that coarse and selfish surface, there was good in him. There remained good in all places, even this. After today, he did not know how he would continue, but for the sake of Bastion, he would find a way. *The evil persists, but so do I.*

Moving to the altar, he kneeled. "In the name of the Father, the Son, and the Holy Spirit, I pray. Guide Guillaume to a peaceful rest. In life, he had many flaws, but he did much good as well. Through grace, all deeds may be forgiven, and I pray he finds such redemption.

"I pray that I may be guided still, that my hand may do the Lord's work, and that we may rid Bastion of its curse. No matter the cost.

"I pray too for Pierre, that he may shoulder the burden of his loss well, and that he forgives for what has been taken from him. That he overcomes his trials, strengthened by them and not beaten.

"I know You are always with me, my God. You hold me by my right hand. For all these things I pray, in the name of our Lord and Savior, Jesus Christ. Amen."

CHAPTER 15

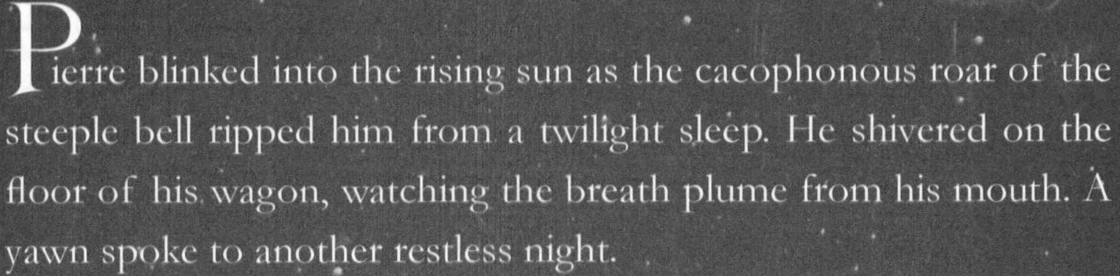

Pierre blinked into the rising sun as the cacophonous roar of the steeple bell ripped him from a twilight sleep. He shivered on the floor of his wagon, watching the breath plume from his mouth. A yawn spoke to another restless night.

He rolled over in his hastily made bed, no more than a pile of blankets laid in a poorly swept corner. Habit caused him to look for Guillaume. When presented with the cataclysmic destruction of last night's ride, his memory returned, and he whimpered in sorrow. For the first time he could recall, Pierre found himself without purpose in the world. He reflected upon his work and within it could find no meaning. Why continue to pretend he could help people? He was a failure, unable to save even the man who taught him all he knew. Nor a single one of the people he had been paid to cure.

Hippo nickered in the nearby stable and the noise caused a powerful desire to hitch the horse and flee Bastion, to find somewhere new. The image of the hung man flashed in Pierre's mind. He pushed the idea from thought. He was stuck as long as the quarantine remained.

He curled into a ball under his mound of quilts. His mind clamored with an inconsolable tempest of terror and grief, feelings he could hardly bear. Eventually, he rose to his feet and searched the wreckage of his home in a frenzy, throwing cloth and debris about as he went. It was not long before he found the medicine he sought, an unopened bottle of very cheap wine. Spirits would bring calm to his grief-stricken heart and unwind his spiraling mind. In a handful of large gulps, half his liquid breakfast had been consumed. Not even the burning tang of vinegar could slow his ambitious consumption. By the time the sun broke free of the horizon, the bottle lay empty beside him.

Wallowing in self-pity and the numbness of drink, Pierre became aware of footsteps approaching his den. Panic gripped through his inebriation and the terror returned from the previous night. He imagined Louise just outside, coming to finish what she started. With his inhibitions softened; he threw the empty bottle blindly out of the wagon. The projectile shattered on the ground nearby.

"Dammit!" came the distant yell of Pascal.

A concerned looking Donadieu poked his head into the wagon. "Pierre? How are you?"

The familiar face eased Pierre's fear but raised his ire. Could he not be left to suffer in peace? "Fine," he slurred.

"Good." Donadieu gave a still worried smile. "Would you care to discuss last night? Perhaps our plans for moving forward?"

"No."

There was a pause. "Rest well, Pierre. I will wait until you are ready."

A calm washed over the doctor when Donadieu accepted the rejection. Guillaume would not have let him get away so easily with such overt defiance.

Guillaume. His heart ripped in two at the thought, even through the haze of alcohol. He decided he must have more. What he'd consumed was insufficient to alleviate the pain of his woe. Reaching for the bottle to his side, he recalled it was empty, and now shattered outside his home. On a stomach empty of all but wine, he clambered to his feet and searched about the place for more.

"You'll do nicely," he mumbled to a dainty bottle of brandy he pulled from a medicine chest. Popping the lid and drinking it down, the potent spirit roasted his throat. The swill had him hacking before it reached his stomach, but when his constitution returned, he nestled back into his corner. With eyelids heavy from exhaustion and drink, he waited in a daze until he fell into a deeply wanted sleep.

Some hours later, Pierre begrudgingly found himself awake and mostly sober. The sun now hung low on the opposite side of his wagon, and his stomach quaked with hunger. His abdomen roared when he caught the whiff of nearby food. Following the scent, he turned his head toward a bowl of stew still steaming at the end of his wagon. Without question, he gobbled the meal.

No longer distracted by want of food, his mind was again obsessed over the previous night. Fearing a return to encompassing misery, Pierre scoured the place in search of more to numb him. This search, however, was less fruitful than the last. He found the broken remnants of two bottles of wine and one of brandy, but nothing intact. Pierre slumped upon a crate and his vision began to blur. A few sniffles burned his nostrils. Just as he thought the pain of his hurt would overcome him, he spotted something almost as good as wine. A coin purse.

Hastily, he brushed aside some debris and retrieved the small leather pouch. He tossed it once to himself; the coins clinked as they fell, and the density of the bag pleased him. Upon peeking inside, he knew by the plentiful silver that this was the coin purse Donadieu had given them as a down payment for the current job.

Ignoring the guilt of using coin from an unfulfilled promise, he clenched his fist around the money and left his disorderly home. While dismounting and walking away, Pierre became aware that Donadieu watched him from the church door. The priest wore a concerned expression but did not accost him as Pierre feared he might.

Wandering through Bastion, it did not take long to find the establishment he sought. It was one of the very few buildings still lively and bright. There was not much to do in a quarantined town, and fewer people to do it. He opened the door and strolled in, only casually looking around.

It was an average tavern, no different from any other he'd patronized. Stools sat by the bar and around low tables. A good portion of them were occupied. Cheap tallow candles dimly burned to illuminate the space, giving off long ribbons of acrid black smoke. More light came from a fire that blazed beneath a large cooking pot and spewed out heat. Already, one man lay sprawled across a tabletop, muttering through unconsciousness. Pierre envied him.

The barman nodded as Pierre entered and the young man found himself a seat at an empty table big enough only for two. He dropped his purse upon the table. The audible thud caught the keep's attention. A few coins promptly changed hands and Pierre's evening was secured.

Mug after mug, he drank through the country ale. As his brain began to cloud, the pain began to fade. Pierre soon joined the mumbling man in indifferent bliss.

A jabbing pressure in his ribs roused him from a dreamless slumber. "Closing time," the barkeep said, holding a broom like a spear.

"Hmmm?" Pierre replied.

"*Out*," said the local, sterner the second time.

Eviction aside, Pierre found himself still pleasantly inebriated and left without conflict. Stumbling over himself, he sauntered through the street and attempted to find his way back to the church and his sorry excuse for a bed.

The evening air felt good against his skin. It was warmer than the previous nights. That, or perhaps the ale warmed him from within. Above, the moon gave only a token effort to light the earth. Through nothing more than aimless wandering and dumb luck, Pierre found his home and resumed his dreamless slumber.

Pierre woke confused. The previous days were nothing but a blur. He recalled the sky changing from blue to black, and back again during the blinks of his bleary eyes.

Now, a blanket of clouds smothered the sky.

Turning his head, he found himself sitting in an alleyway between a pair of old houses. To his right was his mask, to his left was a puddle of purple-tinted sick.

Unlike the sky, his mind was now clear of outside influence. His intentional numbness had been replaced by a blinding headache. Lethargy gripped his limbs; even blinking was challenging and slow. His whole body shook from the repercussions of his bender. This would not do.

With the joint pains of a man twice his age, Pierre reached to his side and produced his coin pouch. Half its contents were now missing, but the remainder would purchase more cure for his pain. He moaned as he rose to his feet. In protest, the world swayed and the wall behind him became a necessary brace.

When both his mind and stomach settled, he pushed free from the support and dragged his feet out into the nearly abandoned street. Those locals who did still walk freely stopped to watch Pierre stumble. His arrival had painted fear and anger upon the faces of the townsfolk. Now all that remained was pity.

As he drifted back toward the tavern, he tried to piece together his missing days. The attempt proved to be near futile. He remembered snippets of thoughts and shadows of scenes, but in his mind, they jumbled together into one amalgamation of drinking in the tavern.

He did produce one nugget from his mining, a fragment of a conversation he shared with Donadieu. The priest had come to the tavern one night, or maybe one day, in an attempt to convince Pierre to return with him to the Dubois'. For what twisted purpose, he could not recall. Just thinking of revisiting that cursed house tangled his stomach worse than excess ale and wine. He quickened his pace, but his speed did not last long. After only a few strides, he heard a call from behind.

"Mister Pierre!" a young girl yelled. "Mister Pierre, I've been looking all over for you!"

He turned and saw Marianne running toward him. Pierre waited for her approach, gently swaying as he stood. "What's the matter, Marianne? Are you alright?" He displayed a strained smile as the child arrived by his side.

Marianne took a momentary break to gasp for air. The noise erased what little grin Pierre had mustered, for accompanying each breath was a hint of wheezing from her lungs. When she spoke, her petite voice whistled with each word, and a gentle cough soon joined.

"Papa sent me to find you," she said. "Well, actually, he wanted Father Donadieu, but I couldn't find him. When I saw you, I knew you would help instead!"

Pierre was almost too afraid to ask. A part deep within him hoped that if he ignored his concern, it may not be true. "Are you feeling alright, Marianne?"

"I'm okay," she replied with more cheer than Pierre felt he may ever muster again. "I think the air is thicker today, though. I can't swallow it as good as usual."

Pierre wanted to both laugh and cry at the child's innocence, but the knowledge of what lay in store for her crushed him. "We'll have to prepare some thinner air for you then. I'll keep my eye out for the thinnest I can find. How does that sound?"

"Great! Thanks, Mister Pierre!"

Pierre playfully rested his hand upon Marianne's head. She quickly batted it off. "Now, what did your father need?" he asked.

"Oh yeah," she chirped. "Last night he was complaining about breathing, too, said he'd find Father Donadieu in the morning. He's very sleepy though, so I thought I'd help by finding him myself. Papa nodded off early last night and he's still sleeping now! I tried to wake him up, but he was so tired he wouldn't get up. Same as Mommy! If he doesn't get up when I go back, I'm going to band some pots and scare him awake. He does that to me when I try to sleep in on Sundays." The girl giggled to herself at the devious plan.

The child's delight did not spread to Pierre. In fact, he had never felt so useless. "I'm not sure I can help, Marianne. I'm sorry."

Her smile faded, replaced by confusion. "You said you were going to help. You have to help. It's what good people do."

The last of Pierre's self-esteem evaporated from his soul. "I'd like to help, Marianne. I really, really would. But I can't. I don't know how. I tried, but it didn't work."

Marianne stomped her foot and scowled at the doctor. "But you have to keep trying, I told you! You're going to come, Mister Pierre, and you're going to try again!"

"I'm not," he replied. A rot spread within him, he could feel it corrupting his soul. Pierre resumed his march toward the tavern.

Marianne responded by latching onto his leg, forcing him to drag her along. He continued for several steps before he stopped and sighed. "If I come and try one more time, will you promise to leave me alone?"

She released his leg, and her bubbly persona returned. "It's a deal!"

"Very well. Lead on."

Marianne led him to her family's home. All the while, Pierre could not help but notice the absence of the youth's usual energetic gait. The house was a standard two-storied dwelling. Shutters on the windows, tile for a roof, and stone with mortar for walls.

"This is it!" she proudly exclaimed. "I'll go get Papa."

Pierre called her back before she got too far. "Maybe it's best you wait here," he said. "Let me go look. I'll be out in a moment."

"Hmmm, I'm not so sure Papa will like waking up to you. You might spook him if you put on your mask."

"You must be hungry," Pierre countered. "Here, take this coin and go buy yourself some breakfast. I'll take care of them as best I can, I promise."

Marianne giggled and snatched the money. "Thanks, Mister Pierre," she said and skipped away. When the child was beyond view, Pierre donned his mask, heaved a deep sigh, and entered the home.

Help the best I can, Pierre thought, *whatever that means.* He breathed the powerful scents of his beak and briefly explored. The dwelling contained necessities and nothing more. Chairs, fireplace, pots, and dust. Nothing unexpected. He ascended to the second floor and quickly found the bedroom. When he saw the couple, he knew any efforts would be fruitless.

Marianne's parents laid upon their bed. Her father looked weak, but altogether whole, having only recently passed into unconsciousness. The visage of her mother, however, sent a chill rippling down his arms and caused the hair on them to stiffen. Pierre's stomach turned as he watched her warily from the door, waiting for her to stir. He remained there for some time but eventually gave in and entered.

The woman retained a fistful of wispy hair, and her cheekbones protruded more prominently, but otherwise she looked nauseously similar to the emaciated husk that had assaulted them a few days past. Terrified and disgusted to find another creature such an affront to natural laws, he hastened his inspection that he may justifiably leave the sickened place. He wanted very badly to return to his alcohol-induced coma.

Devoid of his cane, Pierre grabbed an old hairbrush and started by jabbing each of the two sleeping parties. Neither stirred. Confident he would not be disturbed, he first focused his attention on the father. The mother was simply too far gone. As previously, his inspections yielded nothing. Aside from strained breathing and wakeless sleep, he couldn't find anything wrong with him. Pierre shook his head in defeat and looked for a water jug, finding one nearby. The least he could do was try to keep the man from drying out like the others.

He dipped a cloth into the jug and carefully dripped water into the mouth of the sleeping man. As he focused on the accuracy of his drops, a stirring of motion drew his attention. His heart nearly stopped, and his stomach fell to the floor.

Marianne's mother sat up.

Pierre froze in place, not daring to even breathe. The husk rose from her bed and stood, her white nightgown draped like a sheet on a clothesline. As the creature began to move, he heard the door open on the floor below.

"Mister Pierre?" Marianne's voice called. "Are you still here? The bakery was closed, so I came back."

Still as a statue, Pierre watched the ghoul move. It did not see him, or did not care to see him, and instead shambled toward the doorway.

"Mister Pierre?" Marianne called again.

Brimming with fear over what that creature may do to such an innocent child, Pierre bolted from the room and bounded down the stairs of the home. "Mister—" Mariane began before she was lifted from the ground and carried away in the doctor's hasty retreat.

"What's happening?" the girl screamed as they burst from the home and tore down the street. "Mommy!" she yelled. "My mommy's awake!"

Pierre cast a frightened glance over his shoulder. Sure enough, the ghoul had followed them downstairs and now stumbled into the street. He ran to the east, toward the church. To his immense relief, another look back revealed Marianne's mother shambling in the other direction. This revelation did not slow his steps, however, and he raced through the town as fast as his legs would carry. His lungs strained as they sucked perfumed air through his filtered mask.

"My mommy's awake, Mister Pierre, you did it! Stop running away. I want to see her!" The child jostled aggressively in his arms, but he squeezed her tighter and refused to slow. "I want to see her!"

"I'm sorry, Marianne," Pierre said through gasping pants. "I am so, so sorry, but we can't see your mother right now. We need to find Father Donadieu."

"But why?" As her hysterics grew, so did her difficulty breathing.

"Because," Pierre replied, "she's still unwell. You should keep your distance until she's fully better, so you don't get sick, too."

"But I want to see her!" Marianne wriggled and squirmed and cried as they ran. The church came rapidly into view. When they arrived, the effects of her malady disrupted her tears, and she grew quieter from the strain of her lungs.

"Father Donadieu!" Pierre called as he crashed into the door and tumbled into the building. There came no reply, nor did he see any sign of the priest. Still clutching Marianne's fatigued figure tight against his chest, he peeked in Donadieu's private room and then trudged around the yard, shouting the priest's name. Only when he reached the rear of the building did someone answer his call.

"He left," the gruff voice said.

Turning toward the secluded cemetery behind the church, Pierre saw that it was Pascal, the groundskeeper.

"Where did he go?"

Pascal did not seem to care in the slightest for the urgency present in Pierre's voice. He stood leaning on a shovel and replied in his own time. "Returned to that house o' death. People told 'im not to go, but he still did. Been only me round here since." Pascal paused. "Other than the breathers."

"When…" Pierre replied slowly. "How long ago did he leave?"

Marianne now struggled for air more than anything else, and Pierre set her down.

"Day 'fore yesterday."

The consequences of his multi-day drunkenness collapsed upon the young man. "And he hasn't been back?"

"Nope."

A numbness spread across Pierre. It was not the same mental fog he had experienced as part of his grief. It was not the mist which had clouded his thoughts when he drank. It was a feeling of dissociation, an emptiness that suggested he was not truly there. That it was already far too late.

"Can you look after Marianne for the day?" The words breezed from his mouth with no effort on his behalf. "Her parents are unwell."

Pascal looked at the child and shrugged. "I guess."

"Listen to Pascal, Marianne. I'll be back in a bit." The child whimpered behind him, but she did not protest as he turned to leave.

"Yer welcome," came a gruffer call, but the words did not register in Pierre's ears. He cast a glance toward his horse on the way back to his wagon. It was clear Hippo had been fed and watered in his absence, almost certainly Pascal's doing.

He glided onto the front seat of the wagon and sat. It felt like hours before Pierre was able to organize his thoughts into any sort of cohesion but, judging by the sun, it had only been a few minutes.

The situation continued to grow more dire, that much he was certain, but he knew not how to proceed. Wasting more time in the tavern while the Withering drew more from their slumber was untenable, even to him.

Marianne's mother…she had not chased him nor her daughter. She journeyed to the west, toward the Dubois'. The infected seemed to congregate toward that cursed book, its sinister pull bringing them home, like salmon up a creek.

As revolting and hideous as he found the notion, he knew that he, too, must go. Father Donadieu had left some two days past to achieve the same goal. Had the priest been successful, Pierre would not be readying his wagon now.

Considering briefly whether he should attempt to bring others with him, he decided against it. Only Donadieu had shown resilience to the pestilence of the western wing, and Pierre could not take the risk that new allies might suffer as Guillaume had.

So alone he went, riding through the hollow streets of Bastion, Hippo in front and a mangled wagon behind. He would do one more time what he promised Marianne. He would *try*.

CHAPTER 16

Father Donadieu stood in a tavern, leaning over an ale-filled Pierre. He'd come in hopes the doctor would accompany him back to the Dubois', to help him destroy that horrible text. Instead, he found a feeble young man drowning in his grief. No amount of prodding nor any attempts at conversation could rouse Pierre from his stupor. In the end, he left Pierre to wallow in self-pity and the pungent smell of alcohol. Losing his mentor had crushed the aspiring physician. Losing him in such a horrific way was unimaginable.

As Donadieu returned to the church, he gave thought to how he may best his daunting adversary. He was not well-versed in the medicinal arts, nor did he know much of miasma, or disease, or how best to balance the humors. Though in this instance, he was not convinced such knowledge was what he required. Had this ailment been so easily cured by traditional means, the plague doctors would have already resolved the issue. Whatever haunted Bastion was something *other*.

It had been years since he'd encountered something so demonic, a tangible manifestation of sin. Since the boy. In the face of such evil, his duty to Bastion and to God charged him with divine purpose. He must do anything he could to destroy that tome; he would not let evil win again. The path ahead stood before him like a cave impenetrable to light; and he knew not where to step. The church would not assist, and he could rely on no locals. He would have to act alone and pray that God would guide his weathered hands.

And what of those who lived amongst that horrid tome? Donadieu had not heard a whisper from those that called the old castle their home since he and Pierre made their hasty escape. The thought that all who lived there had been overrun by disease weighed heavily on his soul. Could such people be redeemed? God could redeem any soul. Did Louise even have a soul left to save?

When he arrived back at his church, he made brief rounds to check on the status of his wards. All continued to gasp, and none stirred. He watered their drying lips and then sunk away to his modest room.

Once alone, Donadieu turned his mind to his own kind of research. He scoured about his humble living space and only now realized what a mess it was. Gifts from his parishioners lay scattered about the place, and he had amassed piles of texts, letters, and scrolls.

First, he recovered his bible and placed it upon the small desk. Next, he searched the literary mountains. Donadieu skimmed the pages, looking for any mention of malevolence, possession, or exorcisms. When his bounty had been assembled, he reluctantly lit the candle upon his desk and began to read.

For hours, he consumed the written words. He extracted instructions from firsthand accounts and interpreted meanings from the metaphors. With each relevant script, he jotted notes on a growing list of tools he would need and verses he must recite.

His concentration broke only when his candle reached its end and snuffed itself out. It surprised him he'd allowed it to get so low, never sparing a cautious eye to keep track of the flame.

Satisfied with the knowledge gained and feeling ready for the impending return to that horrible home, Donadieu spent the rest of the evening feeding the ill and preparing his supplies. Scavenging through the church, he collected two small wooden crucifixes, three cross necklaces, four vials of holy water, two bibles, and several candles with a steel to light them. Atop this pile of righteous ingredients sat a handwritten rite of exorcism, an amalgam of all he'd learned. He packed everything into a satchel with care and patted the bulging cloth.

Despite all his preparedness, Donadieu remained wary. The last excursion into the west wing ended in disaster, and this time he would travel alone. Should he succeed, the town would be freed from its blanketing evil. Should he fail—no, he could not fail, for God was surely with him.

In reverence and hope, he prayed for an uneventful night and for the following day to turn in his favor. The priest rose and crawled into his bed. For the first time in as long as he could recall, Donadieu slept well.

When he awoke, he started his day as he always did: with prayer. He withdrew from his bed, bowed his head above his sheets, and he began.

"Yea, though I walk through the valley of the shadow of death, I will fear no evil: for Thou art with me; Thy rod and Thy staff, they comfort me.

"Lord, as I endeavor to do Your work and cleanse this town of that unspeakable text, I ask You watch over those suffering here in Your church. I shall endeavor to return, yet should I not, through Pascal I pray You act on their behalf. This evil is no fault of theirs, and I seek to right this unjust wrong. This I pray in the name of the Father, Son, and Holy Spirit, Amen."

Donadieu lifted his head, and radiance grew within him. He knew he had the support of his God.

After sounding the morning bell, Donadieu grabbed his supplies, bid farewell to his church, and began the long walk toward the Dubois'.

As he strolled through the ever-emptying town, he heard a large commotion growing to the west. The priest quickened his pace, panting long before he arrived at the frenzied crowd.

"I know you fancied her," a man yelled with an accusatory finger raised, "and so you steal her from her bed while she slept? Have you no shame? No decency?"

"I didn't touch your wife," came the rebuttal. "And what of my boy? Did you steal him as revenge for your imagined crime? Where is my son?!"

Donadieu watched with dread as a brawl erupted between the two. Savagely, the men lunged and clawed at one another, ripping at hair and bludgeoning with fists.

The crowd cheered them on.

Placing his hand upon the shoulder of an old woman, Donadieu asked, "Pray tell, what has caused these men to attack each other so violently, and so early in the day?"

"Town's in a veritable frenzy, Father Donadieu, no denying it," the old woman replied in a wheezy voice. "People starting to disappear, it seems. Stolen from their beds while they slept. All the withered folk. People are going mad trying to find their missing family. Can't say I blame them. First time I've been happy my Andre left us those three years back, don't need to worry about no one but me."

Donadieu nodded at the woman and attempted a, "Thank you," but his voice faltered, and he stared farther to the west. "Excuse me," he said before leaving the mob to their violence and hastened again. Whatever this curse was, its pace was quickening. He must hasten as well.

As he traveled the dusty road to the Dubois', the crunchy, dry earth disgruntled Donadieu. It took him a moment to realize why he found the noise so distasteful, but when he was attuned to the problem, it pushed a shiver up his spine. He hated the sound of his footsteps because they were the *only* sound. The evil had driven away every last blackbird and cricket from the forest. Donadieu stopped his march to listen to the deafening silence. He resumed his journey, now placing his feet even heavier into the soil, anything to break the quiet.

His mind spun as he tried to make sense of what was happening to his community, to piece together the puzzle of their suffering.

Donadieu pivoted with every breeze that dared to rustle a leaf in this forsaken forest, terrified one of the withered may be lingering about, ready to attack. Watching the forest instead of his step, Donadieu stumbled as his foot landed in a small divot. Thanks to a lucky tree branch growing close to the road, he caught himself before he fell.

Breathing deeply, he muttered to himself, frustrated he again so nearly destroyed his plans by another misplaced foot. Donadieu tested his ankle for a sprain and found the joint only twisted from the incident. When he pressed on, he more closely watched the ground. That was when he noticed a trail of footprints beside his own. They were the shoeless footprints of a child.

The priest's heart fluttered as he scanned the ground around him. His horror grew as he noticed these prints were not alone. There were at least three more distinct prints of varying sizes, all without footwear. He knew for certain now he was not the sole person on a pilgrimage to the Dubois', but it was likely he was the only one with the goal of ending the contagion.

With God as his shepherd, he continued his holy crusade. The priest remained resolute in his mission, yet his heart thumped all the same. At last, the border of the property came into view. Its iron gates remained open, groaning on their hinges as they swayed under the influence of the wind. The prints he followed continued onto the grounds and disappeared where the earth changed from dirt to gravel.

Standing at the exterior of the fence, he watched for signs of movement within the estate. Despite the certainty of more withered around the residence, there was an eerie calm about the place. The early morning sun fought a losing battle as the sky's blue was slowly consumed by a rolling gray. Donadieu continued through the gate toward the looming home, eager to complete his task before the sun went down.

As he walked along the gravel path to the courtyard, he maintained a wary eye toward the stained-glass window of the desecrated chapel. It hung in the stone at the extent of the western wing, a portal to an evil place. He could see no shadows stir within. Like everything else in the area, all appeared deathly still.

Holding his satchel tight, the priest broke away from the meandering path and trudged toward the doorway at the end of the west wing. His hand hovered above the doorknob and a repulsion overtook him. As always, he ignored it. Donadieu pushed the door open and stared down the empty corridor. Drab daylight flooded into the shadowy hall from behind the priest, his body casting a long shadow down the carpeted passage. All was as he remembered from their previous hasty retreat.

The doorway to the spiral staircase stood open, while every other was shut. Shards of the battered door lay strewn about the hall, the result of Pierre's burst through.

A humble fly stirred in the empty space and Donadieu eyed it with suspicion. After his mysterious assault, the pestilent species worried him. The insect zipped around the air and, after a moment's stillness upon a wall, it escaped up the spiral staircase. The flies of the Dubois' manor routinely appeared as omens of misery to the priest, but now he had no choice but to follow. Ideally, Louise and her ilk would be asleep during the day. Donadieu did not plan to linger and find out.

Although he'd brought candles from his church, he spied an unfired candlestick down the hall. Not wanting to waste his own stock when the house provided, he lit the candle and grabbed its base. Ready as he could be, he marched into the darkness of the spiral stairway. Donadieu's extended arm pushed the flame before him as he ascended. This distance served two purposes. Having the light far in front gave him the best view of the footing to come, and it kept the flame far from his person.

Cool air stirred around him and during his ascension, a gust threatened to extinguish his guiding light, the wick only just retaining its flame. After a flickering of his heart, the flame's power returned. He continued up the steps, taking care to better shelter his light, even if that meant he must hold it closer to his robes.

When he neared the top of the stairs, a scuffling noise cascaded down the surrounding stone. Without thought, he snuffed the flame he had just saved and froze in place, eyes wide as he watched the opening above. For several minutes he waited, breathing no more than puffs of air until a timid squeak gave away the source as a pair of tiny mice. Donadieu's heart slowed, and he released his long-held breath. Refusing to allow further delay or indecision, he summited the stairs in the darkness and strode into the empty room.

Toward the pulsating door, he marched with indefatigable purpose, ignoring the small puddle of Guillaume's dried blood along his way. Stopping just outside the portal, Donadieu held his breath and listened for sounds from within the glowing room. When he heard nothing, he rushed inside, refusing to allow himself even a moment to consider retreating.

As before, the heavy air pressed on him from every side. Along with the air in his lungs, he, too, felt the presence of God forced away from him on entry into the chapel, its desecration so complete as to push away even connection with the Almighty.

Stalwart, his determination did not waiver regardless of how his body suffered. With herculean determination, he breathed in this thickening air. He would bring God back into the once holy space. The discomfort would not stop him, but the sight of Guillaume's withered shell on the floor gave him pause. The physician's corpse still lay where it fell, its chest periodically rising and falling despite its dehydrated flesh. Such extreme decay should have taken weeks, the bandages now loosely draped around his face.

With no assurance that what he saw was real, he turned his head and tried to push Guillaume from his mind. The book had meddled with his perception before, Donadieu suspected it was doing so again. He stopped before the pedestal and its grisly trophy. In his previous encounter, he had not ventured so close. The swirling ink confounded him; never before had he seen such devilry. The mysterious light hovered around the book, its satanic crimson no doubt a remnant from its creation in Hell.

As he leaned forward to observe the tome in greater detail, the crosses worn around his neck began to warm. Then, they burned. The old man yelped in surprise and pain, arching his back to dangle the scalding metal away from his chest. He watched in horror as the symbols of his faith glowed a fiery orange and burned free of their string necklaces. They clattered to the floor, the crosses smoldered and charred themselves black, releasing metallic fumes.

Bestial instincts urged him to hurry, or to flee. The tainted power here was great and should Louise or another of the withered arrive, things would take a turn for the worst. He unpacked his kit onto the front row of the pews and pulled the scribbled rite close to his eyes. He'd read the ritual a dozen times in preparation, but the oppression of the room muddled his memory.

Unable to focus, he followed the directions like a recipe. First, he retrieved a vial of holy water off the pew and emptied it onto the *"possessed person or object"*, in this case, the book.

Puffs of smoke and bolts of brilliant light shot from the tome when the water landed. The swirling ink responded by bounding across the surface of the page in a frenzy, careful to avoid the charred and smoldering dots freshly burned across it. Donadieu shuddered as he watched the ink flee. Its frantic response implied the text itself possessed sentience. Donadieu hated the thought, but the results fueled his purpose; confident his exorcism was working and the evil could be purged.

He followed his first successful assault with the recitation of an ancient prayer. He boomed the performance as loud as he could manage, his commanding voice articulating the dead language with skill.

When he concluded his recitation, he paused, eager to see how his speech would affect the tome. Nothing happened, and the shadow of doubt descended across his mind. Donadieu skimmed over the written work and confirmed he had not missed some crucial verse. Underwhelmed and increasingly anxious, he had little choice but to continue.

The final step was simple: place a crucifix bathed in the blood of Christ upon the troubled entity. Donadieu had prepared this tool the night before, allowing the wooden cross to soak in the sacramental wine for the entirety of the night. He grabbed the symbol from the nearest pew and stared meaningfully at the cross, pensive about what this tool represented. The wood, now a vibrant purple, felt damp in his hand. Unstained, the silver figure of the martyr shone on, despite its overnight bath.

Before he could advance on the book and finish his task, unexpected noises from behind distracted the priest. A strained lungful of air and the rustling of cloth spun Donadieu's attention. As he watched, Guillaume picked himself from the floor and rose to his full height, at least as tall as allowed by his fractured and twisted neck. The doctor's skin had all but mummified, and his motions were disjointed and broken. His head looked over his shoulder, spun halfway around from the neck breaking snap, and his greasy black hair was knotted and protruded in every direction like a jungle of tangled vines. The pulsating red light painted his skin with the presence of every imaginable disease, and snot drained from his nose like a waterfall. The crust around his eyes had all but sealed them shut and a ghastly bruise splotched over his broken neck.

Slowly, Guillaume reached up and grasped his head. With a noise like the grating of cement, he twisted his skull until it faced properly ahead. His neck still bulged from the broken bone.

Panic shot through Donadieu and the shock loosened his grip, causing the crucifix to fall from his grasp. As Guillaume began to shamble toward him, Donadieu stooped low and fumbled upon the ground for his cross. He clasped it between his fingertips and spun toward the pulpit. With only a few steps between the pew and the book, the air felt thicker, and he struggled as though wading through mortar. The decrepit physician did not seem affected by the same hindrance. Before Donadieu could force his way back to the podium, an unnaturally powerful arm grabbed his collar and threw him to the ground.

The impact vibrated through him and scrambled his busy mind. Gasping for air, Donadieu stared at the twisted man towering above him. "Guillaume," he wheezed, "you must let me complete my work. It is the only way I can set you free."

The voice that replied carried the whisper of death, as though it were a conduit straight to Hades. "Your actions cannot be allowed."

"What does that mean?" the priest begged. "You must help me up."

Guillaume's eldritch gaze remained unwavering, his feet firmly planted.

"Think of Pierre, Guillaume! He would be most eager to see you. Why don't we go?" Tentatively, and with his eyes refusing to peel from the doctor, Donadieu slowly raised himself off the ground until he was standing again. "Let's get you out of here, somewhere safe."

The sound of further footsteps grew in the great empty room, but Donadieu did not turn to look. In desperation, he took his purple cross and lunged back toward the book. Crucifix reaching forth, he intended to finish the ritual. All that was left was to touch the cross to the book.

The same firm hand caught him and again threw him to the floor. His momentary descent felt as though it were an eternity. With the loss of his momentum, so too did he lose his hope.

As he lay defeated and gasping, a familiar voice carried in from the doorway. "How very, *very* rude."

CHAPTER 17

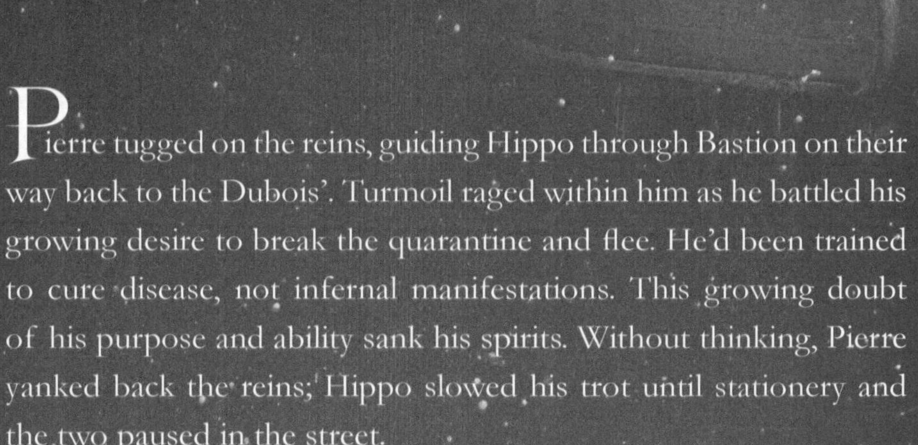

Pierre tugged on the reins, guiding Hippo through Bastion on their way back to the Dubois'. Turmoil raged within him as he battled his growing desire to break the quarantine and flee. He'd been trained to cure disease, not infernal manifestations. This growing doubt of his purpose and ability sank his spirits. Without thinking, Pierre yanked back the reins; Hippo slowed his trot until stationery and the two paused in the street.

The dreary sky did not aid in relieving his mood. Its lingering gray shroud had lasted well into the afternoon and continued even now as the sun began its afternoon descent behind the cloudy veil.

Pierre panted through his mask. His hands shook. The momentary courage that'd initially spurred him forth had abated, and now he sat paralyzed in the quiet town streets.

"Doctor," a voice called. Pierre turned his beak to look down at the man and his heart beat faster; Henri stood at his side.

"Yes?" Pierre asked as submissively as he could. Without the priest to talk the man down, Pierre feared confrontation with the brute would be inevitable.

Henri bowed his head. "I wanted to apologize for myself and on behalf of the others. Emotions and spirits filled us that night when we stopped you and Father Donadieu; your profession does not carry a grand reputation and Bastion was already suffering. Still, I make no excuse for my actions. We are in dire straits here and we know now you have come to help. Father Donadieu speaks highly of you, and I'd like you to call on me for anything you need. Things are getting bad and something must be done."

The tension pulling Pierre's shoulders released, and he tilted his head back in relief. "Thank you, Henri. That's kind of you to say. I'm heading back to the Dubois' now. As far as I know, that's the last place Father Donadieu was seen, and I aim to find him. He was working on a solution."

At the mere mention of the mansion, Henri's skin turned to marble. "That's where *they* have been going, Doctor, you mustn't. And Father Donadieu is already there? Then he is lost to us."

"They?"

"The withered. Have you not heard? They've been waking for days, and many were seen heading to the west. All who followed them have failed to return. What was Father Donadieu doing there? Do you know something of this curse?"

Pierre weighed his options. What did he have to lose? In brief, he explained to Henri all he knew. Should he also fail, someone needed to know of the threat.

Henri nodded along and did not interrupt. Only when Pierre had finished his tale did the man speak. "We've long suspected devilry was at play, but to have it confirmed." He shook his head and then sighed. "Let me join you. The risk is too great for you alone." Before waiting for a response, Henri climbed aboard. The man's bulky frame tilted the wagon as he scaled the vehicle.

Pierre held out one palm to the man and used his spare to steady himself on the tilting wagon. "It's too risky, Henri. I don't have a suit to protect you. I've already witnessed how quickly the Withering spreads, especially in proximity to the tome." The warning did not stop Henri, who instead plopped himself next to Pierre, a wide grin on his face. Pierre continued, "Without a well-fitted mask, you will quickly succumb. You are needed here to spread the news. The people must know what they face, should I not return."

Henri maintained the grin and raised an eyebrow. "Are you going to throw me off?"

Pierre shook his head. The debate was lost. There would be no convincing the brute to stay behind. He jostled the reins and Hippo again began to trot.

"Excellent," said Henri.

"I'm serious," stressed Pierre. "You may ride along and watch the horse, but you cannot enter that home. You must promise me, Henri. You will not survive."

Henri signed the cross above his heart. "I promise, Doc."

Pierre did not believe the man, but he had no choice.

Together, they reached the edge of town. As they passed, the people still braving the open air stopped to gaze upon them. No longer with disdain or pity did the townsfolk look on; now a new expression graced their faces: *hope*. Pierre, too, felt it. It was a warmth, absent since the passing of Guillaume, but slowly it began to return.

Steadily upon their way up the dirt road, Henri turned and asked, "So, what exactly is your plan? How are you going to best this devil book?"

Only then did it dawn on Pierre that he hadn't developed a plan. He rode to a likely demise with emotion alone fueling his purpose. Very unlike himself. "I haven't got that far yet," he admitted. "I was hoping I would find Father Donadieu and he would have an idea. Now that you're here, you can help me come up with one."

"They don't train you for this sort of thing when you become a doctor?" Henri smirked.

Pierre shrugged, playing along. "Not in any text I've ever read. Devilry aside, I've never heard of a physical source of miasma so potent as to infect an entire town from such a distance, especially while being concealed to the nose. It would be a wondrous discovery if not so powerfully evil." Thinking of the text's swirling designs made want to find a dark corner and hide in it. "You locals find talk of that place taboo. Why? What do people say about it? Anything at all may help me or guide me toward a clue."

Henri nodded and then tilted his head back in thought. "I'm not sure anyone knows anything for sure. Mostly rumors passed down through generations. The castle has been deserted as long as anyone can recall, ten generations at least. That is, until the Dubois' moved in. Mothers warn their children that the place is full of monsters. Other than the occasional mischievous dare to touch the exterior fence, people kept well enough away.

"And those are just stories involving the old fort," he continued. "Legends go back longer than anyone here knows involving the hill upon which it was built. When they first decided to erect that stone monstrosity, the locals tried to warn them off. They didn't listen. The English never set foot near that fort, yet the garrison dwindled to nothing all the same. It's been an empty ruin since then.

"The only man I know of who actually went inside was our former priest. He considered our fear an 'indirect worship of pagan gods' and sought to sanctify the place in the name of the Lord. He didn't return."

"An interesting history," Pierre replied, "but I'm not sure it contains anything immediately assistive."

A raven flew overhead, croaking as it went. The men stopped to observe the bird fly; it'd been some time since wild animals had visited the quarantined Bastion. Animals other than the occasional locusts, flies, and rats.

"How would you normally purge a source of miasma?" Henri asked when the interruption passed.

"Well, it depends on what is giving off the bad air. If it's a water source, you would need to find a way to purify it, or simply avoid it. Otherwise, stopping the propagation of the miasma odors would be sufficient."

Henri moved his hand forward to prompt Pierre along. "And how would you do that?"

"Usually you counter the bad smells with good ones. That's why I wear this mask." He tapped the beak. "But I doubt anything so concentrated as that book could be bested for long by some flowers. To purify it would require something more. If our goal was just to stop the spread the simplest way, I would say bury it. No miasma should be able to escape twenty feet of earth." Pierre pulled the reins to steer Hippo away from a hole in the road.

"Would that work?"

"Impossible to know, but I suppose it's our best bet. That is, unless I find Father Donadieu and he has a better idea."

Henri shrugged. "As long as we've got something."

Pierre breathed deep and the spices in his mask tickled his nostrils. His vague idea of "find Donadieu, save the day" now seemed recklessly foolish.

Rescuing Donadieu would still be his primary goal, but the thought of the time it would take to search the entirety of the house allowed him a guilt free excuse to abandon the mission should he not be able to quickly find the priest. Pierre's terror demanded he must not linger in that place, and if Donadieu could not be located between the entrance to the west wing and that accursed chapel, then the search would have to continue another time. At a *safer* time.

No, he would move straight to the chapel and abscond with that terrible text, all the while hoping to avoid Louise and the other horrendous ghouls. Memories of watching Marrianne's decrepit mother rise from her bed crept into Pierre's mind. His breathing grew shallow. A nervous sweat slicked his hands, the salty droplets bit like ants when the stiff wind found its way into his gloves.

Pierre began to doubt his mission and despaired at his hopeless crusade. Just as the doctor was about to stop the wagon in defeat, Henri spoke under his breath. "There it is."

At the extent of their view, the tree line broke, replaced by a wrought-iron fence. "Hand me the reins," Henri said. "I'll park it here and watch over the wagon. You go ahead on foot. I don't think we should ride this contraption right to the front door. It isn't particularly subtle."

Pierre did as instructed, grateful Henri was keeping to his promise to stay clear of the Dubois'. Pierre's mind was already too busy arguing with itself to have a debate the well-muscled man.

Henri slowed the horse a short walk from the edge of the grounds. "You ready?" the large man asked. "We're counting on you, but you've got this."

Henri's prompt grounded Pierre, and the apprentice nodded his beak. The encouragement brought back a semblance of rational thinking. "I suppose I'm ready."

A combination of concern and sympathy rolled across Henri's face. "If you're not back by sundown, I'll come looking."

"You mustn't," Pierre insisted again. "You won't survive. I need you here for my retreat. You swore."

The man threw his hands in the air. "Alright, you win. I'll stay here, but I can't stay forever."

Pierre dismounted the wagon, a small cloud of dust erupting when he hit the ground. "Only stay until sundown. If I haven't been able to grab the book and return by then, I likely won't return at all."

Henri nodded. "Godspeed, Pierre."

"See you soon," the doctor replied.

After saying his goodbyes to Henri and patting Hippo, Pierre grabbed his medical satchel and followed the tree line ahead. When the trunks stopped and the wrought iron began, Pierre instinctively bowed his head and tensed his shoulders as if to hide from view of the mansion. He scurried along and, after he passed through the creaking gate, continued west along the interior of the fence.

He heard nothing as he moved, save for the grass beneath his feet. All the while, his head darted about like a squirrel on alert for a hawk.

As he approached the latitude of the manor, he skulked across the open ground between the fence and the building, still attempting to shroud his head as he ran. Were he an outsider to the situation, the look of a man jogging across an open field, adorned in his robes, would look quite comical. Pierre did not laugh.

He pressed his body against the stone outer wall and caught his breath. Thus far, his mission had progressed without issue, and the doctor fully intended to press his luck. He stood and listened for some time, straining for any sounds from behind the curtained windows. A slight smile tilted the edge of his mouth when the house produced only silence.

Pierre reached the door beneath the stained-glass window; the entrance to the main floor of the west wing they had fled from only a few nights before. His confidence grew with each inhale as he marveled at his successes thus far; and with each exhale, his confidence ebbed at the thought of what lay ahead.

Refusing to allow himself a pause for fear his nerve would break, Pierre's quivering hand clasped the handle and pushed the door. It did not yield. His heart dropped and he pushed again, harder this time. The door was sealed.

Still holding the handle, he looked to the sky and the clouds drifting in the afternoon sky. A restless leg bounced. He would have to enter through the main entrance and sneak his way through the home undetected. His leg bobbed harder.

Pierre loathed the idea of exploring that maze alone, but he had to admit the more of the building he saw, the more likely it was he would find Father Donadieu. That is, if he was still alive. Pierre shook his head, hoping to cast off his doubt.

One long, deep sigh, and he was off. The apprentice snaked along the antiquated stone walls of the west wing, ducking beneath each windowsill to avoid casting shadows within.

The main entrance grew near, and the giant set of double doors blocked his progress like a pair of guardsmen. Pierre could not help the feeling he was about to enter the maw of some great and terrible beast. Caressing the handle, he turned his wrist and gently pushed.

The door silently opened. Pierre smirked at the victory, but its success did not rejuvenate him. Now the truly terrifying part began.

The dull light of the overcast evening slipped its way into the home through the threshold's growing crack; the shadows did not welcome the invasion and seemed to fight it back. The beak of his mask stopped Pierre from pressing his eyes to the opening and surveying for danger. Instead, it forced him to scurry through the door and shut it behind him, only then allowing him a moment to glance around.

Formerly lavish and bright, the foyer now existed devoid of life and color. The room's heavy curtains allowed only a fraction of daylight through, leaving Pierre squinting through his lenses as his eyes adjusted. Without the light or a crowd to indulge in its splendor, the room lost its gilded charm and instead stood a testament to excessive wealth.

But the house should not be empty, Pierre thought. Neither Aliénor nor any member of her staff had appeared in town since his last visit, and several of the withered had been observed shambling in this direction. Pierre relished that his intrusion had been undetected, but the haunting silence of the home summoned a fear that made him half-wish the ill more openly roamed the halls. That way, at least he may see what lay in wait and deliberately avoid it.

Without thinking, he reached into his satchel and wrapped a gloved hand around his largest surgical knife. Hours of work had grooved the wooden handle to fit perfectly in the contours of his hand. The embrace of the weapon brought a semblance of calm, although if push came to shove, he was not certain he contained the fortitude to use it. Its blade extended no longer than the length of his hand, but its edge cut as clean through flesh as it did through water and it would do in a pinch. His hand maintained its place within the bag as he began to move, his fingers wrapped tight.

Cutting forth through dead air, he arrived at the transition where the refurbished home turned to a foreboding and antiquated castle. The plaster walls gave way to the rough unfinished stone, and what little comfort had been given by the ornate decor was lost as the furnishings grew rotten and the gloom denser still. Pierre stared down the length of the corridor and marveled at how short it looked when compared to his memory. He advanced at a crawl, skulking through the shadows.

At the far end of the hall, the door to the courtyard had indeed been boarded shut. This would make his exit equally daunting, if not more so, should he need to retrace his steps with that *thing* in his possession. Worse still, if he needed to bring an incapacitated Donadieu. He pushed those thoughts from his mind. Before he could leave with his targets, he must find them.

Pierre reached the spiral staircase leading up to the empty room and the book. The passageway gaped, its tunnel so black it seemed to suck in light from the hallway and consume it. A bead of sweat started down the back of his neck, sneaking past his collar and tickling its way down his robes. Hesitation gripped him and he swayed from an imaginary breeze which gusted down the stairs.

Catching himself procrastinating, Pierre forced his feet to march before his mind could debate the rationality of that decision. He ascended into the dark, taking great pains to place each foot as silently as possible, all while his spare hand caressed the wall to guide his way up.

Despite the darkness' proclivity to obscure dangerous things, this trait worked both ways. Pierre found himself more comfortable in the darkness than he had been with the light. He still didn't know where his potential adversaries may be, but now they would not be able to see him, either. His logic held strong and steadied his chest until a cackling laughter ricocheted down the stairwell from above.

CHAPTER 18

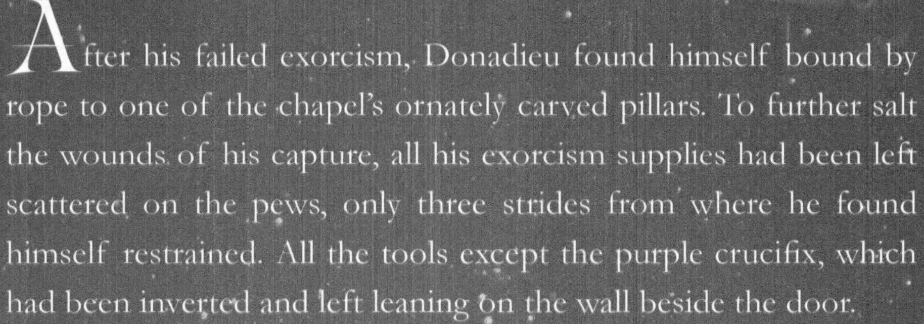

After his failed exorcism, Donadieu found himself bound by rope to one of the chapel's ornately carved pillars. To further salt the wounds of his capture, all his exorcism supplies had been left scattered on the pews, only three strides from where he found himself restrained. All the tools except the purple crucifix, which had been inverted and left leaning on the wall beside the door.

Exhaling frigid breath upon the priest, Guillaume and Louise passed the rope back and forth around his body and added a new knot after every few passes. They wheezed as they worked. Aliénor stood watching them from outside the door.

Donadieu tested the rope by straining his limbs. The more he pulled, the harder the fibers bit back. Convinced of the efficacy of his restraints, he relaxed and addressed his captor. "Why have you done this, Aliénor? Why am I here? Please, let me go." His own voice sounded strange to him, unfamiliar. The density of the room lowered his pitch and warped his words.

Aliénor leaned upon the doorframe in response, careful not to pass the threshold into the chapel. "Leave us," she said, nodding toward the ghouls.

"Yes, my lady," replied the ghouls in unison; their voices echoed hollow, and the words drifted slowly through the air. Hearing Guillaume's twisted speech crumpled Donadieu's nerve. *Thank God Pierre is not here,* he thought. *Heaven only knows what this creature could get him to do with that puppet of Guillaume.*

Aliénor smirked as the withered left. "Now just you and me, Father. Perhaps I should confess?"

Donadieu met her gaze. He could not find even a trace of sincerity behind her smile, but accepted the offer anyway. "Confession without remorse is gossip. Do you regret your actions, Aliénor? If so, it is not too late to right your wrongs and be forgiven."

His captor put on a show of contemplation. She stroked her chin and looked at the ceiling for guidance. "You've caught me," she said, arms lazily rising above her head. "I don't regret what I've done. If you were me, you wouldn't either."

"I doubt that very much."

Aliénor ignored the challenge and continued. "Isn't this place just marvelous? Can you believe this was already here, just waiting to be rediscovered?" her eyes bounced around the chapel in wonder, taking in all the decrepit decor as though it was the first time she had seen it. "Boredom sets in quickly when you have more gold than the sky does stars. I often wandered the grounds after we moved, looking for anything to do outside of interaction with that drab little town. I stumbled across this chapel one sunny afternoon. The doorway had been boarded up, so I ripped the planks down to see what lay behind. Good thing I found it, too, before those troglodyte laborers started the renovations here. They would have destroyed this place before I had the time to discover that stunning book. Isn't it bliss to have its presence radiate around you?"

Donadieu could indeed feel the text's presence. It was impossible not to. Its pressure wrapped around him like eldritch tentacles extending from an unfathomable abyss. But unlike the others in its presence, he did not find the oppression delightful, or convincing, or persuasive. It was monstrous, and Donadieu wanted it to be cast off along with all those who welcomed its influence.

"So, it was always you, then?" he asked. "This plague which has destroyed our home?"

Aliénor shrugged. "I suppose that's one way to interpret it."

Donadieu knew he must break through to the woman that his captor once was. "Aliénor, you're possessed. Listen to me. You've been cursed by something awful and I'm here to help, but I need you to fight back. I need you to free me and let me do my work. Together, we can purge this demon you have inside you."

"A demon in *me*? Maybe. But if there is a demon in me, it's been there long before I moved here. Do we not all have demons inside us? There would be no redemption if there were no sin." A thin, humorless smile crossed her face. "I know something of *your* demons, Martine. I've known for a long time. Before moving cities, I always do my research on the locals; and always first, the priest. There's no better way to divine the region's temperament than by learning of the priest who holds its ear. I wonder what influences the other more? Does the priest change the will of his congregation, or does the congregation alter the beliefs of the priest? What do you think, Martine? Do you bend the will of your flock to match your vision of God, or do they distort your interpretation of an ineffable God?"

"God guides us where we need to be, where we can best support the people, and they us. If we change each other's views, it's because we were meant to."

Aliénor grimaced. "That's hardly an answer. I thought this would be more entertaining." She tapped her foot and looked down to watch it bounce.

While she stood distracted, and with as much subtlety as he could, Donadieu strained with all the force he could muster. Twisting and pushing against the restraints. Friction from the coarse rope burned his flesh, rubbing away patches of skin. Spots on his robes darkened as blood seeped from the burns and his limbs throbbed with pain. His ropes did not yield.

"Please Aliénor," he panted. "What do you want from me? Why am I being held here?"

"Have you ever seen a cat prolong the life of a mouse just to ensure it dies with fear? People condemn the cruel nature of the cat, but no one ever stops to save the mouse. Flaunting victory is in the nature of all your God's creatures, one way or another. Soon you will fall and join me. All will. But while the ignorance of most is acceptable, as long as they submit, I want you to understand why. I want you to behold what you will become. I want you to know what's coming."

Donadieu shook his head in despair. "Just let me go."

"I understand," she replied, gently, as though somehow *sympathetic* to his plight. "You need time to adjust to your new home. I'll leave you for a time, allow you to become better acquainted with our literary friend." She stepped back from the door.

Despite himself, Donadieu called for her to wait. "Don't leave me here," he begged.

Aliénor disappeared into the darkness.

Horror crept through Donadieu. The dread started in his stomach and ascended past his lungs and into his skull. From the corner of his eye he watched the sentient ink squirm, swimming about the page while avoiding the splotches of scorched paper. Before he'd begun the exorcism, the entity's presence was oppressive, but passive. Now, the creature excreted rage. Each pulse from the tome vibrated through the air, shaking his mind like an earthquake. His head throbbed, his consciousness desperate to break free from its skeletal jail.

Donadieu's perception of time began to warp and bend. The book surged with vile intent, tormenting him.

Minutes passed, or possibly hours. With each pulse, Donadieu feared his psyche may break, the strain pushing him nearer to insanity. As the assault dragged on, he longed for the comforting release of madness, anything to distract his mind from his lucid struggle against the book. The priest habitually recited psalms, but each pulse from the book acted as a crisp slap to his face, forcing him back to his despair.

Time passed, though whether he remained secured for a day or a decade, Donadieu's muddled brain could not tell. Relief only came when his tormentor called his name, and the psychic barrage eased.

"Father Donadieu, how are you now?" Aliénor asked from the doorway. "In a chattier mood?"

Desperate for distraction, he acquiesced at once. "Yes, please. We can discuss whatever you'd like." The book ceased all attacks, returning instead to its passive pulsation.

"Let's talk about you, Martine. Let's talk about your past."

Donadieu raised his head and cast a sad, haggard eye at Aliénor. Whatever game she wanted to play, the priest knew it would be painful.

Still not fully within the chapel, Aliénor tapped her hand upon her hip. She wore an elegant gown, the fabric only just darker than her chalky skin. Pretense of innocence abandoned, she observed him with gloating eyes.

"Excommunication," she said, "few priests recover from such disgrace. Tell me about that, Martine. Tell me why they kicked you out, and about the boy and the fires. The whole truth this time."

The honesty which spouted from Donadieu's lips surprised him; he heard himself speak but could not contain the words. They spewed from his lips like vomit and tasted just as rancid. "It wasn't a coincidence they caught the boy," Donadieu confessed. "I told them it was him. It was based upon my word that they saw to the snapping of his neck, and I heard the rope groan as his body swayed." Reliving the memory forced his eyes shut. His failure to stop the fire pulled his head low with shame.

"And why did you do that, Martine? Why did you break the seal of confession?"

"That was no child!" Donadieu's voice took the fervor of courtroom persuasion. "That beast was none other than Satan himself! I swore no vow to keep the secrets of monsters. I had no obligation to that creature or its truths. My only obligation was to the family with which it shared a home. I failed that family, so I saw the creature killed; it would destroy no more."

"But your church didn't see it that way, did they?"

The tide of his anger withdrew, replaced by defeat. "They did not. I tried to convince them of the necessity behind my choice. They cast me out all the same."

Aliénor smiled like a teacher whose pupil had solved a difficult sum. So pleased. "They threw you out like an old rag."

Donadieu bobbed his head. "Like a rag."

"Do you not see how similar we are? Trapped in institutions that abuse us?"

"I'm nothing like you."

"You are. Tell me, why do you think they gave you a new parish to tend?"

"They didn't say, and I didn't ask. I was just happy to serve my Lord once again."

"I know why. Would you like to know? Ask me." Aliénor rolled her head across her shoulders and watched the restrained priest with hawk eyes, waiting for his submission.

Weakness spread through Donadieu. He loathed the idea of playing Aliénor's game, but between his curiosity for her answer and the fear of being left alone with the book, he played along. "Why did they bring me back?"

"It's not because you were wanted, I'll tell you that," she said. "Quite the opposite, in fact. Word traveled fast about your dismissal, and it reached your family before the end of the week. When your eldest surviving brother heard you had been released from your service, he feared you would come looking for a share of the family's estate. He gambled that a modest donation to the Church would be cheaper than supporting you. They accepted and hid you away in the smallest, most backwards commune they could find."

Donadieu narrowed his eyes as she spoke. *Could it be true?*

"Isn't that something?" she continued. "They brought you back because elsewhere you were wanted even less. And you came! Scampering toward your beloved church like a loyal dog. I find you pathetic. You'll grow a backbone when you join me, whether you want one or not."

Aliénor fell silent, allowing the priest time to digest. Focusing on the conversation was difficult, the tome's presence still washing over him, but the words floated in the air, waiting for him to piece their meaning together. When he truly grasped their significance, he found himself indifferent. Better than indifferent; *resilient*. If this was the worst Aliénor could taunt him with, he would have nothing to fear from her unholy inquisition.

"You mistake my allegiance, Aliénor. Yes, I returned at once to the Church, but that was from my devotion to God, not the flawed institution of man. I have qualms with the organization, but none with my God. To be an ordained servant of His is the greatest blessing I have been bestowed, and I would return a thousand times. If your tale is true, it seems time has hardened my brother's heart. We were close once, but that was a lifetime ago. I wish him well all the same." Donadieu defiantly raised his head and met her glare dead on. "You will not break my faith, Aliénor. It cannot be done."

His captor's face twisted into a visage of contempt and rage. She moved as though to step into the chapel, but stopped before placing her foot. Her eyes opened, revealing the bloodshot whites and, biting her lip, she turned and left.

The tome did not resume its assault after Aliénor's departure, instead it seemed content to continue its more passive disruption, the swirling ink resuming its chaotic dance.

Twice during his stay, Guillaume entered the chapel to pour water into Donadieu's mouth and feed him small chunks of fresh bread. No plea by the priest produced a response from the doctor. The ghoul's jaw remained locked. His steely eyes showed no sympathy.

Other than those brief interruptions for food, only the waves from the book kept him company. His wakefulness grew and ebbed between a dreamless sleep and the impact of the psychic siege.

After a length of time lost to the priest, Aliénor returned. This time, Donadieu was cognizant enough to witness her approach.

"How are we today?" she asked, stopping again at the door. She looked calm, ready again to test him.

"Hello, Aliénor. I am well, how are you?"

The cordial response raised one of Aliénor's brows, but her mouth remained flat. "I've found some free time in my schedule, so I came to converse with my guest. I trust Guillaume has been treating you well?"

Donadieu bowed his head as best he was able with the restraints. "I have been fed. Speaking of treatments, how is Claude doing? I'm curious about the progress of his recovery."

Aliénor rolled her eyes. "He's recovering, as expected."

"His condition, I assume that was your doing?"

She tapped her nose.

"Then why summon us to tend to him?"

"I was curious to see if you, or rather—your physician friends, could do anything to help him. Imagine my joy when I discovered their medicine to be as useless as your prayers."

Donadieu hated that she was right. "What *have* you done to him, to them all, and why?"

Aliénor clicked her tongue. "I'll answer your question with a question and guide you to the answer. You mentioned you have qualms with your church. Were you to be given the authority and power, would you not set about correcting what you see as its flaws?"

Donadieu sighed, feeling like a passenger in a wagon to which Aliénor held the reins. Still, anything was better than being alone with that book. "I would try."

"And there is your answer."

Donadieu tried to piece together the intent of those words, but his mind was muddled by the probing tome. He shook his head. "I don't understand."

"And therein lies the problem," said Aliénor, "because to me, it is obvious. To Claude, I wasn't even a pawn. At best, I was a decoration. He married me for my wealth and for heirs. Now, my money is in his vaults, and it seems I am incapable of the latter. My usefulness to him was at an end, and he made sure to let me know. I'll have you know he was even planning to have me killed; marriage was as much a trap to himself as it was to me."

"You'll forgive me if I have a difficult time believing your tales." The priest wiggled his fingers through the ropes. "Especially given my circumstances. But what I believe doesn't matter. All that matters is the redemption offered to us all. No one is too far gone. If you truly do crave the justice, you seek I can tell you with certainty there is eternal justice awaiting. Please, repent. It's your only hope."

She scoffed at her captive. "It's far too late for that now. I've assumed my new position as head of the house, and I believe it to be a marked improvement. No more endless ramblings about architecture or fineries, just progress. I will create my own eternity."

"Progress," Donadieu blurted, unable to hold his tongue. "How could anyone see any of this as progress?"

"*Beauty is in the eye of the beholder*, as Claude would often say. I'm surprised he never locked me away, truth be told; kept like the silver cutlery and brought out only for guests." Aliénor's eyes flashed. "Now that he's my silver spoon, perhaps I'll pull *him* out. You are a guest, after all."

By this point in her tirade, a flush had accented her cheeks. "Look at me blathering on. I hope his presence in my collective hasn't spread his propensity to drone." New footsteps echoed from the room behind Aliénor. "Speak of the devil." With a dramatic flourish, she stepped to the side to make way for the approaching figure.

Claude entered with a candlestick in his right hand, its glow casting an ominous flare to his otherwise neutral expression. He looked no different from when Donadieu and the doctors attempted to treat him, save for his waxed mustache now being bent askew. As Claude strode past Aliénor, she flared her nostrils and recoiled from the flame, a response Donadieu knew only too well.

When the former patriarch crossed the threshold into the chapel, his appearance mutated. The pulses of light eroded away any remaining semblance of health, his illnesses worsening with each strobe. Dried blood decorated the skin beneath his nose and the corners of his mouth. His eyes sank back into the recesses of their sockets, and his left arm began to twitch. Buboes and lesions appeared across his exposed skin and a rash filled the remaining space.

Aliénor curtsied behind her husband. "I know how boisterous men can be, so I'll now take my leave. Don't be too rough on each other. I have plans for you both." With a graceful spin and fading footsteps, she was gone.

Donadieu at once tried to bargain with his new jailor, hoping some aspect of the man remained. "Claude, can you understand me? You must let me go, I want to help you and everyone else that's trapped here."

Claude's sunken eyes did not react. Instead, he bared his teeth in a crater-filled grin. The decrepit man held his flame inches from Donadieu's face, its heat begging to bite the priest's already scarred cheek. Donadieu squirmed and twisted within his ropes, desperately trying to avoid the scorch of the flame. Claude only moved it closer to match the evasions of his plaything.

"Stop, please!" Donadieu cried, and the nobleman obeyed.

Claude placed the candle upon the closest pew and turned back to the priest, balling his hands into fists. The flesh on his hands looked painfully tight and cracking in some spots, disturbingly loose in others. It gave the appearance that Claude's own skin was a poorly fitted suit.

The first blow struck Donadieu's stomach with the force of a kicking horse. Spit and wind exploded from his mouth, and he sputtered and gasped for air. Desperately he writhed his body, attempting to break free, but the second blow took him across the cheek and sent his mind spinning. His head rolled and before he could recover, Claude's ghoulish hands wrapped themselves around his neck. Donadieu's chest spasmed as it tried to suck air through his sealed throat. The trauma worsened as Claude viciously shook the priest, pulling him against the ropes and pushing him back with frantic repetition. Donadieu's already blurred vision dimmed, and walls of black advanced across his sight.

Consciousness returned slowly to Donadieu, his body hanging limp against the ropes. Bursts from the book slapped him awake, and he grimaced at his newfound pain. His head ached like a rat was burrowing within and pushing his brain to the corners of his skull.

When his eyesight returned, he found himself hanging ever so slightly away from the post. Instantly he was alert, his eyes bursting open and his limbs beginning to squirm. The beating had given him an opportunity. With his eyes straining against the tome's aggressive light, Donadieu began to work upon the unexpected slack with a frenzy.

Pushing the left half of his torso against the ropes, he wormed his right hand free and played at the first knot within his reach. The fibers were thick and resisted his efforts, but determination and dexterity won out. The knot released. With the new slack, Donadieu freed his second hand from its prison and together his digits massaged the old rope. Upon release of the final hempen lock, the cords dropped to the floor, and the priest stepped free.

He made it one pace before his knees crumpled and he collapsed. A pathetic cry escaped Donadieu as he fell, followed by a heavy thump. The long restraint left his joints unprepared for effort, especially within the chapel's thickened air.

He groaned but would not relent. He summoned himself back to his knees, and then to his feet where he took measure of his wounds. In what was surely a blessing from God, Donadieu found only a sprained ankle from the fall and a swollen cheek from Claude's blow. Without wasting time, he hobbled toward his purple crucifix. The pain in his joints was nothing compared to the exhilaration of his freedom. He would finish the ritual and end this evil.

"Stop!" came a shriek from the doorway. Aliénor stood glaring just beyond the threshold. A molten fury shone from her eyes, and spittle flew from her mouth as she screamed.

Donadieu froze at the command, a paralyzing fear spreading along his limbs and seizing his joints in place. He was old, he was slow, and he was injured. He would not beat Aliénor in a race to the cross and back.

"What do you think you're doing?" she roared. "You contemptible old fool. How are you still free of my command?" The words betrayed her failure, and her eyes widened at the slip of her tongue, but she could not take them back. "If you won't die with dignity as a man, I'll kill you like a rat."

Donadieu's successes over the influence of the book and his brief escape now seemed hollow victories before his advancing foe. For the first time since his internment, Aliénor stepped through the door. As she did, all her refined elegance washed away under the tome's glow.

Her fair complexion stained into a sickly jaundiced yellow and all hair vanished from her scalp. Aliénor's eyes shriveled like grapes turning to raisins, before falling from her face. Flies circled her head to make a floating crown. Patches of honeycomb-like holes scattered across her leathery flesh, passageways used by the bugs to traverse through her body.

She raised her arms, her fingers spread like claws, and she stalked towards Donadieu. Even her nails were covered in fungus, dripping slimy mold as they reached for their prize.

Trapped, Donadieu paced backward, out of reach of his captor. "Stop, Aliénor, please. You can still let me go."

Aliénor took another step, and Donadieu matched. The priest nearly tripped as his foot came down on the scattered rope. Only a lucky catch on the back of a pew stopped him from another collapse.

Aliénor cackled, speckles of vomit flying from her mouth as she laughed. Snot ran freely from her nose and dripped from her cracked and blistered lips. A serpent's tongue extended and collected the salty treat before her crowing continued.

The hideous laughter, loud as a church bell, echoed through the house. It echoed through the empty rooms, it echoed across empty halls, and it echoed down a spiral stone stairwell.

CHAPTER 19

Pierre froze as the maniacal cackling bounced around him, and his body shook with terror. Dread swallowed his spirit. What if his enemies' vision was not as impeded by the black as his own? Even If he had not yet been seen, Pierre feared his discovery was inevitable, thanks to the drum thumping within his chest.

After a quarter minute of unexpected but welcome survival, Pierre found the courage to inch forward. Despite the success of his continued existence, his jittering did not abate; instead, it grew. His limbs quivered with the knowledge that the path ahead would not be as solitary as he had hoped.

Reaching the door at the top of the stairs, he poked his beak into the empty room and panned. Guillaume's blood still stained the floor, and the doorway pulsed ahead, the occasional shadow flitting across the light.

Muffling his footsteps by placing his feet on the edges of his soles and rolling them in, Pierre crept toward the chapel and the horrid glowing book. His breath spasmed in and out of his chest, his fear so great he did not even smell the mask's pungent bouquet.

He withdrew the surgical knife from his satchel and held it to his chest. Even with the stability of his torso, the instrument bounced helplessly in his hands. He would have to rely solely on the sharpness of the blade; a skillfully clean cut would not be possible with his jumping palms. In this accursed place and against his eldritch foe, there would be no second chances.

When at last Pierre made it to the chapel and looked within, it took every ounce of will he had to not flee. Down the center aisle stalked a ghoul in an off-white dress. The creature moved with its back to the door, its hunched shoulders and bald head obscuring the pedestal beyond.

With bravery that surprised himself, Pierre stole into the room and snuck along the wall, always watching the creature for fear it may turn. If he could hide amongst the pews, perhaps it would leave without his discovery and the book would be his. Another bout of laughter erupted from the creature. Pierre threw himself to the floor as quietly as so rapid a descent would allow. With a tilt of his head, he strained to hear if the creature approached.

Instead of footsteps, there came the sounds of a struggle, rustling fabrics and gasps for air. Whatever sick ritual that entity was performing, Pierre wanted no part of it—until he heard the victim scream.

"Aliénor, please!"

The voice echoed within his head like a gong, and he peaked above the pews. "Father Donadieu?" he whispered, but not quietly enough. The creature stopped its sinister work and turned to Pierre. Donadieu dangled by his throat from one of its skeletally thin arms. The ghoul was hideous yet, somehow, unmistakably Aliénor Dubois.

"Pierre," Donadieu sputtered, but the creature's grip crushed tighter, choking out the rest of the phrase save for a few disjointed syllables. The priest's face was covered in scratches and swelling bruises that resembled a victim of an animal attack, wounds to make him suffer but not yet die.

Aliénor's toothless grin split her face in half as she twisted her torso to fully face the doctor. With two grand steps, she blocked Pierre's escape and confined him to a corner within the chapel.

Donadieu turned purple in her grasp, but Pierre's fear drew his gaze back to her soulless eyes. Then the taunting began.

"What are you doing here, you cretinous child? Can't you see I'm busy?" Aliénor proudly displayed her toy, holding Donadieu aloft as though he weighed no more than a doll. "If you wish to join my menagerie, you'll have—"

Pierre did not wait for the end of her goading speech. With a lightning maneuver fueled by purpose and terror, the doctor lunged forth and buried his blade deep into the ribs of his tormentor, then yanked to across her torso with all his strength. The resulting wound split through Aliénor's abdomen, leaving a gash the length of his forearm.

Aliénor shrieked in unbridled agony. She ripped the knife from her side, sending it clattering across the floor. Torrents of black bile and blood erupted from her wounded side, and she sprayed the interior of the chapel with her gore. Pierre yelped in disgust as a burst of the corrupted fluids coated his mask and his clothes. Like the knife, Aliénor cast Donadieu aside, throwing him into the rows of pews.

Pierre dove after his scalpel, retrieving the weapon and rolling onto his back, brandishing the stained blade. He was ready to pierce his assailant again, but he did not get the chance. Aliénor fled the room, wailing curses and promises of destruction before her voice was lost to the corridors of her mansion. For the briefest moment between Aliénor's exit and when she disappeared from sight, Pierre could have sworn her hair had regrown from her head.

Father Donadieu's gasping yanked the young man's attention back to his accomplice, and he hurried across the room to tend to the priest. The man's mutilated face was covered in superficial slices and lumps, but Pierre sighed in relief to find there were no injuries beyond recovery.

"Hold still, Father, I've got you."

From his satchel, he retrieved a small tub of cream and rubbed the poultice on Father Donadieu's face. Donadieu recoiled in pain at the contact, but once the shock had passed, he eased and allowed Pierre to continue his work. While he toiled, Pierre's head swiveled over his shoulder like a ticking clock, watching for another attack. Satisfied once the poultice was applied and some bandages wrapped, he patted the old man's shoulders and helped him to his feet.

"Thank you, Pierre. I owe you my life," Donadieu said. "But now, I have work to do. Watch the door."

"We need to get you out of here," Pierre contested, terrified that the same madness which muddled Guillaume now afflicted, or would start to afflict the priest.

"Have faith, the time is nigh to complete our task. Together, we will end this. Fetch me my crucifix." Father Donadieu pointed to the far end of the room. "Bring that to me and then watch for more of those *things*. I will banish this evil."

Pierre did not entirely believe him. Not after what befell Guillaume. But if they had a chance to end it all now, he knew they must try. That, and the thought of having to return another time made him sick. He read Donadieu's face; the priest looked sincere and whole.

"How is it that you're still well?" Pierre asked as he fetched the cross. "Guillaume fell in minutes to this disease. You've been here for days."

"Truth be told, it seems not even the witch herself knows how I resisted its influence; it was not her design that I be spared. Regardless, we have a job to do." They exchanged the crucifix and Donadieu turned to the book. "Ready your blade," he said over his shoulder. "Leave the rest to me."

Donadieu's resilience awed and inspired Pierre. A lifetime of piety and service had left the old man with a will stronger than steel. Pierre hoped his own profession could equally temper a soul. His eyes lingered on the back of the priest longer than he intended. It took deliberate effort to look away and stand watch at the door.

As he waited, staring into the darkness, Pierre could not help but feel as though the air in the chapel nudged at him, trying to push him out. He feared should the room be successful, he would not find the strength to re-enter. Once, the chapel very nearly succeeded, but the commencement of Donadieu's ritualistic chants snapped him back from the edge. Although the apprentice did not know the dead language in which the priest spoke, the passion with which Donadieu recited it made him wish he did.

Maintaining a vigilant watch, he was distracted only once when Donadieu splashed the text with holy water and puffs of smoke and light erupted from the surface of the book, its pages flapping wildly in response. Waves of psychic pain slammed into Pierre, and he squeezed his eyes shut. The torrent ripped at his mind as though his brain were splitting in two.

Pierre only regained composure when Donadieu yelled louder still, above the confusion and through the ringing in his ears. There was strength enough for them both in the priest's resolve. When he returned his gaze back to the doorway, a familiar face approached. *Quickly.*

"Guillaume?" Pierre asked in wonder. He squinted through the gloom. Pierre addressed him again, more jovially this time. "Guillaume, you're alive!"

His mentor did not respond. Then, in the flashing light, the broken bone in Guillaume's neck became visible where it jutted out against his flesh. The master sped his approach and barreled toward the doorway. His grotesque gait was half a shuffle and half a run.

"Stop!" Pierre called, but to no avail. He raised his knife at arm's length. The steel shimmered with a barbaric red glow, caked in the drying blood of its former victim.

The gap between student and master closed rapidly. Pierre was out of time. The knife in his hand shook as his nerves frayed, and then…they snapped. He lowered the knife. Pierre would not stab his mentor, but that didn't mean he couldn't slow him.

I only need a moment, he thought, and cast the knife aside. Just as he and Guillaume were about to collide, Pierre lunged to his side and cast a leg across the path. The slight caught Guillaume mid-stride, and he descended to the ground with a revolting crunch as his face met the floor.

"Guillaume!" Pierre cried, his loyalty to the man overwhelming him with guilt. Guillaume was not still for long. Before Pierre had finished calling his name, the man was already crawling toward Father Donadieu, leaving a trail of blackened blood smeared behind him.

The former doctor's features had changed after he entered the room, now appearing an amalgamation of the worst diseases Pierre knew, and some he didn't. His eyes widened at Guillaume's possessed determination, and before his rational brain could stop him, he jumped on the man's back.

"Hurry, Father!" Pierre called as he tried to use his weight to slow Guillaume's advance. The young man bent his head low and whispered into his mentor's ear, "Stop moving, let us help you!" Guillaume groaned in response and dragged himself further along the floor.

Pierre raised his worried head toward Donadieu, whose voice had grown even more dire. Donadieu's arm raised high above his head, the crucifix held triumphantly in his hand like a trophy—"*In nomine Patris, et Filii, et Spiritus Sancti,* Amen!"—before he slammed it down upon the cursed tome.

A blinding flash of ruby light exploded from the book and an ear-splitting hiss forced Pierre to squeeze his hands against the hood covering his ears.

When the chaos abated, darkness swallowed the chapel. Pierre lowered his arms. The air had thinned. Only the light of the hollow moon and its surrounding stars entered through the chapel's stained-glass, shining a faint array of tinted color into the otherwise abyssal room.

Caustic odors settled about the space, even worming their way through the densely packed beak of Pierre's mask. He scrunched his nose to refuse their entry. Beneath him, his human mount began to spasm, and the jostling threw Pierre from his back.

"Father?" Pierre called out in terror when he hit the ground. "What happened? Help me hold down Guillaume; he's convulsing."

"I'm here," came the reply. "Stay where you are, and I will find you. We'll tend to him and leave this place."

The sound of Guillaume thumping on the floor sickened Pierre, but not so much as when it stopped.

"Guillaume?" he asked, his voice barely above a whisper. He tested the darkness to feel for his mentor. Patting the floor before him, he found the body. Its flesh was already cool and the muscles still. A salty tear settled on his lips and his breathing shortened to periodic gasps. Pierre tugged at Guillaume's clothes, desperately trying to pull him close, but the stiff man was heavier than a boulder and moved no more than an inch.

"Please, Guillaume, get up!" he begged, rocking the stone-cold man and weeping above the unmoving flesh. "How could you come back just to leave me again?" In the darkness, a hand brushed along Pierre's arm before clasping around it. The young doctor wailed in fear and sorrow.

"It's only me, Pierre," Donadieu said before a long pause. "Guillaume is at rest, then?"

Pierre could not bring himself to reply. He would not speak the words. He'd abandoned Guillaume once already, and to condemn him again would be the ultimate betrayal. Instead, he wrapped himself around the body, praying his own heat would infuse into Guillaume and bring back warmth to the man's cold skin.

"We can't stay here, Pierre. We must return to town. We can inform everyone the curse is lifted, that Guillaume sacrificed himself for that cause. Then, we shall return with sturdy men and carry Guillaume to a proper burial by the church in the town that he saved."

Donadieu's hand cupped the bottom of Pierre's arm, and a gentle tug helped the young man to his feet. "What do I do now, Father?" Pierre lamented while he sobbed. "I have nothing left."

"You have everything left. We've won. Let's return to the church and discuss more there. There is nothing to be gained from wallowing here in the dark. I've got what remains of the book. Let's dispose of this evil relic and be done with this ordeal."

The surprise of Guillaume's continued life, and the shock at his second death fractured Pierre's mind, but Donadieu's words comforted him some. Guillaume had died in service to the people of Bastion, and he should be remembered that way. Pierre allowed the priest to guide him from the room as his tears slowed. He would see Guillaume become a martyr to this town. They owed him that. Through the darkness, the pair found their way to the door.

As they exited the chapel and turned to shuffle toward the staircase, a voice called from behind them.

The voice was gravelly, spoken through shattered teeth and swollen lips. Despite the distortion, Pierre recognized it instantly.

"Wait, Pierre. Don't leave me." The words crawled toward them, each syllable sluggish and grating from the unseen lips.

A bolt of fear arched between Pierre's vertebrae at the voice. He wanted nothing more than for Guillaume to be alright. To leave with them now. But there was something off about this voice, something wrong.

"Guillaume?" he replied, frozen in place.

Donadieu tugged at his robes, attempting to pull him along through the darkness. "That's not Guillaume, Pierre. You *know* that. We need to go."

"Come back, Pierre," the voice moaned. "Help me."

Pierre started toward him, but he was jerked back by Father Donadieu. "No one could have survived what was done to him, you know that."

"But what if he did? He's tough, stubborn." Pierre pleaded, mostly with himself. He needed so badly for Guillaume to be alive.

The voice called again, louder and clearer this time. "Come back, Pierre. Help me stand. I want to live."

Pierre thought of Guillaume and the time they had spent together. He thought about when they met at the university, when Guillaume had shown an interest in the young man, brought him under his wing and shared with him all he knew of the trade. He remembered the first patient he diagnosed under Guillaume's supervision and of the past summer they'd spent together in study.

Then he remembered the crack of Guillaume's neck as Louise's decrepit hand ripped his spine apart. He remembered the bulge in Guillaume's neck from the dislocated bone.

Father Donadieu was right. This was not his Guillaume.

"Alright, let's go," Pierre whispered.

A terrible roar surged in the darkness, wild, like a wolf caught in a trap. Pierre heard the scrambling of Guillaume rising to his feet, all the while threats spewing from his abused mouth. "I'm going to drag you back here, you little worm. Leaving me to die like a mosquito swatted with no regard! Is this what my tutelage meant to you? A discardable devotion?"

This perversion of the man who Pierre once called his friend revolted him to his core. He charged toward the staircase, fleeing from the voice that called after him. He ran with one arm reaching and the second dragging Donadieu behind. His wrist slammed into the far wall, sending a shockwave up his arm. The pain caused his hand to turn limp, but he did not slow in his escape down the stairwell. He released the priest and used his good hand to guide him.

At the bottom of the roundabout, he tore into the hallway, frantically scanning left and right for further threats. A speck of starlight snuck through the curtains and supplied just enough light to guide their way to the windows.

The darkened sky sunk his heart into a well of dread. With the sun having fled, and the ghostly new moon risen to take its place. By now, Henri would surely have left. Adrenaline was a powerful motivator, but Pierre worried panic alone would not allow the pair to outrace the horror which pursued them. With no other option, they would have to try.

Pierre threw himself at the closest windowpane, its glass shattering on impact and sending him tumbling out of the home. His heavy robes cushioned his fall, and his mask remained intact.

With a hearty tug, Pierre yanked Donadieu free from the building and back to his feet.

"What was that?" Pierre screamed as they tore across the courtyard. "I thought you exorcised whatever evil held this town?"

Donadieu examined the tome he still clutched in his free hand. "The book is blackened to a crisp, as though burnt in an inferno," he said, showing Pierre. "I don't know what now possesses Guillaume, but I doubt it was caused by this."

Pierre stopped his retreat. "If the book is no longer corrupting him, could that actually be Guillaume? Did we abandon him again?"

"I don't know. Maybe? No. He can't be alive, not after all that. Perhaps he—"

From overhead, a noise caught the attention of both men. It was faint at first, but it grew louder with each passing second. A vibrating sound, coming from an amorphous black cloud in the sky sailing over the far end of the mansion. It seemed to be heading directly toward the pair.

"What is *that*?" asked Pierre through squinted eyes, which bulged as the object came closer into view. It was no cloud, but a monstrous swarm of flies. Protruding at the tip of the swarm, sticking out like a figurehead at the bow of a ship, was Aliénor Dubois, her sickly state displayed in full horror.

"Run!" Donadieu yelled. It was his turn now to pull at Pierre.

Still gasping for air from their hasty escape, the two resumed a frantic sprint across the Dubois' grand estate and out onto the road. With elation, Pierre cheered as a familiar whinny graced his ears, and a homely carriage caught his eyes.

"Father Donadieu?" Henri called from the wagon. "You're alright!"

"Hurry, Henri!" Donadieu yelled back. "Turn the carriage around. The ghouls are after us and we must flee at once."

The joy fled from Henri's face, as did the color, but he wasted no time in maneuvering Hippo to the task. Pierre reached the back of their covered ride first, lungs burning in his chest. He turned back to pull Donadieu on board, and with a hasty yelp, they were off as fast as Hippo could move.

CHAPTER 20

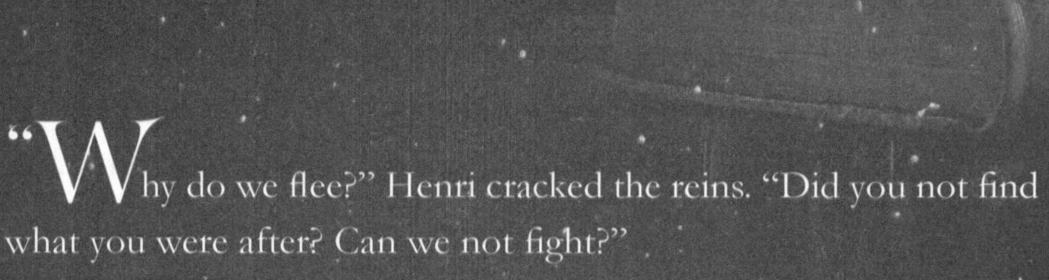

"Why do we flee?" Henri cracked the reins. "Did you not find what you were after? Can we not fight?"

"Focus on the road ahead," Donadieu urged. "We'll explain as we move."

Like a disobedient child, Henri turned back. "What in God's name is that?" he asked, mouth agape. Aliénor and her swarm had made it to the dirt road, and they followed in frenzied pursuit.

"Look ahead," Donadieu commanded. "If we crash, we'll all be victim to her whims." He waited until Henri complied and then continued. "That thing in pursuit is Aliénor Dubois. It was she who conspired to destroy our town."

The thunderous beating of hooves filled the air with dust and flung back clods of dirt and small pebbles. The cracking and shattering of glass testified to the undoing of whatever tidying Pierre had done since the last frantic ride.

Gradually, the distance between their carriage and Aliénor grew;

Aliénor's swarm could not match the speed of their galloping mount. Donadieu thanked God for that.

The wagon swerved along the old country road, dodging potholes and stones with remarkable grace as their pilot coaxed dexterous maneuvers from their steed. "Why does Aliénor wish to destroy us?" Henri asked, his voice vibrating from the ride. "What have we done to her?"

Beyond their flying foe, back at the gate to the Dubois' estate, a mass of the withered began to spill onto the dusty thoroughfare. Much slower than either their master or the wagon, Aliénor's army had risen in full, and toward Bastion, they marched.

"Her reasons are her own, and indifferent to us," replied Donadieu. "I can explain the details when safely within town. For now, focus on your task to make sure we get there at all."

Aliénor shrieked. She navigated through the dying branches of the forest with ease, her swarm impossibly agile. It was a miracle her flies were slower than their horse, but they were only just. Donadieu studied their chasing pursuer as they bounced along the road. Aliénor's countenance now fully reflected her sickly soul.

Donadieu cast his eyes to his trophy, examining the charred shell that had been the evil tome. In the abyssal night, he could discern no details upon the scorched pages. He passed the book to Pierre.

"Have a look at this. You have young eyes, surely sharper than mine. Can you make out if any devilry remains?"

Pierre reluctantly accepted the unholy text, almost pulling his hand away before he grabbed it. The paper crackled as it changed hands, small pieces of char breaking off and floating away.

"Looks like a burnt book to me," Pierre said after a few moments of examination. "Nothing remarkable left at all." The doctor handed the text back. Just as Donadieu made contact with the tome, Henri's expert navigation failed, and the wagon struck a crater. The pages tore between their hands and slipped from their grasps. The awkward handoff sent the relic toppling down the road behind them. Pierre nearly leapt from his seat to grab the thing, but a firm restraint from Donadieu held him inside. Panic froze the two.

"Have I just condemned us all?" Pierre asked.

Donadieu did not know, and together they watched as Aliénor closed the distance between herself and the small black spot sitting on the dusty road.

Aliénor could not have missed the tumbling book, even in the murky gloom, but her pursuit did not slow, nor did she stop to collect the ruined thing. Donadieu exhaled, and he heard Pierre do the same.

"It seems that tome is of no more use to her," Donadieu said. "Thank God."

"If that's so, how does this plague continue?" Pierre asked.

Donadieu shook his head. "God only knows."

"I can see Bastion," Henri cheered from the front. "We're almost there. Where should I bring us?"

"To the church," Donadieu replied, calling through the wagon. "All my supplies are there. With luck, the hallowed ground may repel her sickly ghouls."

"I can do that, Father. Leave the—"

Donadieu knew their driver was not one to hold his tongue. He placed a hand upon Pierre's shoulder and instructed the physician to alert them should anything change behind. Donadieu climbed through the jumbled wagon and sat beside Henri.

When he emerged by the driver, he understood the hesitation. Scattered tentacles of orange burst from the rooftops throughout the town. Bastion had been set ablaze.

Donadieu's breathing seized and his scars bit his nerves anew. "Find anywhere that looks safe," he managed to sputter out. A wave of panic washed over him, his pupils dilated, and unwanted memories demanded their place at the forefront of his mind. The priest stared down at the old scars on his arms, surprised to discover he was not alight.

The reins snapped beside the priest, urging Hippo to continue his sprint. Only the faintest strip of blue hovered above the horizon; blackness claimed the rest.

Donadieu's head tilted high and his hands clasped together. He gazed into the moonless sky, looking for God, and the strangest of sensations struck him. What had been phantom pain burning across his scars transformed into a radiant warmth, like the sun on a winter day. He still remembered the smell of his searing flesh before he'd lost the ability altogether, but he also recalled his ordeal within the dining hall of the west wing, how badly he wanted a fire then. Slowly, control over his breathing returned. The fires ahead grew brighter, but his fear did not. He had come too far to let old hauntings stop him now.

The now distant Aliénor posed only a minor concern when they crossed the boundary into town. Compared to the pandemonium which raged around them, her pursuit seemed inconsequential.

The streets of Bastion, all but dead since the onset of the Withering, now spilled over with people who clamored and screamed in fear and revulsion. Over two dozen of Aliénor's infected puppets, awake from their comas, patrolled the city streets. They attacked the healthy and brought them low, converting them to the sickly hoard. Each ghoul displayed a varied assortment of afflictions, all of them grotesque.

Those not beset by corrupted attackers wandered around the street in a panic, shouting after loved ones or to God. The foul odor which permeated the town caused retching from those who had yet to clog their noses with fabric or mud.

Donadieu thought back to the charred tome abandoned on the dusty road. Whatever spell that foul book had used to conceal the plague must have been shattered upon its destruction; now all could see and smell the evil which permeated through their homes. The stench of Aliénor's miasma wafted in every nook of Bastion, watering the eyes of the unprotected. As Henri gagged, Donadieu handed over his handkerchief, grateful his nose could not smell the rot.

Hippo's pace slowed to a crawl as people ran by in the disorderly streets. "We'll have to leave the wagon here and continue ahead on foot," Donadieu said. "It'll be harder for Aliénor to track us through the alleys, and we'll never get a horse through such chaos."

Without protest, the party dismounted and waited for Pierre to hitch the animal. They left Hippo by a small garden and, when the coast looked clear, they snuck into the nearest alleyway. The walls of the homes pressed in on them as they marched, unable to stand shoulder to shoulder in the confined space. Before progressing the length of a single home, a ghoul brandishing a dagger emerged at the end of their enclosed path. Donadieu recognized the creature covered in pocks. A teenage boy from his congregation. "Marc," he said, "put away the weapon. We just want to pass."

The child hoisted the blade before him at the extent of his boney arm. His face carried a sinister smile, which revealed blackened and rotting teeth.

Donadieu held up both hands and begged the boy, "Please, Marc. Bastion needs no more violence tonight."

Despite the pleas, or perhaps because of them, the youth charged. When it became clear he would not slow, Donadieu accepted his fate. He closed his eyes and indulged in a deep inhale, ready for it to be his last. He prayed the others would use the distraction to flee and complete what needed to be done.

Heavy hands grabbed Donadieu from behind and the subsequent yank sheared his thoughts of death. Only when his feet again touched the ground and he found himself staring into Pierre's mask did he realize what happened. Henri swapped places with the priest.

The boy's wild howl and Henri's grunts battled for supremacy while their limbs did the same. The two combatants crashed into each other, wrestling upright and bouncing between the narrow walls. Donadieu watched in horror, helpless to assist when their limbs danced faster than he could follow.

In a surge of bestial strength, Henri threw the boy against one of the houses. The child's head cracked upon the stone exterior, and the body fell limp to the ground. After a tense moment of waiting, it became clear the boy was done.

Elated at the unexpected triumph, Donadieu began to thank Henri. His relief turned to dread when he beheld his champion. Henri swiveled back, his right hand pressed firmly against his ribs, blood spouted from between his fingers. Henri clenched his jaw, and his lips opened into a scowl.

"Pierre," Donadieu gasped while beckoning to the doctor, unable to say more.

The apprentice rushed to Henri's aid, but when Pierre pulled up the stained shirt and hesitated, it told the priest all he needed to know. The physician wrapped the wound to hinder the flow, and the trio shared solemn expressions, all aware this would only slow the inevitable.

"Let's continue," Henri said through gritted teeth. "We can't wait here."

Cries of pain from the civilians and growls from their attackers echoed through the town. Donadieu led the way, Henri secured the rear. They pushed on through the darkened paths and, as they approached the next break in housing, a woman ran past their limited view. Shortly after, a man followed. The pursuer's face oozed with pus and blood. Donadieu knew them both. They were Charlotte Allard and her husband, Louis.

The trio halted when the Allards ran by, stopping to read each other's faces, each wondering if they would break their mission and attempt to help the beset wife. After a few seconds of silence, Donadieu offered the wanted excuse, "We can save the most by stopping this all."

God forgive me, he prayed. When they crossed the exposed thoroughfare, he looked for Charlotte. Although he could not see her, he could hear her scream. "I need a moment," Donadieu gasped when they reached the safety of the next alley. "Those things are everywhere, and the people need our help." From elsewhere, a gunshot cracked; Donadieu flinched at the noise, his weary legs almost giving out beneath him.

"We need to find somewhere to collect ourselves," Pierre said. "Somewhere we can take a moment's rest and decide what to do."

Henri stumbled forward. "My friends," he gasped, "I don't have many moments left to spare. Whatever we're going to do, if you need me, we best do it soon."

To compound their dire situation, a voice crashed over the town from above. "Find them," it screamed, louder than any human had boomed before. The buzzing of Aliénor's flies gave her away as she circled the village. With her soldiers on the ground and her aerial vantage, it would not be long before they were discovered.

Pierre's beaked mask darted from side-to-side with increasing rapidity. "What do we do?"

As if to answer the question, a voice cooed beside them. "Quickly, quietly, in here." A woman called to them from a cracked window on one of the houses. The window opened more, and she beckoned them to crawl inside.

"Camille, a seamstress," Donadieu assured Pierre as he nearly vaulted through the window and into the home. The curtains rustled behind him, and shortly after Pierre followed course. Together, they heaved Henri through, who whimpered as they pulled him inside.

The cramped home contained a small group of townsfolk, each shivering from cold and terror. There were twelve hiding within, fifteen including the new arrivals. A small candle in the center of the room cast the only light, but from what Donadieu could see, everyone appeared free of disease.

"What is this, Father?" Camille asked. "Is this the rapture? Why have we not been called to heaven?"

Donadieu struggled to craft a satisfactory explanation of their plight. "This is not the end of days, or the anger of God, Camille," he said. "This is the wrath of man, empowered by unknowable and ancient evil. Our enemy is Aliénor Dubois. She has found a way to harness infernal power and is channeling that sorcery to corrupt our homes and the ones we love."

"And where is God?" Another woman asked from the corner of the room. "Are we abandoned here to die?"

"We are never forgotten, never alone. God is with us, always. If it is in his plan to do so, he will see us through this terrible night."

"How?" demanded another.

Donadieu shook his head. "I don't yet know." He stared into the center of the room, into the paltry light. An idea dawned in his mind. "Or perhaps maybe I do." Shuffling broke the silence as the survivors leaned in toward the priest.

"Return to your homes, or those of your neighbors, and gather whatever sources of light you can find, be they torches from the streets, lamps from your shelves, or tallow candles from the table, but most important of all, keep them dark. Conscript any others you find unaffected by the disease and tell them the same. Then, we must all meet by the old barn at the edge of town. Pierre, surely you passed it when you first arrived. Do you recall, and could you find your way there?"

Pierre's beak bobbed up and down. "I think I do, and I believe I can."

"Excellent, follow the road east out of town and you'll find it without trouble. Everyone should travel in pairs. I will meet you all there. For now, I must return to the church. There is much for me to gather, but it is too far, too exposed to ask any of you to join."

A teenage boy yelled in rebuttal. "We can't go out there! We'd all die! Surely, you've seen those monsters. They attack on sight." A murmur of agreement spread through the meeting.

Henri groaned as he climbed to his feet. "I can distract them," he said.

Donadieu's heart turned to lead when he beheld the haggard man. Despite his herculean frame, Henri slumped against the wall. He looked so pale, and his shirt was now more red than anything else.

"Let me hear no more of your plan," Henri continued. "I am not long for this world, and I fear when I fall, they will have me. Pierre, lend me your robes and mask. Aliénor seems to despise you and the father the most. I'll lead her hounds away so that you may all make your escape."

Silence spread across the room, broken only when Pierre released the clasps on his mask. "Bless you, Henri," Donadieu said. The others shared their thanks. Pierre assisted Henri with his exterior clothes, and in a few short minutes, the bleeding man crawled back out the window.

"Allow me my final moments to lure them away, then make your escape. Godspeed, all." Holding his side, he limped into the night.

Donadieu stared at his wrinkled hands. Never had he felt so old.

"Are there any other concerns before we disperse? We must not let Henri sacrifice himself in vain."

"I'll be your second on the journey to the church," Camille said. "My daughter is there, and I need to ensure she's still alright."

The mother's steely eyes told Donadieu any rebuttal would fail, not that he'd refuse the extra help. "I'll gladly accept the company." The remaining heads scanned the room, waiting for any complaints.

"Alright," Donadieu broke the silence and reached for the candle in the center of the room. He puffed out the light, shook the wax on the floor, and tucked the stick into his robes. "We wait another minute, and then we move."

Before long, a monstrous scream echoed through the town, "There!"

The priest muttered a quick prayer for Henri, and the party dispersed. One by one, they slinked through the window and out into the street with a subtle clack when their shoes hit the cobbles.

Donadieu patted Pierre on the back as they parted ways. The young physician gave him a paltry but reassuring smile before following another young man into town. The priest watched Pierre go until Camille tugged on his robes.

With the exception of a distant ghoul sighting, Donadieu and Camille arrived at the church without confrontation. All their foes, it seemed, were distracted and in rapid pursuit to the west, toward their decoy.

Together, the pair approached the church's door. As Donadieu reached for the handle, a furious roar boomed from the west.

"Was that a cannon?" asked Camille.

"Henri bought us much time," Donadieu replied, "but I believe that means our deception has been discovered."

With a short breath through his nose, he pushed open the doors and entered his home. The hinges strained from the weight of the heavy wood and a warm breeze came from within. Donadieu almost hesitated to look around the holy space. Thoughts of the castle's disgraced chapel flashed through his mind, and he could not help but imagine his own church in such a sacrilegious state.

Donadieu forced himself to look. Handfuls of candles illuminated the nave and a familiar, almost reassuring, wheezing filled his ears. The church was intact, and his wards still lay sleeping upon the pews. Everyone. He could not hide the smile that spread to his ears, nor did he want to.

The sounds of old hinges brought his attention to the side door where Pascal had just entered. The groundskeeper lumbered in, clay vessel in hand, and began to drip water into the mouths of the ill.

"Josephine," Camille cried out and ran to her child.

The sudden shout caused Pascal to yelp and throw his cup into the church wall. It shattered with a crash. The groundskeeper sputtered and swore at the surprise. "What'cha doin' sneaking up on a man like that, what with devils about 'n all? Scared me half to death."

Camille was too busy weeping over her daughter to hear Pascal's lament. Before that night, mothers had cried in horror when their children sank into a withered sleep. Now, Camille cried in joy that her daughter hadn't awoken to join the fiendish throng.

Donadieu approached Pascal in her stead. "I'm sorry for the start. Thank you for taking care of them in my absence. It means the world to me. I've just come round to grab a few things. I'll be off again shortly. Should the sickness end but I not return, find someone who can write and ask them to send for a new priest. Until the new father arrives, continue to care for them. It's important they remain safe here."

Pascal's expression changed from anger to sorrow. "Where you going, Father? You're not coming back?"

"I'm off to the old barn to meet a few others. I'll do my best to return, I promise; just taking precautions in case I don't. You've been a great friend, Pascal, but it's crucial I be on my way." Donadieu extended his hand to shake, but the surly groundskeeper pulled the priest close and hugged him with a laborer's strength.

The priest blinked away a tear and patted Pascal's back. When the embrace ended, he retreated to his room and grabbed an empty sack. Into the hempen container, he collected every spare candle from around the church he could find and readied himself to leave. He circled the nave, saying a quick prayer for those warded within, finishing with young Marianne.

"I'm taking my leave, Camille," Donadieu said while heading for the door. "Aid Pascal in caring for the ill, water is kept outside and the pot—"

"I'm going with you," Camille cut in. "I can't do anything for Josephine here, but if I may be of any use to her by following you now, then together we go."

Donadieu adjusted the sack on his back. "I was hoping you'd come. Grab a torch by the door. Three or four if you can manage. The more we can get, the better."

Camille obliged, and the two set off toward the barn.

The ghost of the new moon hovered high in the sky, its faint shimmer illuminating only the brightest of colors on the ground below. With heads hung low, they stole along the abandoned road out of town, hidden by the dreary night.

When they arrived at the decrepit barn, they joined a party of some thirty locals. "Thank you all for coming," Donadieu said, smiling widely when he saw Pierre among the crowd. "These numbers will do us well."

"We found many more," Pierre said, "but they would not leave their homes or join us here now."

"Not to worry," Donadieu replied as he set down the sack and clasped his hands. "This group will work fine; my plan is simple. I'll light a torch and stand before the barn. I shall lure Aliénor with a holler and then coax her within. After that, you must seal the doors behind me and hold them shut. I'll set light to the old building. I doubt even that infernal disease could withstand such flame. Should something go awry during my attempt, you each have a light to take my place. No matter what, she must be forced inside that barn. She must burn."

CHAPTER 21

After a series of denied appeals and no better idea proposed, the townsfolk agreed to Donadieu's plan. Pierre had been its most ardent critic, even volunteering for the mission himself, but Donadieu recited his age and insisted it must be him.

Repulsed by the proposal, Pierre could not bring himself to move. He detached from the world and ignored the others preparing around him. At what point was the cost of victory too high? They had already paid too much. Even should their efforts succeed, he would be left with less than nothing to live for. Pierre stared at the ground. He envisioned Guillaume's jovial face, and then its disfigured end. He pictured the barn ablaze, and he heard the screams of his pious friend. Pierre retched.

A glowing light approached from behind, and a friendly hand squeezed his shoulder. "It's time we begin, Pierre. Are you ready?" The young doctor withdrew from his dream and looked around. "Hidden well, aren't they? It's time you join them."

What he said was true; Pierre could not see a single one of the scattered villagers. They hid around the abandoned property, skulking in ditches and behind overgrown shrubs.

His daze ended when he saw Donadieu holding the torch. It all became very real. "Please, Father. You're my last friend. You can't do this. Suicide is a sin."

"I don't wish to die, and suicide is certainly a sin, but self-sacrifice is something else altogether. I merely follow the example of our Lord and Savior. Besides," Donadieu gave a coy smile and a wink. "I think Pascal and Marianne would be mortified to hear you don't consider them friends."

Pierre suppressed tears and hugged the priest, who nearly dropped his torch in the embrace. After a moment's recovery, Donadieu wrapped his free arm around Pierre's back, pulling tightly for a man of his age. Pierre held on as long as Donadieu would allow, but a gentle pat told him it was time to move.

Pierre blinked hard, sending a salty trail down his cheek. He slinked into the darkness and took his own hiding place in a dusty irrigation ditch. Under the hollow moon, their obscurity was all but assured. Lying alone in the dark and knowing what was soon to come, his sorrow morphed into panic. His heart quickened until it bounced off his ribs and his hands grew clammy and slick with sweat.

A great, heaving sigh floated across the field and Donadieu called.

"Aliénor," he yelled, the man's old throat croaking from the strain. "I'm done running. Come, find me here." Donadieu raised his torch to the sky, a beacon of light in a field of black. The priest maintained an iron composure and stood unwaveringly still. Defiant against corruption until the end.

The silence that followed was agony, every breeze the implication of a dead man's breath chilling the nape. Pierre nearly sprung from his ditch when a bush rustled close to his side. "Quiet," chided someone in response, and a harsher, "Shush," topped them all.

Again, he faced the horror of waiting. His imagination ran wild with all that could go wrong, and he glanced at the crudely constructed lance by his side. The unlit weapon was a pair of roped-together brooms topped with oiled rags. He had already proven knives would not work, not forever.

In the field, Donadieu raised his free hand to his mouth and cleared his throat. Before the priest could utter a follow-up call, a hum broke through the silence.

The noise grew louder with alarming speed until it climaxed with a heavy thud. Donadieu fell, tumbling to the ground, his torch flying from his hand and snuffing out on the ground. The flame reduced to a glowing smolder. Aliénor hovered above him. She raised the weapon used to club the priest—the broken and battered corpse of Henri, her boney fingers clasped about his ankle as a handle.

"I've played your little game, Martine, and I killed your sneaky fox." With careless disregard, she flung the body into the field, the bones crunching as they landed mere feet from Pierre. Despite the grotesque condition of the body, Pierre could swear he heard the faintest wheezing. With the speed of a slug, he pulled his torch closer and eyed the dying embers of the priest's own.

"But now," she continued, "it's time to end this."

Her buzzing fog plunged slowly toward the earth. When it nearly reached the ground, Aliénor emerged from the flies as though descending the steps of a staircase. Her shoeless rotten feet clumped upon the field's hardened soil and her swarm retreated into the air above, hovering like a low hanging cloud. She looked as hideous as she had in the chapel, perhaps even worse. While no longer bleeding, the side of her dress was stained black and red from the bile and the blood. He wished he'd stabbed her more.

Beneath Aliénor's hostile scowl, Donadieu crawled backwards toward the barn. The plague witch towered over him and matched the pace of his creep, her steps unnervingly dainty and refined for such a hideous and deformed creature. Pierre saw the panic in Donadieu's eyes as the priest flicked his gaze between his advancing foe and the fading salvation of his light.

"It's not too late, Aliénor," Donadieu pleaded. "Redemption is still possible. God welcomes all who truly repent." His voice wavered as he crawled slowly back, a good twenty feet before he would reach the barn doors.

Aliénor cackled. "You should repent to me after what you did to my book. I will not make the same mistake again. This time, I'll kill you myself."

Donadieu's torch's final embers began to flicker and fight for survival. Should its heat die, their plans would be for naught, as would Donadieu's sacrifice.

"I'm sorry," Donadieu said. "I failed you. I sought to release you from your curse, from whatever evil possesses you. But I did not succeed."

Sill grinning, Aliénor kicked at Donadieu. "Do you want to know why you failed, priest?" She kicked him again, hurrying his backward crawl. "Why you never had any chance at all? Your exorcisms could not work on me, for I am not possessed. I was offered more than you could fathom, and I claimed what I was owed. I am a willing host, Martine. Sickness, and the potential it holds, are older than your religion. While your faith may grant access to powers enough to destroy an old relic, those abilities will not work on the chosen, like me."

Donadieu's face contorted in confusion and fear. "What has happened to you, Aliénor? Why would you choose such blasphemy? Why would anyone?" He huffed as she kicked at him again.

"Did you not listen before when we spoke? I was a servant to my husband. A decoration. Now, I am the master of the house, his lands, and more. I have become pestilence itself, more powerful and omnipresent than any old fable or tale. I have the power to bend all to my will, and with the spreading of my plague comes the spreading of my kingdom." Her grin deepened into her toothless smile. "I have the power to conquer all, and I plan to use it." Ribbons of amorphous text began to glow upon her flesh. They danced across her dried skin as had the ink on the now destroyed tome.

"But your book," Donadieu continued, stalling as he crawled back, "it was destroyed. We came so close to freeing you and the town. Why are you still bound?"

"Oh? Does it look like my influence or power has waned?" Aliénor threw her arm west, toward the town. What Donadieu saw momentarily stopped his crawl. Pierre turned to follow Donadieu's gaze and understood why.

The witch had summoned her legions, and across the field they marched. At first silent in their approach, now the mob howled in macabre delight. Some carried torches, many more carried improvised weapons. From within their wretched ranks, Pierre recognized several. Louise, Claude, Guillaume, and dozens more. The army had only just left the town, but when they arrived in full, every hidden survivor would be discovered…and hopelessly slaughtered.

Aliénor stopped smiling, transitioning instead to an expression of impatience and anger. "That book was the means to gain my powers, not the source of them. Things may become more difficult with its illusions gone, but my control remains. There's no getting rid of that, Martine."

Donadieu stopped crawling when he reached the gaping entrance to the decrepit barn. "Please, Aliénor, hear my final plea. Repent to God, confess your sins. Come back to the light."

"No more crawling. You can't escape me." With the flick of a wrist, her buzzing cloud funneled to the barn's entrance. Now a vibrating wall of insects stood where the open door had just been.

Pierre starred in disbelief. With the barn sealed, he did not know how they could succeed.

"You know, Aliénor, despite it all, I believe we have one thing in common," the priest said. He laid back on the ground, his head no more than an inch from the humming wall.

Aliénor sighed and looked back at her approaching hoard. They had gained considerable ground and numbered as many as fifty. "What else could you possibly have left to say? If I haven't killed you by the time they arrive, it's only going to be worse for you."

As Pierre laid there, spying from his ditch, something changed within him. His fear turned to frustration, and his frustration turned to rage. They had come so far, and they had lost so much; he would lose no more. A jolt of urgency sparked within, and Pierre Laflamme grabbed his lance and crawled from his ditch toward the dying flame.

Pierre shared a glance with the priest, and Donadieu raised his voice to cover the creeping man. "I, too, used to be afraid of fire. Don't lie; I saw you recoil when Claude brought the candle."

Pierre reached the dying embers and coddled them in his hands. Frantic puffs of air failed to bring the fire back to life, his breathing too strained to produce a constant supply.

Donadieu continued, louder than before. "But this past week I have remembered its light and its warmth. If something destroys, but also creates, is that not holy? What more perfectly represents the sacrifice and triumph of our Lord thy God, Jesus Christ, than a sacred flame?"

Pierre blew harder still, and his heart nearly skipped a beat when a flicker of orange relit upon the charred end of Donadieu's torch.

He pulled his own torch close and held the old against the new. He blew, and a magnificent yellow flame erupted from them both. The fire lit his face, and he held the flames aloft.

At the sight of their radiant cue, the villagers leaped from their hiding spots and sprinted toward the Pierre, each wielding their tool waiting to be lit. They ran by him one by one, each lighting their own flames and moving to surround the malevolent witch while her attention was consumed by their priest. Only when they began to encircle her did she regard their approach.

"What treachery is this?" screamed Aliénor, her bugs vibrating angrily as a unified mass. Her encroaching soldiers joined in the anger, cacophonous roars erupting from within their ranks.

When the first man reached Aliénor, she grabbed him by the throat and flung him with the strength of a catapult, right into the midst of ghouls. The poor man's screams were short, and the sound of ripping flesh and splattering blood carried far in the still night.

The volunteers did not stop, for they knew that if they did, their fate would only be the same. The number of flames continued to grow and march toward their foe. Before long, Aliénor found herself within a blazing half circle, trapped against the barn door.

A few flies broke from the wall and moved to Aliénor, but their journeys ended abruptly when batted by townsfolk's flames. When Pierre joined the mob and raised his incendiary lance, blocking the sky, Aliénor scowled.

In all the commotion, Donadieu rose to his feet, stuck between Aliénor and the vibrating wall. "I had hoped for a calmer outcome," he said.

Aliénor's confusion turned to fury again. "You worm," she cried, and leapt to tackle the priest. With anticipatory readiness, Donadieu dove and Aliénor smashed through her insectoid wall.

Without needing command, all but Pierre threw their torches to the ground and heaved the barn doors shut. They pressed their bodies against the old wood and held with all their strength, the largest two men bringing a drawbar into place to help hold the witch inside.

Pierre launched his spear through one of the barn's windows. At once, a glow began to grow inside the old barn. Every spare candle from the church's inventory lay hidden within the mounds of dry hay. The blaze spread quickly, and flames burst from between the barn walls, recently reinforced in the trap's hasty preparation.

The advancing withered army quickened their pace and increased the volume of their roars. If the flames did not claim the witch soon, the defenders would be slaughtered down to the last man.

Screeches of pain erupted from within the barn. Flies vacated the trap through every sizable hole. Many carried the embers upon their wings, illuminating the sky like a swarm of scattering fireflies.

The doors heaved as though being charged by a furious bull. One particularly powerful impact sent a woman flying from her position. The next assault stumbled a man backward until he tripped over his own legs. Each impact sent a shockwave through Pierre, but after each jolt, he threw himself back against the door. Donadieu too held the line, and despite it all, Pierre could not help but smile to see his friend still among them.

Another assault against the door, and another flying warden.

A nervous leg bounced beneath Pierre, and he turned to look at the field. The disorderly nature of the withered ones' sprint unsettled him, as did their rapidly closing distance. He pushed with all he had against the barn doors, but the rising heat blistered his palms, and the seeping smoke scorched his lungs. Two of the townsfolk lost their nerve and fled into the night.

Aliénor's voice dimmed in strength, but the pounding attacks doubled in frequency and power. Every other impact sent someone flying from their post, but just as quickly, they would rise again and rejoin the line. An acrid metallic odor seeped from the cracks in the wood, and Aliénor's jailors coughed from the stench and the smoke.

The throng of the approaching withered broke into a frenzy as the fastest of the lot charged to rescue their broiling queen. The quickest two within their ranks, Roland and Louise, readied their cleavers only steps from the townsfolk. Camille broke from the defensive line and flung herself into the attackers' vanguard. Her unexpected launch toppled both the ghouls and bought the defenders precious time.

When the next closest withered arrived, it raised its axe, ready to hack the audacious mother. Before its blow could land, an ear popping roar exploded from within the barn. As it grew in strength and sorrow, the shout became shared by all the marching ghouls. They dropped their weapons and grabbed their heads, crying in harmony.

The fire turned from a roaring orange blaze to a hellish red. Bolts of crackling energy shot from the windows, and voices deeper than the darkest mine roared from within. Pierre's skin screamed in protest from the heat, which at last became too great to bear. The door guards retreated from their post, moving instead toward the screaming line of their corrupted kin.

An explosion blew within the barn and quaked the earth, snuffing out all the fire with its shockwave. In unison with the burst, the fetid combatants collapsed. Their haggard breathing ceased.

A silence spread across the victors. They looked over the battlefield and, in the distance, a bird began to sing in the night.

All at once, they erupted. Some cheered with joy as loud as they could scream, others ran to the crumpled dead to weep over their fallen friends. Donadieu knelt to the ground, feverishly thanking his Lord.

Pierre saw the corpse of Guillaume amongst the pile of Aliénor's dead soldiers. Pins and needles poked at his heart, but he was not overcome as he had been before. He had mourned Guillaume twice; his peace was made. Instead, he walked to the line and extended his hand to Camille. A courteous yank had her back on her feet. Pierre had never seen someone so relieved.

As the cheering died down, curiosity spread through the survivors, and they all turned their heads toward the empty barn. Only wisps of smoke seeped from within. Together as a mob, they moved to see the charred interior. Pierre led the group and, when he peered inside, he gasped at the sight.

There was no charred corpse within the barn. Instead, written in glowing embers upon the floor, there was a series of symbols arrayed in strange geometric patterns. He recognized the letters from within the former fortress of Bastion.

Most distressing of all, the symbols moved.

CHAPTER 22

"Please bow your heads and let us pray. Heavenly Father, we rejoice at the sun and the warmth You have brought us. You have seen us through the Withering, and You have gifted us a short winter. As we return to the fields and the woods with thanks to Your early spring, we know we are blessed, and we feel Your love in our hearts. Oh, Lord, let this weather help birth a new and purer version of ourselves, as the flowers themselves are reborn. In all we do, we strive to bring You glory. This we pray in Your name, Amen."

The booming *amen* from the congregation echoed through the rafters, its noise quickly muffled by the swishing of clothes as the parishioners began to rise. After so many months of the church being only a wheezing ghost, it elated Father Donadieu to see the pews so full once again. The survivors of the Withering remained a thankful lot, and church attendance now exceeded even pre-Withering times. Although healing from the sickness had been slow, a complete recovery was made by all who had not fully succumbed to Aliénor's plight.

With small steps and minding his stiffening knees, Donadieu descended from the pulpit and joined his pious crowd. The warmth of his congregation surpassed even that of the spring air, and the casual conversation brought Donadieu more joy than he would have ever thought possible.

As he made his way through the church, he caught a glimpse that poked a sliver of pain in his otherwise happy day. Sniffling by the votive candle rack was a young girl, her father standing by her side.

Compelled to try to soften the pain, Donadieu nodded at the man before kneeling beside the girl. "Good morning, Marianne. Why so glum on such a sunny day?"

"I miss my mommy," she whimpered, her sorrow spreading to the priest.

Donadieu turned to watch the flames, many representative of those lost to the putrid disease. "As you should, she was a wonderful woman. She was loving and kind, and you're nearly a spitting image. Although it might be hard now, it's important to remember she lives on in the Kingdom of Heaven, and you will see her again."

"I want to see her now," Marianne said.

"I know, my child, as does she. She will watch over you as you grow, and she will love you all the same. But, important as it is to reminisce about the past, you must not let it stop you from growing into the future. The Lord loves you too, Marianne, and He has envisioned great things for you. Remember that."

The girl stared at Donadieu with a blank face, the words passing clear above her head. She turned, confused, to her father, who took her hand. "Thank you for your kind words, Father," he said, before leading Marianne out into the day.

Pushing off his knees, the priest rose again to his feet. He sauntered to the door and bid farewell to the last of his lingering flock. When only he remained, Donadieu walked to the center of the church and breathed deeply, ingesting the solitude and the quiet. After months of the choked, gasping breaths of those who would not die, the silence couldn't be sweeter.

Donadieu decided the buoyancy in his chest would do well to carry him on a stroll, and he emerged into the morning, beaming as vibrant as the sun. He could taste the freshness in the air, the budding leaves and flowers palpable on his tongue. His nose longed to be able to smell the spring air, but this setback would not ruin his day.

Had his legs been able, Donadieu would have skipped down the path to the street. Along the way, he passed Pascal, who was busy pulling weeds along the walkway. The surly man dropped his spade and waved at the priest, but in Pascal's usual fashion, he refused to smile. Donadieu happily returned the gesture and continued his way through the town. He marveled at how quickly Bastion had been rebuilt. Only scarce traces remained of the fires and carnage from the season before.

A handful of times on his journey, he stopped to engage with the busy citizens going about their day and pleasantries were shared.

When Donadieu reached the edge of Bastion, he gazed out across the open fields. Even long dead trees were beginning to blossom once again. He squinted and the blurry shape of his destination came clearer into view. The old barn.

Donadieu patted his robes to ensure he carried the flask and marched through the recovering countryside. His legs ached even before he arrived and, when he did, he pressed the palms of his hands into his tender flesh. His muscles protested, but the brief massage did him good.

He approached the barn and peered inside. The letters were glowing again. Donadieu shook his head and retrieved the flask from his pocket. With his thumb covering most of the opening, he splashed the holy water about the blackened room. Hissing and sputtering erupted from the earth as the letters lost their light and stopped their dance. The text recovered slower after every purge, and Donadieu prayed it would not be long before they stopped forming altogether.

The yellow smoke tasted strangely metallic on his tongue and he spit in protest. Whatever evil still lived here, he would keep it banished as long as he was able, lest that unholy plague return.

Donadieu retreated from the barn and stared at it for a long while. With great dismay, he could not help but marvel at how resistant the structure had been to destruction. After that fateful night, the timbers had become stronger than stone, strengthened in the inferno.

The same could not be said for the Dubois' home, which had suffered a catastrophic fire over the winter. No one reported the blaze, so no outsiders came to investigate. The Dubois' had no heirs, and their estranged families had not yet learned of their fates. Although much of the building lay in a charred ruin, the skeletal remains of the old fortress remained. The hilltop that once held the mighty walls of the fort of Bastion was again relegated to a site of myth and taboo.

A shiver forced its way through him. It was time for him to return to the church.

When back in town, Donadieu visited the grassy lot. Hippo watched indifferently as the priest walked by and poked his head into the back of the covered wagon. Pierre was busy packing reagents and storing foods; the artisans of Bastion had been generous in helping the physician repair and improve his traveling home.

Donadieu waited patiently until he was spotted for fear of startling the busy man. "Just about packed, I take it?" he asked.

Pierre hopped out of the wagon and placed his hands on his hips to breathe. "Just about. Winter's broken and there's no one left here in need of my aid. It's time I continue Guillaume's legacy and get going."

"You're more than welcome to stay, Pierre. I know many of the townsfolk would be happy to have a resident doctor."

"I appreciate that, Father, but no. I must be off. There are too many diseases and not enough doctors to handle them. That's not even accounting for demonic plagues!"

Donadieu chuckled. "You have everything you need?"

Pierre surveyed the mounds of his cargo. "More than enough. You've all made sure I'm healthily supplied."

"Good, good. You'll have to come back and visit us from time to time, whenever you're in the area. You'll always have a place here."

"I promise I'll come back to winter in Bastion every year. Until you get sick of me, that is."

"Marianne will be thrilled." A silence settled between the two. Donadieu stepped closer and placed his hand on Pierre's shoulder. "How are you doing, Pierre, really?"

Pierre's gaze fell to the ground. "I miss him." His voice scratched on the final word.

Donadieu pulled Pierre toward himself and they embraced. "He would be so very proud of you, Pierre. For his work to carry on in hands as capable as yours is the greatest legacy he could leave. Don't forget that. Ever."

Pierre sniffled and stepped back. "Thank you, father. Thank you for looking after me." He took a deep breath and stood straighter. "Well, I best get back to packing. Can't have all my supplies shattering before I get wherever I'm going."

"Of course," Donadieu replied. "I'll leave you to it." He watched Pierre resume with a smile spreading to his cheeks. The boy would go far.

When satisfied with letting the doctor work, Donadieu twisted and walked toward the church's side door.

Halfway there, Pascal hobbled by with a wheelbarrow full of soil and stones. "Got one waitin' for ya in there," the groundskeeper mumbled.

"Thank you, Pascal," Donadieu replied.

The priest entered the church and, as Pascal foretold, one of the confessional curtains had been pulled shut.

Donadieu stopped to ponder the sight of the closed confessional. He lamented the days when a closed curtain had filled him with dread and worry. Those days had passed, and he was happy to provide his spiritual service. With a light heart, he strode toward his task, unburdened by the world.

ACKNOWLEDGMENTS

To be honest, I didn't think I'd get this far. Writing can be daunting at times, and I am not always a patient man. Without the support of a great number of people, I'd have given up long ago.

I owe my greatest debt to my wonderful partner, Talia, and to my family. They always read what I shove their way and insist I continue, even when I am not so sure.

What I consider my best ideas then spill onto the plates of my friends. They have been relentlessly supportive, and I can't thank them enough for their encouragement.

Finally, I must extend gratitude to the team at Graveside Press. Thank you, Hannah, for pulling my manuscript from the pile and seeing the potential. Thank you, Kala Godin, and especially Kelley York, who read through my meandering submission, helped me to polish it into something respectable and put up with my frequent questions.

Thank you all.

J. Brian Ballinger is an aspiring new writer with a taste for the historic and the macabre. He writes both novels and short stories and is best known for skin-chilling tales that take you back through the centuries. He lives in Canada and loves bewildering coworkers and friends with his wild tales and unique style of horror and nonsense.

If you'd like to read more,
you can find a collection of his works at
jbrianballinger.com

Content Warnings

Please note: it should be assumed that basic horror tropes will apply. These include death, gore, and violence.

death of a loved one

child illness and death

self-harm

suicide (off-page)

substance abuse

THANK YOU!

Thank you for supporting Graveside Press and our authors.
One of the biggest ways you can help is to leave a star rating or a
review wherever you purchased your copy!

Stay spooky.

graveside-press.com

www.ingramcontent.com/pod-product-compliance
Lightning Source LLC
Chambersburg PA
CBHW031030310726
48969CB00007B/1928